Praise fc

"Readers who enjoy a rollicking adventure firmly rooted in family interactions ... will find that *Navigating the Storm* comes steeped in a battle between love and loyalty in which Kat reconsiders her ultimate goals."

—Diane Donovan, Senior Reviewer, *Midwest Book Review*

"I absolutely adored *A Merry Life*.... If possible, *Navigating the Storm* is even better than the first instalment in Kat's tale. Branson isn't afraid to rip your heart out or to make you laugh."

—Sally Altass, author of *The Witch Laws* and reviewer, Reedsy.com

"This is an incredibly impactful, emotional, entertaining, funny, heart-tugging book."

—Martha Bullen, author and owner, Bullen Publishing Services

"*Navigating the Storm* is not your typical pirate book. Rather, it is a blend of science fiction with steampunk and cyberpunk interlaced with realistic human emotions and experiences set in the twenty-fourth century. Action is high paced and riveting. Kat matures as the book progresses; hitting rock-bottom makes her stronger and savvier, and puts her on firmer ground to face whatever lies in the future."

—Cindy Vallar, editor, *Pirates & Privateers*

"Sarah Branson's novel, *A Merry Life*, is a rousing page-turner. Her tough-as-nails heroine is relatable and genuine, and the plot is action-packed from start to end. Great for any reader ready to buckle in for a lightning fast ride of a book!"

— Andrea Vanryken, author

"Swashbuckling, vengeance and heart - all wrapped up in one heck of a strong woman."

— Sally Altass, author of *The Witch Laws* and Reedsy.com reviewer

NAVIGATING THE STORM

Pirates of New Earth
Book 2

SARAH BRANSON

To Rebecca—
The motorcycle....

Sarah E Branson

SOONER STARTED PRESS

Pirates of New Earth:
Book 2: Navigating the Storm

Copyright © 2022 Sarah Branson

SOONER STARTED PRESS

Published by Sooner Started Press
For more information, visit www.sarahbranson.com
Edited by David Aretha and Andrea Vanryken
Cover design by The Book Designers:
Ian Koviak and Alan Dino Hebel

ISBN (paperback): 978-1-957774-03-9
ISBN (ebook): 978-1-957774-04-6

Printed in the United States of America

For Rick who makes all of this possible.

"I am not afraid of storms, for I am learning how to sail my ship."

Louisa May Alcott

District Ⅰ   Banking, Financial, Theater
Distract Ⅱ   Light Industry, Business
District Ⅲ   Mining (Clay & Glitter)
District Ⅳ   Harbor
District Ⅴ   Mining, Manufacturing (Bricks & Glitter) also a developing artist community
District Ⅵ   Agricultural (Grains, Livestock)
District Ⅶ   Agricultural (Vineyards, Orchards)

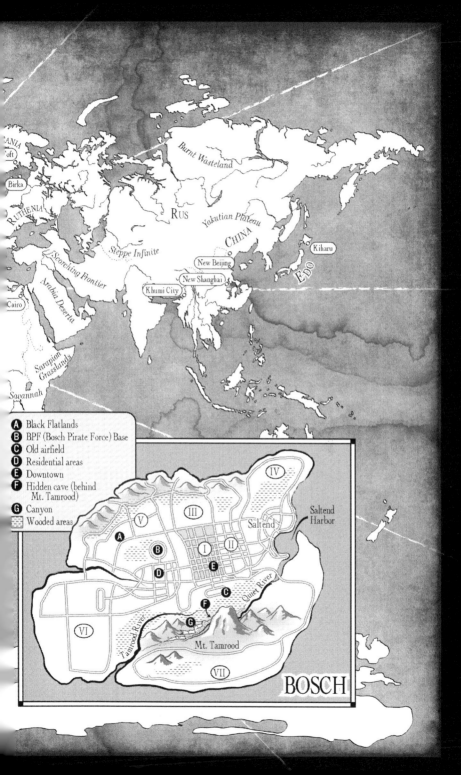

Contents

Part I

ONE

Safe Haven

I keep my weapon clasped close to my breast, at the ready.

The late afternoon sun beats down intensely on my head as I crouch behind the large rock. It is unseasonably warm for October, especially for Northern Edo in the foothills of Mizueyama. These hills usually cool early in the fall, but not this year. I feel sweat accumulate in my short curls and on my brow as I press myself against the cool stone and listen carefully, knowing my fully armed assailants are circling on the far side of the boulder. I can hear them jabbering back and forth with each other in their own language. They are armed as well, and they're gunning for me, but I'm ready to fight back.

Just take your time, Kat Wallace. There are only two of them. You can wait until they are distracted. I take a deep breath and start to move but freeze as I hear a yell in the distance. *Dammit. It's their leader.* She is particularly shrewd and will organize the attack. I rethink my strategy. Three armed and now organized opponents. There's no way I'm getting out of here without taking some fire. Suddenly there is palpable silence. They are closing in. It's time for me to move.

I leap around my rocky refuge, aim my weapon, and begin

to fire as I yell, "Avast, me hearties! Dead men tell no tales!" I hear their cries go up, and then I am hit, once, twice. They continue to fire, and I know I am done for. But I won't go alone. I fall to the ground and wait, panting, my finger on the trigger. As they approach, I push onto my elbow, point my rifle, and begin to empty its contents onto them.

My shots are, even now, accurate, and I hear screams from my attackers, but they, too, are unrelenting, and I find I am hit again and again.

"Mama! You are getting my hair all wet!" Grey shrieks at me through her giggles.

Kik and Mac throw their water pistols aside and simply jump on me, cackling with toddler chuckles. "We got you! We got you!" I am soaked through, but it feels good in the heat.

"Yeah, you did." I wipe a wet curl from my face. "But then you approached while I still had ammo, so I got you!" We are all talking and laughing at once.

Grey turns and puts her little five-year-old hands on her hips as she castigates her just-barely two-year-old brothers. "Told you! We are supposed to wait a safe distance." I smile as she repeats the lessons I have taught her.

The boys, one sturdy with brown curls and green eyes and one slighter with straight dark hair and eyes to match, though, are joyously wet and muddy and don't listen to their sister's scolding. They suddenly see their grandmother, Takai's mother, who had brought Grey over to the park from school, and they run toward her for a hug. She's going to hate getting all that mess on her. I hop up and scoop Grey into my arms, kissing the dark brown waves of her hair that are now dripping with water as I move to run interference for Yumiko.

"Thanks for bringing Grey over." I smile at the stern,

unyielding face. My rough and rowdy play with the kids has never impressed her. *Too fucking bad. We have fun.* "Boys, don't get mud on your grandmother." I provide lip service for them to behave, but in reality, I kinda like seeing them fluster her and mess up her impeccable self. She has never warmed to me, and the events last month in Bosch have made her even colder still.

She breathes a disapproving inhale through her nose. "Is this really an appropriate way for you to play with my grand-children? They aren't pirates, you know. The boys are far too small for such roughhousing, and I really think Grey should stop this brawling and start something more suitable for a young lady, like ikebana." She looks disapprovingly at the children. Grey has climbed down from my arms, and she and the boys are now engaged in finding rocks to throw into the creek on the way home.

Yumiko has never disguised her dislike for all things Bosch. I usually try to defuse things, but today I decide to poke the bear. "Grey's a bit young for ikebana now. But there's no reason she can't be a flower-arranging pirate someday. And the boys started roughhousing in the womb. They'll make fine Bosch-doan pirates." I wait for this comment and my portman-teau to land and am rewarded with the gratifying look of disgust that crosses Yumiko's features. "Boys, give your grand-mother a quick kiss. We need to go get dinner ready. And remember, Papa will be home tomorrow." Black-haired Kik and blond-brown Mac begin to clap and chant, "Papa comes home!" as they smear two muddy kisses on Yumiko's cheeks. "Do you want to join us, Yumiko?" I offer as graciously as possible. *Please say no.*

"I cannot. I have important work that I need to accom-plish." She draws herself up as she mentions her work. Edoan diplomats, such as my in-laws and husband, are proud to the point of hubris about their profession. But I also think she is giving me a dig as I cannot do the work I love. Not for a whole year. Not until my banishment from Bosch is over.

"Mother, you've made your feelings about Kat very clear for years." Takai frowned at the older woman sitting in the chair across from him. Her shoulder-length, deep brown, almost black hair was pulled back in a tidy ponytail with a thick fringe of hair cut into neat bangs that accentuated her dark eyes. She wore a very proper, yet very fashionable, Edoan tunic with a high neck and full sleeves in a deep marmalade color, highly appropriate for the season. She had small and elegant gold earrings that complemented the gold chain around her neck. Takai shook his head. "But she's my wife, and she's the mother of my children: your grandchildren. You must accept that she is here to stay."

"My son, Kat Wallace is a pirate. You can't trust pirates. They refuse to even be part of the FA. How do you even know if you and the children are safe with her? Takai..." And here Yumiko Shima leaned forward meaningfully. "She killed her own father!" This she said in a loud whisper that was almost a hiss.

Yumiko had made this statement in much the same way almost every time she had seen Takai since he, the pirate, and the children had returned from Bosch a few weeks earlier. Now her son stood and looked balefully down at Yumiko. "Enough." His handsome face, so like his father's, was stern. "I don't pretend to fully understand why she did what she did, but I know our children are safe and well and loved when they're with Kat."

Yumiko's lips pressed together and formed a straight line.

She audibly breathed a puff of air through her nose as she glanced down and away from Takai. It was the expression she always took on when she knew she had lost an argument. She paused for only a moment then stood, quietly turned, and picked up the light knit throw from the side of the chair, carefully shaking it out. She folded it neatly, putting it in its place on the chair back. "I expect you are right about the children. They'll be fine." Yumiko kept her back to Takai as she continued. "But dear, what do you expect her to do when she invariably discovers your assignations while away on diplomatic missions? What do you think a pirate would do?" She turned her head and smiled a small, knowing smile at her son, watching his deep brown eyes that had just a hint of laugh lines in their corners as he took in her words.

"What? Mother, I don't have any idea what you are talking about." Takai's eyes went wide ever so briefly, and he nervously brushed at his hairline near his ear with his right hand. Yumiko kept her expression unchanged, but inside, she gave a laugh. She knew she had been correct. After all, she knew her son best. She knew all his tells when he lied, whether it was about a broken plate when he was a child or his adult penchant for romancing the loveliest woman in the room, wherever that room was. She had thought about this behavior extensively and had decided that Takai would never be settled until he found a woman very much like her. She would see to it he did just that.

"Takai, dear, the diplomatic corps of New Earth is not large, and while we keep confidential those things we must in our work, what happens at events never stays quiet for long." She turned and put a hand on her son's arm and looked at his face with its strong jaw, arched cheekbones, and bronze complexion. "My boy, I do not fault you at all. You are far too handsome, intelligent, and charming to not attract lovely women. But I do worry about your safety if your pirate wife becomes aware of certain events."

Takai looked at his mother. She could see him appraising the situation by the way his eyes studied her. "I think it best..." He paused and glanced involuntarily over his shoulder. "... that information stays private. Though Kat would not behave recklessly." She saw his eyebrows drop briefly, and she knew she had planted a seed of doubt. Good.

She squeezed his arm. "Well, you know best, certainly. And I would never intentionally say anything." She let the word "intentionally" hang in the air for the briefest moment. Then she moved her hand from his arm and began maneuvering about the room, straightening the living area that was already neat and tidy. Then, almost as an afterthought, "Oh, I wanted to ask you if you could talk with your wife about Aika Grey coming over on Tuesdays after school. I believe she is the right age for me to instruct her in ikebana. But her mother seemed reluctant when I brought it up."

Takai closed his eyes and sighed. "Yes, Mother. I will see to it. Expect her next Tuesday." He walked over and leaned toward her as she proffered her cheek for a small goodbye kiss.

"Wonderful. Have a safe walk home." She raised a hand in farewell as her son opened the door and stepped out into the October sunshine. Then she paused as she watched him walk down the path to the road. Walking home to that cabin. There were so many isolated areas on that path. Her brain started to whir. She hadn't had enough information the last time. This time she would ask an Edoan to handle it. They would not fail the way the outsiders had back when Aika Grey was an infant.

∽

Takai walked along the road from his parents' home that meandered through the village. Just like always, he felt like he would never measure up to his mother's expectations. It was amazing that she could make him, a grown man, a trained FA officer, a diplomat, a scholar, a family man, feel like a naughty child. He sulked a bit over the injustice of it and toyed with a few conversations in his head that he knew he would never actually have the nerve to have with Mother. That was one of the things he admired about his wife. She had backbone and didn't hesitate to say what she thought.

Takai smiled to himself as he thought of the first time he had seen Kat: That fire and the devil-may-care attitude intrigued him then. It still did. He believed she could do anything. He had seen her work as a pirate, and he had wanted her ferociously. It still stood as one of his greatest achievements that he had made her his own. While he hadn't originally intended to procreate, the children he and Kat had brought forth were the lights of his life, and he was careful to curb his expectations for them. He knew how distressing that could be. And Kat was an astounding mother. She was gentle and kind with the children and encouraged them to explore the world while creating a safe home for them to return to.

He thought of his mother's comments on his behavior while on diplomatic missions. He shrugged. He had always appreciated beautiful women, and beautiful women seemed to be drawn to him. Ever since secondary school, he had enjoyed acquiring them into a collection. In his mind, his women were part of a carefully arranged bouquet, each a flower in it, unique and exquisite.

Kat was now the center of his bouquet and always would be. A sturdy perennial that he now compared all other flowers to. He had so hoped he had successfully transplanted her to Edo. Before the old man had convinced her to do the unthinkable, she had seemed happy and settled in their cabin. They had even talked occasionally about another child. The only silver lining Takai had seen to Kat's role in the old Master Commander's death was that she would be banished. Bosch would be off the table forever. But the eleventh-hour testimony of the doctor changed that, and the Kat who had returned to Edo was different: unsettled and eager to step back into her pirate life.

It had taken him quite some time to convince Kat that they should marry. He had attempted in the first year of his marriage to be monogamous, but it was not his way. Of course, he sought other women out when Kat was unavailable due to pregnancy and child-rearing. And of course, he collected many diplomatic blossoms during his travels. How could he be expected not to? He had even tried to be honest, making a suggestion once to Kat that he might be interested in seeing other women. He thought about how fierce she had become then, her eyes flashing as she ferociously forbade even the idea. Then he smiled when he recalled their lovemaking after he had made the suggestion. Perhaps he should bring the idea up again. He paused and considered, his mother's words echoing in his ears. Kat would never harm him. Would she?

Jiro's comm rattled in his pocket, and he surreptitiously pulled it out and glanced at the screen. He smiled to himself and looked at the men sitting around the table in the small restaurant snacking on gyoza and edamame and talking business. He addressed the older man at the head of the table. "Tsukasa-san, if you will excuse me. This is a comm I need to take."

Kenichi Tsukasa, a strongly built man in his sixties with deep black hair set off with the occasional silver strands, cut conservatively, nodded at the dark, tousled-haired man some thirty years his junior and went back to speaking to the man on his left. Tsukasa-san was head of the Koshijiya-rengo family, the current dominant yakuza family in Edo. Jiro was a kobun. He was not a foot soldier, but neither was he really an executive. Too many not-old-enough-to-die waka gashira stood in his way. As Jiro stepped toward the door, he did not see the small nod that Tsukasa, who in his view was getting old and making poor judgments, gave to Riki, a large, impressive bodyguard.

Jiro walked down the narrow street, which really was more of an alley, lined with shops and tiny restaurants with paper lanterns strung high up, zigzagging back and forth across the street. Of average build in Edo and with a rather plain face, he was a man who could blend in. People didn't notice him. Until it was too late. He pressed the comm to his ear. "Yes, ma'am. I understand the assignment. Have you sent the funds to the account number I gave you?" He listened to the woman as she affirmed the transfer and then reviewed, again, the details. "Yes, ma'am. It will look like a robbery." He listened again and rolled his eyes. "I understand. Please be assured I am skilled in this." Jiro nodded as he listened. This woman obviously did not know Jiro's skill set as she continued to warn him about the target's abilities. "Thank you, ma'am. I appreciate the details you have given. The task will be completed by next week." He smiled. "Good day to you." He ended the comm with the woman and decided to follow up on a different job, placing another comm. He listened to the distant buzzing sound.

"Abernathy Enterprises, how may I direct your comm?" A pleasant, Western voice finally stopped the buzzing.

"I am Jiro Yamagata. I was asked to contact Mr. Abernathy's office by—"

"One moment please," the pleasant voice cut him off, and he frowned. "I'll transfer you."

A different tone sounded this time, definitely more pleasant than the standard one. "Mr. Yamagata, it's Casey Sutton, Mr. Abernathy's assistant. I believe we spoke a few days ago."

Jiro cringed at the FA-style honorific. *How can Abernathy's people not even attempt to be respectful of Edonese customs?* But then he considered the markers to be made and the influence the relationship would bring if he could nurture it and set his pride aside. "Yes, Mr. Sutton. I am available for the job you and I discussed. As it turns out, I will be in the general area you had mentioned in the next few days."

The assistant responded, "That is wonderful news, Mr. Yamagata. Mr. Abernathy is very keen on having his property returned to him. If you could locate it and secure it for him, he would be most grateful. And his appreciation for this will extend beyond the markers we discussed. As you know, Mr. Abernathy is quite influential."

Jiro nodded. There would be competition for this job, even just for the markers, which were plentiful. But the influence, that could go a long way. "Yes, Mr. Sutton. And I appreciate being considered for this job."

"I'll forward you the detailed description of her. All payment will be made upon receipt of the thrall. Good day and good hunting."

Jiro smiled and turned his comm off as he pivoted to return to the restaurant and his place at the table with Kenichi Tsukasa. How fortunate to be able to do two jobs so close together. He hoped the funds he was collecting and the contacts he was making from these various side hustles would give him the power and *influence*—there was that delectable word again—to break off and create his own family organization. Tsukasa was getting old. Jiro had been in touch with the

Western traffickers as well as the Chinese ones. They were eager to do business with him and to restore thrall trade within Edo. He knew it would be deliciously lucrative, and he intended to cut himself a large slice of that pie.

His comm vibrated again, and he saw a message. It was the target's description from Abernathy's assistant. He paused in the doorway of a ramen shop as he read through it, astonished by its inexactitude. No photo. The height, weight, and hair color could be any Central Continent woman, though, he had to admit, just that narrowed the field. Distinguishing characteristics: thrall brand, possibly obscured, and a neck scar. That one helped. He was determined to be the victor in this hunt. He would find and return the thrall. He dropped the comm in his jacket pocket and headed past a few more shops as he returned to his official work.

As he slipped back into the restaurant, he collided with the largest of Tsukasa's bodyguards who was just stepping out the door. He looked sharply at the big man. "Be more careful, Riki." He rolled his eyes. *Foot soldiers*.

"A thousand apologies, Jiro-san." The bodyguard nodded his square head on his almost non-existent neck.

Jiro shook off the collision and headed to the table, his mind planning his trip to Northern Edo, unaware that his comm was no longer in his jacket.

I head out into the dusk of the warm October evening from the physicians' offices where I help out most Tuesdays. I have started staying longer now that Grey goes to her grandmother's for ikebana lessons, and Aiko generously offered to come down from the temple and watch the boys since Takai is on a diplomatic mission—again. I stretch as I walk home along the quiet dirt path. The work here is not exciting, and the pay is low, but it does require that I have to shower beforehand, and I do get to talk to adults, so those two things are enough to make up for any shortcomings. The walk is about three kilometers, and I could hustle, but I am enjoying the serenity and stillness. This half-a-bell walk between the offices and home is my time to think, and I don't want to hurry through it. I take deep breaths of the air as I head up into the foothills where the trees are putting on a show with their yellow, red, and orange leaves. I can hear the little stream that parallels the path, happily bubbling stories of its travels to itself as it skips over rocks. I love the peace of this journey.

The path narrows as I slip into the woods, and the light dims even more. The sounds of the stream recede as I move away from it. Takai and I had a conversation before he left, and I am rolling that about in my mind. He doesn't know why I want to re-enlist. What was it he said? "I'm not speaking ill of the dead, Kat, but Teddy is the one who grounded you. Why would you go back to that rough, boorish life?" He says we can just visit once the banishment year is up. I don't think he understands how important...

My head jerks back. I feel another person behind me, and something around my neck tightens as my air is cut off. I instinctively put my training into use, leaning my body back into my assailant and reaching up with my left hand and grabbing what feels like a small, but strong, beaded chain around my neck. I pull it forward to relieve some of the pressure, and I feel air pass into my body. I quickly pivot and strike what I now see is an Edoan man with the ball of my right hand first at his groin, then at his ear.

He drops his hands, and the garrote falls from my neck, but the man recovers quickly and lashes out at me, using the garrote as a whip. I feel the very end bite into my thigh and jump backward, losing my footing on some rocks at the edge of the path and tumbling to the ground. I swiftly hop up, getting my feet under me, and see him come at me with a push dagger. My hand drops to my thigh for my double-edged knife that Teddy had given me, and then I curse inwardly as I have become complacent here and have started leaving all weapons at home when I go to work. I won't make that mistake again.

I grab a handful of dirt and throw it in this man's face, which slows him enough to allow me to twist out of the path of the dagger that is bearing down on me. I open my hand and tighten my fingers together, so they are like a blade, and bring it down hard on his forearm, putting my full body weight into it. He yelps with pain and his hand releases the knife, which falls into the shadows and is lost from view.

Out of the corner of my eye, I see a large shadow come out of the trees and begin to bear down on us. Two of them. *Okay, then.* I'll take care of the little one first. My assailant gives his arm a shake, and I am shocked as he reaches across into his coat and pulls out a short-muzzle gun—it looks like a Chinese ZHP-59 with a suppressor. *Shit.* Does this guy have a cannon hidden on him somewhere as well? This may end badly for me.

I shift slightly out of the shadow and raise my hands and my head, trying to buy a little time. For some reason, he doesn't fire. He stares at me, his eyes now flitting from my neck to my face and back. His face looks confused, and I hear him murmur, "Scar?" I see his eyes widen, and he drops the arm holding the ZHP ever so slightly. This is my opportunity.

I reach and grab the inside of his wrist with one hand and the slide of the ZHP with the other, leaning my head and body out of the line of fire in the same move. The gun fires past my shoulder, and I feel the slight kickback and then him resisting my grasp and attempting to pull the weapon back toward him.

I move with the direction he is pulling, giving an elbow to his chin, and then I twist his hand until he cries out as his finger is wrenched. When the barrel is pointing at his middle, I jerk the gun back and pull it into my hand, immediately chambering a round. Without hesitation, I fire into his gut. He drops to the ground, moaning, and I pull the slide again, turning to defend myself against the second approaching opponent when I hear a familiar, deep voice: "Are you okay, Kat-san?"

"Riki?" I squint and his face comes into view. My hand drops to point the gun at the earth, and I move my finger from the trigger. I am confused; Riki is one of Kenichi's bodyguards. A huge man by any standard and particularly huge in Edo, I know Riki would never harm me. I take a moment to catch my breath. "I'm fine. Well, a little banged up, but fine," I reiterate. "What are you doing here? And who the fuck is this?" I kick the writhing man on the ground, who moans a bit louder.

Riki gives a short, dry laugh. "He is, I am grieved to say, a member of our family who took on an outside paid job."

My eyes widen a bit. I know that is a huge breach of the rules in the yakuza family Kenichi heads. I look up at Riki who, while immense, is just half a head taller than I am, which makes him tall for an Edoan man. He has an open, honest face with his black hair in a bowl haircut and a van dyke beard and mustache. He stands with his arms crossed in front of him, and his biceps look a bit like tree trunks. I bet if I had pulled the trigger, the bullet would have bounced off his titanic chest. I am really glad I never have to fight Riki. "A paid job? Like, to kill me?"

He nods his massive head.

I sigh loudly. "It's gotta be Abernathy. Damn. I heard him mention my scar." My fingers automatically move to stroke the tiny rise of flesh that runs from my left ear to my right collarbone. I glance at Riki, but his face is passive. He won't reveal anything he hasn't been instructed to. I will have to talk with Kenichi about this, but for now, I look at the man on the ground. This won't go well for him. I am glad. I get offended when people try to kill me. "I guess you can't come home with me and see Grey. She'll be disappointed to have missed you."

Riki's face lights up at the mention of my daughter. He plays with all three children, but he and Grey have had a special friendship ever since her baby-dimpled smile charmed him at the Winterfest when I first met Kenichi. "I will come back. I am sure Tsukasa-san will want to talk with you about this." He motions to the man.

I nod. "Most definitely." I tuck the gun into my belt. Then I extend my arm in friendship to Riki. "Thank you."

He reaches out and grasps my elbow gently. My arm looks like a child's next to his; I can't even reach his elbow. "I will always look out for you and your family, as will Tsukasa-san."

He releases my arm, then picks up the would-be assassin and tosses him over his shoulder as if he weighs nothing. Riki heads toward the village, and I start to walk toward home but then pause. "Should I expect anyone else?"

Riki smiles. "No. This was, foolishly, a one-man operation."

I nod, then spy the errant push dagger half-hidden in the leaves and reach down to pick it up. Riki and I look at each other and then part ways. He heads back toward the village of Kiharu with a soon-to-be-dead man on his shoulder, and I head back into the foothills on my once-again peaceful commute home, now heavier by one dagger and one pistol. Perhaps Edo is not the safe haven I had thought it was. I consider what that could mean for my family and my babies, and this thought sobers me for the rest of the walk.

TWO

Mergers and Acquisitions

NEW DETROIT, OCTOBER 2360

"So, we understand each other then?" Rob Abernathy looked intently at the dark-haired man across the large desk from him.

Alejandro DeLeon worked his jaw for a moment before looking back at the tall, handsome man whom he knew was intent on regaining his position as senator of the Federal Alliance. "Indeed. I shall continue as the face of the business, but you are now my employer and as such will direct its management."

"And I will pay myself accordingly. Though don't worry, Alejandro. As the other cartels have discovered, my business acumen will translate to sizable profits for us all. You will be living a life you only imagined before."

DeLeon's mouth turned up slightly, and he nodded. "Yes, the reports from other businesses have been...positive. I hope you don't think I was reluctant—"

"Not at all," Abernathy cut him off. Rob knew that DeLeon was the last holdout for a reason. His thrall cartel was the most profitable, and DeLeon had been looking to expand his reach before Rob quietly entered the thrall business several years ago after his trial. "The business will thrive as all mine do, and you, sir, will be a rich man. My assistant will contact you with the paperwork and all directives. You will seldom hear directly from me, and as you know, I am never to be mentioned by name with any of your associates. It is a pleasure doing business with you." Rob motioned to the door.

DeLeon hesitated for a moment in his seat, then stood. "Good day, Mr. Abernathy. And I wish you the best in your upcoming Senate campaign. I have no doubt as to the outcome." He smiled tightly, turned, and saw himself out.

Rob leaned back in his comfortable leather chair with its high, winged back and narrowed his eyes. DeLeon would need to be watched closely. His right hand went automatically to his side desk drawer, pulling it smoothly open, and passed over the small pistol he kept loaded and at the ready and the cache of writing utensils until it found what it needed to touch. Rob stroked the disembodied braid of hair he kept in the drawer and smiled. He thought about how he would have to thank Mary/Katrina for putting him on this path. With the acquisition of the DeLeon cartel, he was now the semi-silent partner for all the major thrall enterprises across the globe, and he was making a fortune trafficking people to those who were willing to pay. The thrall business had given him even more markers and power than he had acquired before the trial, and it was all a result of Mary/Katrina's finger-pointing.

He would find her and bring her back to him. He had the assurance from Casey, his assistant, that operatives were scouring the Western continent. Casey had even arranged for some Edonese operatives to search for her, a task made essential after that yakuza boss had banned his people. He had gone as far as sending the bodies of Abernathy's own men back to him after Rob had ignored the ban. That man would have to be

19

dealt with eventually as well, but that was not the priority now. She was. She would be found. He caressed the braid. He thought of her face and her body and how she made him laugh. He would lovingly thank her. Then he would kill her.

THREE

Heave-To

I set the cups of tea on the table for my guests. Kik and Mac are flying kites with their grandfather, Shigeo, for a few hours on this breezy early spring day. I am sure, since the boys are two, this means Shigeo is flying a kite and the boys are watching, or more likely, wandering. Grey has her regular Tuesday after-school ikebana work with her grandmother, Yumiko. I have taken the day off from the physicians' office so I can have my two friends over to my small cabin in the foothills of Mizueyama. One walked carefully down the mountain path, and the other was flown here from the nearest city-ship. His bodyguards stand outside holding the tea I delivered to them. I know Riki has asked to come so he and Grey could have a visit. I love watching the big burly man sit and play delicate little girl games with her.

My friends are seemingly disparate: Aiko is an old priestess of The Way from the Mizueyama Temple. Most of the villagers, including my husband, are a bit terrified of her, but she and I have been friends ever since I was pregnant with Grey, and I came upon her on the mountain path one evening. She had twisted her ankle, so I brought her to my cabin and wrapped

21

it. She and I visited for several hours, and she developed quite a taste for the Warner Wine I had brought from Bosch. Takai was surprised to find us singing and laughing when he arrived home that evening. I had her stay the night wrapped up in blankets on the couch. We have been friends ever since. I am still uninterested in The Way, and that seems to suit Aiko just fine.

Kenichi Tsukasa is the head of the top yakuza family in Edo. I don't discuss his family's business dealings with Kenichi. He and I spend our time together discussing mostly Old Earth books and theater, though I have little time these days for either. I have introduced him to westerns, and he has introduced me to Kabuki.

I was astonished to find that these two friends of mine were acquainted from many years before. They are quite evasive when I ask them about how they met and know each other but were both delighted to reconnect, and now we try to meet up at my cabin regularly.

"It's your move." The slender man with slightly graying temples and a strong bearing gestures to the older woman sitting across the Shogi board from him.

"Give me a moment to think, Kenichi. I am old."

"Ha. Crafty, more like." He rests his elbows on the table, showing the elaborate tattoos on his arms. A red and green dragon spirals along one arm, and on the other, a brilliant orange koi fish frolics amid waves and seaweed, each scale carefully drawn. Kenichi's tattoos are usually covered by his jacket as most Edoans disapprove of them. But now that jacket is tossed casually across a chair in my little cabin's front room.

The priestess of the Temple Way laughs like a schoolgirl, tucking a strand of her still coal-black hair back into the red and white scarf that holds the long tresses back, and moves her

Kakugyo. "There. Promoted." She neatly flips the piece. "Ryuma! Watch your Osho, Kenichi."

The leader of the strongest yakuza family in Edo eyes her under his brows and says with the hint of a smile, "I am the Osho."

Aiko laughs heartily. "That you are."

"So why are there no queens in Shogi?" I ask as I watch the game unfold. I am in line to play the winner. "I like chess where the queen is the most powerful."

"You would," both Edoans say together, and the three of us laugh.

I sit back in my chair and consider an issue I have been contemplating. "Seriously, though. What is it with Edo, and for that matter, Bosch? I knew in the North Country that as a woman, I was of less value than the men and boys. That was told to me from the time I could understand speech. I didn't like it, but at least I could work around it. Be the girl who could work like a boy, who could run a farm and plow and plant and harvest. People liked that. They could hire me to work and get, frankly, better and faster work, and then pay my dad less than if I was a boy. Since I went faster, I could work two or three farms while my brothers took their sweet time on one and got to split the pay with Dad. A couple of farmers' wives used to sneak me a few coins, so I actually had real money to keep." I smile at the memory and run my fingers thoughtfully over the raised scar in the shape of a circle with a "T" inside on my forearm. The brand sits next to the black and red tattoo of a flying pirate vessel with crossed daggers below it that I received when I graduated from the Bosch Pirate Force.

"When I was a thrall, it was clear that being a woman was far more dangerous than being a man—no surprise there. In Bosch and in Edo, though, everyone talks about equality between men and women, but there's always a 'but.'" I look up at my friends.

Kenichi smiles. "You are as good a fighter as any man I know. No 'buts.' You are as capable in performing the tea ceremony as this priestess." He gestures at Aiko who nods graciously. "And you are an expert negotiator, hence the marked decline in our family's involvement with New Earth traffickers." Here, he puts the first two fingers of his right hand to his brow in a salute of honor.

Aiko looks at me with a thoughtful expression. "What qualifier would you add to that?"

I give a rueful smile. "I don't know. Those things are true, and I love that you see that in me. But..." I grin and then lean forward and rub my brow. "It's just...maybe it's the chaos of having small children, but I often wonder, when will *I* get to decide the direction of my life? I mean, Teddy signed me up to enlist in the Bosch Pirate Force after I escaped Bellcoast. He managed my career. Tommy trained me to fight and shoot. My brothers got me into the ring, and the three of us made a bundle of markers for a while. Takai got me to come to Edo. Then a group of old men decided what I could and could not do to serve when I was pregnant. Hell, then Teddy arranged for me to kill him and blow him up, landing me banished, and back in Edo." I half-grin, shake my head, and blink back the tears that begin at this too-recent memory.

Kenichi politely looks away as I compose myself and asks, "And after your year of banishment is up in the fall—what will you do? What do you want?"

I take a deep breath and continue my inventory. "What I want? Well, I want to go back to Bosch and re-enlist in the BPF and try to end trafficking. I want to settle the score with Abernathy. Those two goals have never changed; they've just been forestalled by...life." I make a tight fist and then look around at the homey cabin and relax it. "But Takai brought me to Edo. He rented this cabin. We have lived here for years, had our babies here." I point to the spot in front of the fire where I gave birth to all three children. "He says this is our home. We are settled here. His work is here." I look at my yakuza friend. "And you, Kenichi, you tell me I need to stay in Edo under your protection—under your direction—so Rob Abernathy can't come for me again. But Sweet New Earth, that is a battle I would welcome." Kenichi Tsukasa gives me a side-eye and shakes his head, his eyebrows drawing down. "I mean, I get it. You are all people who care about me. But sometimes I feel as if I am a sailing ship, cutting through the sea but never choosing the course. That I am just being buffeted by the winds around me. Navigating the storm and heavy weather and then just tiding over when the winds briefly calm. Then repeating the cycle when the winds rise again." I look at my two older friends at the table, and they look back at me, their dark eyes holding thoughtful expressions. I smile and sigh a deep sigh and shrug slightly.

Aiko has been listening quietly. She returns my smile and reaches out a wrinkled, age-spotted hand to pat my arm. "Sweet Kat. If you wish to choose the course of your life, stop being the ship and take the helm. Be the captain of your life."

I consider this and nod. As I start to respond, I hear a noise at the door, and it is pushed open as Kik and Mac barrel in. From behind them, I hear Shigeo call, "Tano, Kita!" He only uses their Edoan names. "Wait for me!" By the time he appears at the door, the boys have leaped onto me and are both talking at once about their kite-flying adventure. Moments later, I see Yumiko appear as well, but no Grey. She and Riki must be playing in the yard.

"We need snack!"

"When dinner?"

"Wanna see my kite?"

"Not yours, mine too!"

I look at Aiko and grin. "I am the cabin boy/scullery maid on this cruise. These boys are two of the three captains!"

She laughs and reaches out to take Kik into her lap. He joyfully goes to her, jabbering about kites and all the small things he saw with his grandfather. Mac gives me a wet kiss and then climbs over to Aiko as well, adding his views of the day. I look over and see Kenichi slowly putting on his jacket, his magnificent colored tattoos going back into hiding as my in-laws glower at him.

He smiles at me. "It is time for me to go home, my friend." Then he does something odd. He looks at Yumiko. "I am happy to know that there have been no further calls. Excellent. Let's keep it that way." At this, the superior glare she has on her face shifts momentarily to one of surprise that borders on panic, and she looks quickly away from him to the ground.

Shigeo looks confused. "What do you mean?"

Kenichi simply smiles as he adjusts his jacket and reaches for the door. "Good day, Shima-san. Kat, always a pleasure. Aiko, we will complete the game next time."

"And I will win as usual, you old fox."

He laughs and steps out, motioning to his men. I walk to the door and see Grey joyfully riding on Riki's huge shoulders, picking lilacs from the large bushes that grow in the sun and tucking the flowers behind his ears. He sets her down and receives a hug and a kiss on his massive cheek, and they part ways, my daughter turning and running toward me, undoubtedly hungry for dinner.

I turn to the kitchen to start my scullery tasks. Maybe I'll be promoted to captain. Someday.

FOUR

My Turn
_____

"Dammit, Takai. It's been a year. I want to go home!" I lean forward and slap my hands on the sides of the chair I am sitting in.

Takai responds in his infuriatingly calm diplomat tone. "But, Kat, isn't this home?" He gestures around the cozy cabin with its fire ablaze and warm yosegire quilts on the edge of the sofa.

I shut my eyes and put my hands to my face. "It is." I move my hands and look at my husband. "And it isn't. You know I'm Bosch. It will always be home."

"Actually, Kat, you've lived here in Edo almost as long as you have ever lived in Bosch. You speak the language. You have work. The people here have come to like you. Our children are asleep in their room in our home. *Our children.* Who were born here. In this cabin." Takai's voice is still calm, but I can sense an edge to it, and his features are becoming unyielding.

I let my head fall back as I take a breath, then I look at him and say, "I know. I love it here. I do." I see his face soften. "But I'm not Edoan, I'm Bosch, and I need to see my family!"

27

His face goes taut again. *"We* are your family." He jabs three fingers to his chest and frowns. "Go visit Bosch. Fine. But we live in Edo." He says this with a tone of finality.

How can two people have the exact same conversation this many times? I throw up my hands and stand. "I'm going to go work out. I need to hit something."

"You know, a run would probably calm you down far more than some violent—"

I turn toward him, incredulous. "I'm still a pirate, Takai. I am Bosch." I stomp off to change and box, leaving him shaking his head.

I am freestyling and hitting the bag high and low with all the power I can. I've had this workout room here since just after Grey was born. It's my getaway, like the basement study is for Takai. The kids love to come out and watch me, and I've made them some little gloves so they can hit the bag and mimic my moves. I've stressed to them to only hit the bag, never each other or anyone else, but Grey has some pretty impressive kicks that make me think that she has the makings of a fighter. I keep this to myself. I remember how horrified Takai's mother had been when Grey had stacked a dozen of Yumiko's floor pillows up and then scattered them with a roundhouse kick. Yumiko had looked at me aghast. I'm sure that went on her list of why I am not worthy of her son and her son's children. I had to explain to Grey that kicks and hits needed to be limited to the workout room. But I was proud. I smile. *It was a solid move.*

He really thinks I am going to stay in Edo forever. My breath hisses out as I land a hook. *I've been telling him for most of the year that I want to go back. I need to go back.* Hiss, an uppercut. *I am Bosch.* Hiss. A second hook. *I am Kat Wallace.* Another hook. *I am a pirate.* Hiss. This hook goes to the body. *I will re-enlist.* Hiss. Uppercut. *And he'll just have to deal with it.* Hiss. Hiss. I give the bag a powerful jab-cross. I pause, panting. I look at the world clocks on my personal comm. It's morning in Bosch. I take in a deep breath and make my decision. I have two comms to make. Miles will just be getting to work, and Mama will be up and around.

I put in the number for the MC office. Betsy answers, "Master Commander of Bosch's office. How can I help you?"

I revel in knowing I am finally talking to someone from Bosch. "Hi, Betsy." I let my voice sink in for her.

"Oh, Kat. It's so good to hear your voice." I can hear her smile through the device.

"It's good to hear yours as well. I'm hoping to be there soon to catch up. Is Miles in?" I can feel my voice quiver with emotion.

"I'll transfer you to him," she says efficiently, then, "I can hardly wait to see you!"

Miles' hearty voice comes across the comm. "Kat Wallace! You wasted no time getting in touch. I just got in two minutes ago. So, tell me, are you ready to come home and re-enlist?"

"Yes, sir, Master Commander. I am ready."

My eyes pop open. What time is it? I look at the clock. Sweet New Earth, it's eight bells. I swing my legs out of bed and hear all the little voices coming from the kitchen. I call out, "Takai, I don't know how I overslept. I'll be right there, and you can get to work." The kitchen goes silent and then erupts in giggles, and I hear Takai shushing the kids. I pull a tunic over the leggings I slept in and run my fingers through my cockeyed hair as I dip my feet into my slippers and hurry to the kitchen.

Takai stands with a steaming cup of coffee in my favorite green cup, smiling at me in a way that tells me something is up. Grey giggles and grabs my hand, tugging me toward the front room. "Close your eyes."

"Okay, okay." I take a quick sip of my coffee and then abandon it on the counter to avoid hot spills before closing my eyes and letting Grey and the boys hustle me to the front room.

"Okay, Mama! Open them."

I open my eyes to see several duffels and bags all stuffed full, piled near the front door. The children all start to talk at once at maximum volume. "We go to Bosch!" and, "We see Mama M!" and, "Are you surprised?" They are clapping and laughing and bouncing around the room.

I turn to look at Takai who has rescued my coffee. He comes up, hands it to me, and wraps his arms around me from behind, whispering in my ear, "I thought a visit back right away would ease your heart a bit. Go take a nice long shower while I negotiate with our tiny terrorists and then you can fly us all to Bosch."

I take a big enough swig of the coffee to make my next move safe, and I turn and pull Takai to me in a one-hand/one-cup hug. Then I kiss him and whisper back, "You're the best." And I receive a very nice kiss in return before I scurry back to our room to get ready for our first trip home post-banishment.

"When are you planning on telling him you re-enlisted?" Mama comes and sits next to me at the table in the family home, where I am blinking sleepily. Everyone else is in bed since our bodies are on Edo time. I had a small nap but want to make the most of my time with Mama.

I blow air out through my cheeks. "I don't know. I don't have to report until December…." I suck air in through my teeth and close my eyes. "Maybe never? Do you think he'd notice?"

Mama looks at me askance. "He'd notice, Kat." She takes a sip of her evening tea that smells of cinnamon. "Are you two okay?"

I shrug. "Remember when you told me that relationships moved like the tide?" She smiles and nods. "I think we are just at an ebb. Little kids. Busy life. Also, he is pretty clear about not wanting to move to Bosch. But it's his turn, dammit. But he did plan this trip, which is amazing." It feels good to have Mama to talk with again.

We spent the first half-bell after I stepped in the door holding each other and crying, both of us mourning Papa and my part in his death. Even though it's been a year, I never got to mourn with my family. I still can't with Peter, Paul, and Mimi. Mama says they aren't quite ready to see me, and I understand. I killed their father. It was at his request, but still, dead is dead.

Mama and I, though, have generally fallen back into our comfortable, talk-about-anything relationship. I run a hand through my newly trimmed curls. Mama took care of my scraggly hair before we had our early dinner.

"It was very sweet of him, yes. But turn-taking is something to be agreed upon together, dear, not just assumed." Mama stretches her hands out toward me on the table.

"Well, I have said it enough times. He knows what I want." I crinkle my brows and shrug while taking her hands.

"And what do you want, Kat?" Her warm smile is such a gift to have back.

I squeeze her hands and lean forward. "I told Aiko I wanted to be the captain of my own ship. I want to be in charge of my own life. Does that sound odd?"

I see her smile shift and her eyes take on a far-away look. "I remember when your brothers and sister were small. At times, I felt like every day was simply made to survive. My mother would tell me to 'enjoy every minute. Children grow so fast.' Easy for her to say. She didn't have to deal with the three little ones. But I would try to make a point to stop and breathe and let go of my own ambitions for a time. Eventually it was the season for me to blossom. So, no, Kat, it doesn't sound odd, just...challenging. It sounds as though you are ready now."

"I am." I am earnest in my response. "And I've told Takai that."

"Telling and agreeing are not the same. He has been traveling quite a bit this year, hasn't he?"

I shrug. "Well, 'the diplomatic corps must be visible.'" I chuckle as I quote my father-in-law. And then I nod. "Yes, he has. And I don't see that changing."

Mama smiles at me and pours me a small glass of wine that will put me to sleep. "Is it hard with him gone?"

I give a melancholy smile, thinking of all the nights alone in bed and all the days taking care of the children and the house and dealing with my in-laws. If it hadn't been for Aiko and Kenichi... I nod and feel tears prick in my eyes. But then I take a breath. "It will be fine. But I think I'll wait until we are back in Edo to tell him."

Mama tilts her head to the side and puts her warm hand on my arm. "Don't wait too long, dear. No one wants to feel duped."

FIVE

Return

There's only the hint of wind, so the flakes fall steadily, covering any brown or green that still remains outside and mounding on the windowsill in a soft, rising curve. It's been falling almost daily, which is unusual for mid-November. It is so peaceful in the house. The boys actually are napping, which, at three years old, is a sporadic event at best. I just checked on them, and they are curled with their heads together as if they fell asleep whispering to each other, which is likely exactly what happened. Grey is tucked in on the big bed, wrapped in quilts, reading to her favorite stuffed moose, and Takai sits in front of the fire quietly reading a book on China in the twenty-first century in the front room. Me? I'm about to detonate a bomb.

"Hey, love. Are you in a place you can pause?" I sit down near my husband's knees on the big, padded ottoman that opens to hold blankets and quilts, settling the explosive neatly on his lap. Takai looks up from the research tome he is studying and smiles. I wonder if he holds a grudge against the Chinese for imprisoning him years ago. I would. I mean, it worked out. I rescued him and we had our first kiss. And our second and third...I refocus on my incendiary.

He closes the book, marking his spot with a slip of paper that Grey has drawn pink flowers on, sets it on the nearby side table, stretches, and yawns. "I need to take a break. I may make some tea. Interested?" He starts to stand.

"Um, maybe. But can you wait for a moment? I wanted to tell you something." I fiddle with the detonation cord. He sits down, looking at me with anticipation written on his face. It's a friendly look. We have been back in flow since our trip to Bosch, and things have been comfortable and loving.

"Sure. What's on your mind?" He smiles warmly at me, and I see love in his eyes. I set the blasting cap.

I take a deep breath and look back at him. "I re-enlisted in the Force. Recruitment classes start in two weeks, and I've arranged for us to rent the little white house from Mama, who is also willing to help with childcare while I am confined to base during the week." Boom.

Miles hands me a glass with whiskey. "Is this some of Teddy's stash?" I ask as I gratefully accept the glass.

"No. He put all his best stuff somewhere else after he retired. I expect you know the likely places." He grins at me as he sits down behind the big, mahogany desk.

I laugh. "I have some ideas. I'll go looking after graduation." I take a sip and nod approvingly.

He wrinkles his brow. "So, how are things with you and Takai?"

"He is willing to speak to me again as of this morning. I suppose that's something." I shrug and set the glass on the desk. "Of course, what he said was that he had accepted a three-year captaincy on the colonial settlement ship *FA Venturer*. He leaves the week before graduation." I cross my arms and sit back in my chair.

It has been ten days since I announced my plan and leveled our life in Edo and five days before my enlistment begins. As I attempt to take control of my own life, I have begun keeping a mental tally of my good decisions and not-so-good ones. Enlistment: *good*. Delay in informing spouse: *not-so-good*. Though in my defense, when Naya Clark had tossed me that lifeline of a one-year banishment instead of the lifetime one I had anticipated, I knew I would return to regain my Bosch citizenship. This was never a secret. I suspect Takai really hoped I would forget Bosch and my "pirate ways and soldier games" as he often calls them and stay settled and peaceful in our mountain cabin in Edo.

"Is this like a *separation* separation?" Miles leans forward, his face clouded with what I imagine is worry. I chuckle to myself. He's taking over all of Teddy's jobs, not just the Master Commander one, and it makes me feel warm inside.

I tip my head backward and close my eyes. "I don't know. Maybe? But it's not like I don't want to be married to him. I just have to be here and do this as well." I lean forward, pick my glass back up, and take a long drink.

Miles studies me for a long minute, and I watch as the creases around his eyes shift as he considers what I've said. "Stuart and I separated once. I mean, he's an artist. He doesn't get the whole 'duty to battalion and Bosch and the BPF' thing." He shrugs.

I give a sympathetic laugh and nod. It is not an uncommon story for the Pirate Force. Miles continues, "What helped was when I made an effort to make space for him. That's when we bought the place out in District Four near the beach. Fixing it up all these years has been a great connector for us."

"But you were both in the same country, which I think helps. I think I pretty well fumbled my first attempt at taking charge of my life post-babies and banishment." I lean my face on my hand with my elbow propped on the desk, swirling my whiskey in my glass and studying its motion.

Miles claps his hands together, which makes me jump a little. "How about this: How about I arrange for a pilot and vessel that can take you and the kids for visits to his ship after graduation? Those colony ships are behemoths and will have plenty of room for a vessel to land."

I stare at the MC. "That'd be great but a bit over the top, especially for a zero-recruit returning from banishment." I am gratified and astonished by the offer and its generosity.

"Nonsense. It's what Teddy would have wanted, and I still take orders from him! And no one really knows about the banishment thing."

I laugh and then look at Miles skeptically. "One: It's good to know someone other than me is still taking orders from Teddy, and two: You are crazy if you think the rumors aren't going to be more extravagant than reality when it comes to Teddy's death and my part in it."

Miles laughs as well, and we sit quietly for a few minutes. I am thinking of Teddy and the times I spent in this office with him. I imagine Miles is as well.

I hear him clear his throat, and I look toward him. "So, I have a recommendation for you."

"Let's hear it." I am coming to really appreciate Miles' friendship and counsel.

"I think you should plan to attend Officer Training School after recruitment." His face is open, and he looks totally serious about his statement.

"Miles...," I start.

"Listen, Kat. I know it's an extra six months of training, but then you'd be a lieutenant and could move up the ranks." He nods at me, and he is in earnest.

I down the rest of my drink and stand up, grinning. "Not a fucking chance, Miles. I am not qualified to be an officer."

"What do you mean? After OTS, you will be." His hands and arms are turned over as if to show me how easy the choice is.

"Miles, I can't be an officer in some fancy vest and buttons." I see him straighten his vest as I say this. "I'm not a pain in the ass." I put my hands on my hips and give a nod of finality.

Miles stands up and stares at me for a moment, and his face is unreadable. Then he starts to laugh. "Excuse me?" He is laughing so hard, he can't get words out. He takes a deep breath. "Kat Wallace, if that's the main attribute needed to be an officer..." More guffaws. "...then I have never met anyone more highly qualified than you!" He bends over with a new fit of laughter.

I refuse to even smile. I simply eye my future Master Commander and turn my middle finger to him, causing him to cough and sputter as he laughs. He is wiping tears from his eyes as I walk out the door, and I can still hear his deep laugh echo as I make my way down the hallway.

It's the first Saturday night since recruitment began, and I had hoped to be home before the kids went to bed, but I didn't leave the base until late because the officers wanted to caution all the young recruits against too much drinking and partying in the city. I had heard the same lecture years ago and was pretty sure it was falling on deaf ears now as it did then. And anyway, it didn't apply to me. My Saturday night was going to consist of walking home, peeking at my sleeping children, taking a long bath with a glass of wine, and hoping not to reignite The Climate Wars with my husband.

I come downstairs after fulfilling the first three parts of my night. I peer into the kitchen, dining room, and living room: Takai isn't to be seen. Then I hear bumping coming from the spare room off the living room. I open the door, and there is Takai, pushing a desk into position near a nice wooden bookcase.

"It's a nice room," I venture. "Can I help?"

He glances toward me. Very little has been said between us since we arrived in Bosch and he then announced his plan for the next few years. "It is a nice room. I think I'll claim it as my study. The books I am not taking to the *Venturer* can go on the shelves, and there's a cabinet I can keep my research materials in."

"Good idea." I move toward him and touch his arm gently. He pulls away and I step back. "Are we ever going to be okay again?" I'm practically pleading.

He starts to put books on shelves, not looking at me. "Kat, you got what you wanted. You are back in Bosch and back to your pirate ways and soldier games. Did you have to completely uproot all our lives to do it? Yes. But, hey, at least we aren't on the list of the family members you are willing to blow up."

I stand stunned by the harshness of his words. I consider turning and walking upstairs and simply going to bed. But then I hear myself lob a salvo. "Well, you haven't exactly suffered mightily the past few years. You've been happy to live off the markers those 'pirate ways and soldier games' earned while you've learned to dress up, sip champagne, and rub elbows with the diplomats from a dozen nations or sit in a library and read for hours on end. And I'm pretty sure some of those markers have paid for those 'quiet' dinners you have with some of the more attractive lady diplomats."

His head turns quickly to me, his hand brushing the hair near his ear, and his voice is elevated. "Still on about that, are you? Don't come at me with your insecurities, Kat Wallace. My friendships are simply that. Friendships. Maybe if you weren't so reckless and reactive, you might have a friend to have dinner with too!"

I come closer to him, and I say quietly in my deadliest tone, "I am reckless, and I am reactive, and if I ever find out that there was more to those 'dinners' than food, you and whoever was at your table will be on the list of people I plan to blow up." I glare at his wide eyes and turn on my heel and head to bed. Boom.

SIX

Reenlistment

Colonel Gialani Ka'ne adjusted her uniform and her jacquard vest and picked a small piece of lint off her sleeve before she approached the woman at the desk just outside of the Master Commander's office. "Good morning, I'm Colonel Ka'ne. I have an eleven-bell meeting with the MC."

"Good morning, dear. I'm Betsy. He's running a few minutes behind, so just have a seat and he'll be right with you."

The Colonel took a seat in one of the brocade-upholstered straight-back chairs in the office. She had come into the Bosch Pirate Force a decade ago, an early part of the wave of women being actively recruited to serve and to integrate into the Force. There had only been eight women in her recruitment class, but that was apparently double the number from only a few years before that. And of the eight, four had decided to attend officer training. Gia and the other three women from OTS still got together occasionally to have a glass of wine and talk about the Force and their part in it as well as share how their families were doing.

For her part, Colonel Ka'ne had her eye on a commandership and had worked hard to move steadily up in rank over the past ten years. She had made Colonel last year and now was looking to put together a flight unit that would shine, attracting the necessary attention needed for her to be elected Commander.

Gia was descended from peoples who escaped the drowning of the low islands in the Great Sea generations upon generations ago and was proud of her heritage. She felt it melded nicely with the pirate heritage of most of the other Bosch citizenry, including her husband. She was taller than her ancestors, muscular, and fit. Her long, full, dark hair was typically kept in a bun, and she had deep, dark eyes and a ready smile when she was off work talking with her husband and children, but she kept the smile under wraps with the recruits, the non-coms, and the junior officers, instead using her expressive eyebrows to send messages of approval or disapproval. It was a technique that had served her well through the years.

"Some tea, dear?"

Gia looked up and saw the MC's assistant (Betsy, wasn't it?) holding a steaming cup out to her and smiling. There was something about her smile that made Gia feel safe and at home, and she broke her own rule and smiled warmly back, gratefully accepting the cup.

"Thank you. It's a bit chilly out." The Colonel nodded to the older woman. As she took a sip of the rich, fragrant drink, the heavy wooden door opened, and Master Commander Miles Baldwin-Bosch came toward her. His winter uniform was very much like hers, with a long-sleeved black tunic and a pocketed black and red vest. Of course, he wore man's pants while she wore leggings, and the brocade and buttons on their vest denoted their ranks, with his sporting the gold edging and embroidery befitting his office.

She quickly set her cup on the nearby table as she stood and saluted, her fist to her chest.

He smiled and returned the salute. "Thank you for your patience. I had some comms that ran a bit long this morning. Please come sit down and bring your tea. Betsy, could I...?" The MC turned and found his assistant already holding a cup of warm tea for him to take. "You are nothing short of a magician, Bets."

"The magic is in the licorice tea on these chilly days." Betsy smiled.

The MC accepted the cup in one hand and motioned the Colonel toward his open door.

"Please, take a seat, Colonel." The MC indicated a comfortable-looking chair in front of a rather magnificent inlaid desk as he moved behind it to sit.

"So, I understand you are putting together a flight unit, and you've got Tom Pikari. He's quite an engineer." The Master Commander looked over the table to Gia.

"Yes, Master Commander," Gia began.

"Please, call me Miles in here. If your past progress in rank is any indication, I imagine it won't be too long before you are sitting at the General's table."

Gia straightened and raised her chin at this compliment. "Well..." She felt slightly hesitant, but he had invited the familiarity. "Thank you, Miles. I don't know if the General's table will have a space for me, but truth be told, it is on my professional agenda wish list."

"Good. Now tell me about this flight unit."

"It's almost complete with top-notch people. I am only short a pilot. Which I know is the linchpin. Unfortunately, Captain Warner is not interested in switching units, so I am looking for new talent."

Miles nodded. "And where are you looking for this new talent?"

"It's been challenging. I won't lie. But I understand there are some very capable fliers running cargo routes." Gia shrugged. Finding a good pilot willing to quit their unit had been an ongoing frustration for her.

"Those pilots have to be not only capable but also willing to cope with the isolation that comes with those long flights. Not exactly fighter pilot skills but likely could be taught," Miles said evenly.

Gia decided to take the opportunity in front of her. "Do you have any other suggestions?"

The MC leaned back and looked off to the ceiling, rubbing his chin with his hand as if he was deeply considering her question. "Well, now…" She watched as he tapped his lips with the first two fingers of his right hand. "What about the recruit class?"

Gia was sure she heard him wrong. "Excuse me?" She had to consciously keep her eyebrows neutral, though they were fighting to drop to a disapproving crease.

"This new recruit class. Sergeant Cowper has mentioned there are some very capable recruits. Perhaps you should take a turn on duty with the class and use that time to scope out any talent that might be appropriate." Miles was now leaning his chin onto his clasped hands with his elbows on his desk, his face open as if the statements he was making were entirely reasonable. Gia wasn't sure what to think, but she knew how to be political.

"I think that is a very intriguing idea, MC—I mean, Miles." She smiled at him, though she thought perhaps he was either putting her on or his mind was slipping. Recruits had to complete about eighty bells on the simulators before they even touched a real vessel, and the recruit class had only been in session for four weeks, so they were barely off the simulators.

Miles hit his desk gently with two fists and smiled as he began to stand up. "It's decided then. I'll let Sergeant Cowper know you are going to take the next two-week shift as the officer-in-charge. That should give you ample time to see…to see if there is any talent that might work."

Gia now let her eyebrows drop. This seemed to all be a ruse to get another OIC for the recruits. It was not a duty many officers were particularly fond of as it required them to stay several nights on base and patrol the dorms. "Miles…" She relaxed her face and sighed as she, too, began to stand to leave. "Thank you for the opportunity. I will let you know if I discover any prodigy." She saluted.

The Master Commander smiled and saluted.

This time, my recruitment class has sixty people, and over half of them identify as women. That delights me. It's a huge shift from the four out of fifty-three in my first class. It's also a helluva lot easier going through recruitment a second time. In the first place, I don't have to be "the worst recruit ever" this time. In fact, I've started watching who the sergeant earmarks as "the worst" and subtly giving them a boost where they struggle—either through a classroom review or some tips when we fly, fight, and shoot. I try to stay in the background, positioning myself carefully in the invisible middle, but I'm secretly delighted when the sergeant or the classroom instructors are surprised by a recruit's improvement. And secondly, since I already know almost all the basic classroom information, I now get to absorb details.

As I walk to the mess for lunch, I can hear new recruits

quizzing each other on these details. I play a game with myself as I pass the amiable groups, trying to see how quickly I can answer all the questions posed by the time I have passed them. I smile and wave a bit but don't even try to join them. I tell myself it's because they are too young, but really, I like doing things my way, though I can hear Teddy's grizzled voice in my head telling me to "make connections."

The afternoons and evenings are dedicated to understanding the various missions the Bosch troops will run. I remember when Teddy first schooled me about the history of the Bosch and central product of the Bosch economy. "Our forebearers, enslaved after the floods and fires of the 22nd century, became seafaring marauders having taken over the ships where they were held as thralls. They pirated and freed others who were enslaved and formed alliances with other newly free seaborne thralls. The tales of the Golden Age pirates had been recalled and spun and we embraced the code. With our own adjustments, of course." Here he had winked at me. "Under Master Commander Hizir Bosch the fleet came ashore to this island almost a century ago, and while mining clay for bricks, discovered in the surrounding peat bogs, veins of a sparkling material they named Glitter. Someone decided to smell it and taste it and discovered, as the records tell us, 'twas better than the rum and spirits for easing pain and celebrating'. Then we discovered what the rest of the planet would do for a taste of it. The original Bosch saw the trade as a way to accumulate markers without having to plunder. A win for everyone."

The Bosch are still pirates. Teddy told me when I initially arrived in Bosch that while marauding was no longer part of the culture, a little push and perhaps a subtle show of weaponry during Glitter negotiations could certainly increase the markers collected. And if there were treasures that could be quietly liberated, all the better.

The second type of mission is my favorite, though. New Earth is not without its petty—and occasionally, not so petty—conflicts. The FA and China in particular have a tendency to stir up all sorts of disputes that we Bosch want no part of. However, a Bosch unit—or as I prefer, a solo trooper—could "happen to be in the neighborhood" and perform an extraction or partake in intelligence gathering for a price. And again, if a quality bit of booty could be lifted…well, we are pirates.

I know that extraction and intelligence gathering are highly lucrative parts of the Bosch Pirate Force economy. Back when he spoke to me, I would often say to Takai that this was where the real diplomacy took place, and he would chuckle as though it were a joke and shake his head. But I have actually seen both short- and long-term conflicts resolved with Boschian negotiation during these types of missions.

One thing non-Bosch often don't understand is that we are clear on what is wrong and what is right. I remember a conversation I had with Phil Reston during the Abernathy trial.

"Phil, the Bosch will not tolerate evil!" This phrase is so common in Bosch, I've seen it stitched on wall hangings and once even saw a coffee mug with the saying on it at a knick-knack shop in District Four.

I must have been on the twelfth time of saying it when Phil breathed out with exasperation. "Isn't that a bit rich for a people whose major economic export is a drug? And who think nothing about barging into other countries and taking things and people for a price?"

I laughed. "Well, we are pirates, Phil. But we have a moral compass your government may want to borrow on occasion, particularly when they are outward-bound. Savvy?"

He didn't say I was wrong.

All the missions, whatever the type, require skills beyond being able to fly, fight, and shoot. Recruits need to develop cultural understanding, tactical abilities, expert recon skills, and excellent prowess in world languages. And there are no hard and fast rules, no matter what anyone says. In fact, once, when an instructor was preaching on the inviolability of some set of rules, I leaned toward a group of fresh-faced recruits and said, sotto voce, "Well, they're more like guidelines, really." Then I gave them my best pirate's wink. They laughed nervously and immediately went back to taking copious notes, leaving me to finish my comedic routine in my head. Moral of the story: I don't need rules. Just decent judgment. And I have that.

I complain to Miles one evening after surreptitiously slipping away from the dorms to have a whiskey with him in the office. "These are a bunch of green kids for the most part. It seems damn unfair for me to compete with them."

Miles scoffs. "You'd be at the top of the class with our most seasoned commanders, Kat. Focus less on that and more on, say, leadership. That's what Teddy would have wanted."

I roll my eyes. Still with the leadership. "I don't really want to be a leader." *At least I don't want to be told I should lead.*

"Too bad, Kat." He shrugs. "You have always led. Your units, your missions, your family. It's what you do. You just need to find a way to do it without leaving so many bodies in your wake."

I consider these statements. I did like leading my teams on the *Kingfisher*. I should call Dale. He always has good advice. I conjure an image of Takai walking the deck on the *Venturer* as its captain. Three years. Is my marriage one of the bodies in the wake? I hope not. My watch gently buzzes, pulling me from my thoughts. I glance at it and then stand quickly. "Yikes, gotta get back to the nursery." I finish my whiskey with one quick swallow.

"Ever the diplomat…. Making friends, are you?" Miles chuckles as he calmly watches me from his seat at his desk.

"Friends? Are those the ones that become the bodies I leave in my wake?" I quip as I grin at Miles and slip out the door.

I go to the back side of the dorm, where the heat pumps are set up. This is my escape hatch. Fred, Rahim, and I used it a few times back in the days of my first recruitment when we were late coming back from the gym. None of these kids have figured it out yet, and I do not plan to have that be my contribution to the class. In my head I tally: *good decision.* The screen comes away easily, and I just need to jiggle the window a bit. It is cold out here, and I didn't bring a coat. I am intent on my task when I hear someone clear their throat. My head comes up, and I take a breath in.

"Excuse me, Troop?" It's Colonel Ka'ne. She has just come on today as the OIC. Shit. I turn and hop to the ground.

"Colonel Ka'ne, ma'am." I stand at attention, sort of. I keep one hand at my face, my finger across my mouth. I had a couple of whiskeys with Miles, and I'm sure my breath reeks of it. I see her thick eyebrows go up briefly, and she is not smiling.

She gives me a disparaging look and says, "Troop. Attention."

I drop my hand and assume the proper attention pose. My feet are together, and my left hand is at my side with my right in a fist clasped to my center chest in the Bosch salute. I decide

I will just hold my breath. As I do so, I feel those whiskies in my knees and hope I don't have to hold this posture for long.

The Colonel looks at me, and her dark eyebrows cock to the side. How does she do that with them? She leans a bit toward me, so her face is right next to mine, and waits. And waits. I am determined not to breathe out on her. But I can only hold my breath for so long. We keep the pose, me like a mouse in the military and Colonel Cat is toying with me. The image and the situation make me start to smile, and finally, I let my breath out in a steamy whoosh that likely smells like the back of a bar, then take a fresh one in.

She pulls her face back quickly, shaking her head at the scent of whiskey that emanates from me. "Wow," she begins, "out of the dorms without permission *and* drinking. Where off-base did you go?" Her eyebrows are down in a way that states deep disapproval. I try to copy them, but I am sure I just look confused. I wonder if she could teach me how to make mine do that.

"I did not go off-base, ma'am."

"There is no liquor on base, Trooper Wallace."

Well, great. She knows my name. I imagine she figures she has caught me in a lie. But generally, I don't lie. I just omit things and distract from those facts that are more awkward.

I step into an at-ease stance and gesture with my hands. "Well, now, that's not entirely accurate. There's none for sale, that's true, but there is liquor if you know where to look."

"And where would that be?" She doesn't look like she believes me. Ah, well, the truth will out.

"Master Commander's office." I give a little shiver. I'm cold.

Silence. Her brows are very still. There is a long pause, and I attempt to focus on her and on keeping my body from swaying. *When did I get this drunk? Must have been that final gulp.*

"You are confessing to breaking into the Master Commander's office? And stealing his liquor?" The Colonel's eyes go wide.

I am feeling very bad for her. I really love having a woman as the officer in charge. So, in what I believe will go on the tally sheet as a good decision, I confess fully and blurt out, "Oh, no, ma'am. I was invited, and I drank with Miles as usual."

Silence. She narrows her eyes, but it doesn't seem to be in anger. They shift to the left and then right and then run along the ground. She is remembering something.

"You are the old Master Commander's...what?" She pauses. "Adopted daughter?" Another pause. "Friend?"

Don't forget assassin, I think grimly but nod. "Yeah. Both, really."

Colonel Ka'ne looks intently at me, and there is an audible pause before she says, "I see. Please accept my condolences on his loss. I know it's been over a year, but I still remember when my mother died, and it's been several years. It's hard." She looks at me curiously, then adds, "Whatever the circumstances." She shrugs with her right shoulder.

No one has ever said anything like this to me in the past year. At the time, no one, other than Mama, ever considered that I was grieving the loss of Teddy. Instead, the concern was what I did and how I would be punished. Even Takai was more concerned with getting back to Edo and away from the chaos of Bosch. I am touched in a way that is unexpected, and I feel tears well in my eyes. "Um…" I look at the ground and blink fast, then look at the Colonel, whose face has softened. "Thank you. I… It has been hard."

She nods and then her focus shifts. "So, about this." The Colonel uses her finger in a gesture that encompasses the window and the heat pump.

I shrug. "This recruit class is great. Lots of women." We

both smile and nod at this statement. "But they are pretty young. It's nice to talk with someone who you share some history with—hence, Miles. He is an old, dear friend. A mentor."

The Colonel looks at me. "Walk with me." She motions away from the dorm, toward the officer in charge's office and quarters.

"One sec…." I see her look a bit shocked, but I can't just leave the window half-jimmied. I quickly hop back up, fasten it, and replace the screen. I am careful to make no sound as I do so, then I hop back down. "All set. Lead on, Colonel."

I see her face twitch slightly, and I hope it is because she is suppressing a smile.

So, it turns out Azizi has a delivery service from his grocery, and Gia and I—she said I should call her Gia instead of Colonel—are laughing as I describe some of the antics of the twins. We are on the second of the three bottles of wine that we had delivered. Gia has two daughters, fairly close in age to my kids, and we have been swapping stories about them.

"So, given what we do, how do you deal with arguments and fights between the kids?" I am leaning back in a straight-backed chair with my feet up on a fairly small desk—not exactly Master Commander-type decor for the OIC.

"What do you mean, 'What we do'?" Gia reaches for the bottle again.

"Well, we fly, fight, and shoot. Aren't those the skills we are told to hone? How do we tell our kids not to fight when that is such a big part of our lives?"

"We don't fight them…."

I laugh. "No, but I had a space in Edo for working out, and

the kids always loved the heavy bag. Especially Grey." I think wistfully of my babies. I hate not seeing them every day. There are three empty spaces inside me longing to be filled with their faces and voices. Mama and Mimi are helping Takai take care of them through this recruitment time, and then when Takai leaves... My thoughts trail off, and I look up toward the ceiling. Then I plumb the depths of my wine glass. "How do you keep your marriage together?"

Gia looks a bit surprised by this pivot in topic. I can tell by the way her eyebrows come up. Those eyebrows are really a great feature. "I don't know. Red and I want the same things for our family. Also, he knows what I want career-wise, and I know what he wants. We push each other to get there."

I laugh ruefully as I get up to pour more of the dry, ruby-colored wine. "That is not the best news. My career is the source of virtually all our fights." I consider what I have said. "Well, that and all the women Takai seems to have 'friend-ships' with." I make air quotes with the hand that is not holding the wine.

"Does he cheat?" Gia is looking at me with her brows drawn deeply down between her eyes.

I tip my head at the question. It certainly is one I have asked myself before numerous times. Mostly, I just try to ignore the messages from and the stories about the 'lovely young diplomat' from...pick a country, any country. I love him, and I want this marriage to survive. "No?" I look off to the side. I look back at Gia. "Maybe?" I sigh. "We have been so deep in child-rearing the past seven years that we hardly have time alone together. And he gets to travel and meet new people, see new things, and I am in the cabin in the foothills of Mizueyama and simply have been grateful to shower once a week. I can see where attraction might wane."

"Are you insane? It's not about the kids. He is married to you, and those are his kids you are raising…"

"Takai is a great father. There is nothing he wouldn't do for our babies." I hear the start of a defensive tone in my voice.

She looks at me with incredulity written on her face.

"I know." My voice softens and I can feel a flush of both anger and shame start in my neck. "I want a marriage like Miriam and Teddy had, like you and Red have. I'm just not sure how to get there. Maybe I shouldn't have agreed to be married. I get so angry when I wonder if his friendships are more than that, but then he tells me that it is all part of the diplomatic dance and I am overreacting. And I do have a tendency to do just that. So, I have chosen to believe him. But coming back to Bosch has created a whole other set of issues, and his solution is to run away and captain a ship in the Southern Sea." I take a long drink of my wine and sit down with a huff.

Gia twists her face slightly. "You deserve to follow your path too, Kat. I can't believe you are having to do recruitment twice." She shakes her head. We talk a bit about how I ended up in the recruitment class at this point in my life. It seems the bones of the "Who blew up the Master Commander?" story are pretty accurate: Some adopted child took him up in a vessel, and "boom." Said child was banished for a year and is now back. Please fill in details as desired.

"What did you do on base before the babies and the banishment?" Gia tilts her head to the right and looks at me expectantly.

"I flew missions—Glitter and extractions. Did a pretty good job of it too." I say this with a combination of wistfulness and nonchalance. I can't wait to get in a real vessel again.

There is a pause, and Gia goes quite still looking at me. Her voice drops slightly. "You're a pilot?" There is a second pause. "With experience?"

I nod. "Mmm-hmm. A pretty skilled one if I do say so myself. And I do." I grin at her.

I see her re-animate and start to chuckle, and then she leans forward and shakes her head. "Master Commander Miles Baldwin-Bosch is one shrewd man."

I'm not sure what she's referring to, but I remember what he had said to me. I rub my hands together—a thing I do when nervous and thinking. "He says I leave bodies in my wake. Maybe that's why I have very few friends." I chuckle, not knowing why I feel so vulnerable. "So...I get it if you want to steer clear of the danger that is me." I gesture at myself and grin nervously.

"I'm pretty good at taking care of myself and others. I'll be okay." She grins back.

I hear the clock on the green chime two bells as I open the third bottle. I am going to be tired and have a headache in the morning. But I have made a friend as well.

SEVEN

Graduation

BOSCH, JANUARY 27, 2362

Graduation day is chilly with bits of sleet in the air, but the recruitment class is exuberant, nevertheless. Mama and the children are here at the ceremony, and she and Gia have arranged for Gia's husband, Redmond, or "Red" as Gia calls him, to bring their daughters to meet up with Grey, Kik, and Mac to see if they get on. The ceremony is very traditional, and each of the five generals speaks, then Miles gives a moving speech about commitment and loyalty. I only half-hear it now as he had asked me to listen to him rehearse it last evening, making me miss the smoker once again. I've never made it to one yet. This graduation is particularly special as it includes the unveiling and dedication of a statue. I watch as Miriam and Peter, Mimi, and Paul come forward after the speeches, and Mama pulls the cord that releases the crimson fabric. There on the pedestal, just a bit larger than life, stands the old Master Commander, Teddy Bosch. The sculpture was initially underwritten and commissioned by an "anonymous donor." It so happens the anonymous donor was a certain banished person. When word leaked about the project, contributions were received from all over Bosch, both the city and districts, because Teddy was, well, Teddy—well-known and well-beloved.

The graduating class, most of whom are tremendously hungover, all stand on the stage at attention. Each graduate is then named and walks across the stage, where they are bestowed with a three-corner hat and a sash in blood-red in keeping with the pirates of the ancient times. My name is one of the last called, and I feel tears well as I receive my hat and sash for a second time. I stand and wait for the ceremony to conclude as I contemplate the hat and sash. As Miles dismisses the class for a week of leave, I smile and walk to the newly dedicated statue. I know my next move. I climb up the pedestal and boost myself until I am almost eye to eye with Statue Teddy as he stands with his hands on his hips and overlooks the parade grounds.

"Here." I lean toward him and say in a loud whisper, "This is for you, you old bastard." Then I smile as I place my hat on his head and wrap my sash around his middle. I gaze at my handiwork, stand on tiptoe, and kiss his statue nose, then shimmy down. A sizable crowd of people has gathered to watch this exchange between a newly graduated recruit and the statue of a recently dead Master Commander. I look back at them as they look at me, perplexed expressions on their faces. I smile, shrug, and go to find my children.

I see them close to the front, holding Mama's hands. Mimi, Ryann, and their three kids are there as well. Mimi and I reconnected several weeks ago and it has been wonderful. And what's more, I see Paul, Elise, and their kids. Neither he nor Peter have wanted to see me since I've been back, so this is monumental.

My heart leaps at the sight of my babies. I watch them start to bounce and pull at Mama's hands as I start to jog toward them. Suddenly, the boys break free of their Mama M's grip. I watch as they run to me, gamboling about like spring lambs until I kneel to wrap my arms around them. We are a mass of hugs, and we overbalance and fall backward. Kik, Mac, and now Grey, who has caught up with her brothers and is squealing, throw themselves into my arms as we cuddle on the chilly, frosted ground. I kiss them each dozens of times and hug them fiercely, listening to their stories from the past week. I clamber up, trying to keep contact with each of my babies. Paul is standing in front of me and reaches down to help me up. We don't say anything, but his eyes are glowing, and I have to imagine mine are as well. We hug and then hug again. The children now are gravitating toward their cousins, content that I am home. I see Mimi watching with a smile. Then Mama comes up, grabs my hands, and looks at me with teary eyes. "Oh, Kat. Well done. Papa would be so proud. I love that you gave him your hat and sash. It makes him look quite dashing." She looks over toward the statue and gives a sigh. "When Takai told us that you wanted to commission the statue with the markers of yours the Council surrendered to us, we were so astonished. And so pleased. But we kept it quiet as you asked."

"Papa always joked about having a statue made," Paul says, speaking for the first time.

"Right? It seemed like the thing to do." I smile over at him, and Elise comes and gives my hand a squeeze. Tally sheet: *good decision*.

I look at Paul. "I'm so glad you are here. I've missed you." I look for my other brother. "Peter…," I trail off.

"He's not quite ready, I guess. I thought he might come." Paul shrugs sympathetically.

I glance around the green and see Peter and Sharon standing and talking intently near Teddy's statue while their girls are making a beeline for their cousins. Makes sense he would be the holdout. I mean, I did promise him years ago I would never hurt Mama and Papa and look what I did.

EIGHT

The Unit

BOSCH, FEBRUARY 2362

Gia nabs me as I walk through the base gate just off the road to the old airfield on Monday morning. "I told you I'm putting together a unit. And we need a pilot."

"And you apparently want the best." I grin at her.

"Well, you need to convince the rest of the unit. Hope you can be a little charming."

"It's been known to happen."

"I've been piloting and navigating with the unit while I waited for your graduation. They know I've been shopping for the position. You would be perfect. Then we'd have two women, two men, and one middle."

I grin at her pirate egalitarianism. And she continues, prepping me for what I can tell is an important meeting for her. "They're all officers, and only one is a non-com, so try to be a little polite."

"I'm always 'a little' polite."

Gia stops her hustling walk with me and looks at me askance. "Seriously?"

I laugh. "Hey, I can be both charming and polite. But more

than that, I can fly the shit out of whatever vessel you put me in."

"Let me guess, in your previous life, you used to mostly work alone."

I nod in agreement. "Meetings are easier that way."

"Listen, Kat, I need a team of people who can work together. And get along."

I look at my officer-friend and say with all sincerity, "I know, Gia. And I know this is important to you. I will be on my best behavior. Promise."

"Okay, then." Gia gives a sigh of what I imagine is relief and grins at me. She returns to her quick-paced walk toward the airfield, and I shift gears to keep up.

We arrive at the hangar, and I pause for a moment and take a deep breath, pulling in the unique smell of working vessels. "Smells like home." I smile at Gia as I see her eyebrow cock back and forth as they do when she is curious.

She shakes her head and gives a small chuckle, then points over to the far side near the coffeepot where three people stand. "There's the rest of the unit. Showtime, Kat." We walk over, and I stand, relaxed, while Gia makes the introductions. "Major Bailey Alexander, left gunner; First Lieutenant Atama Pikari, flight engineer; and Sargent Demery Ludlow, right gunner. Bailey, Tom, Demery, this is Trooper Kat Wallace. She's auditioning for pilot today."

My head swivels toward Gia at this. I'm not sure I heard that correctly. "Auditioning?" My voice is incredulous.

"I think that given your rank, you ought to be grateful for the opportunity, Troop." Sergeant Ludlow is probably just a year or two older than me and has a smooth, rich voice.

Major Bailey Alexander leans toward me, looking at my face with their dark eyes. "You seem a little old to just be a trooper."

Oh, for fuck's sake. I look back at them and deadpan, "I'm a late bloomer."

Lieutenant Pikari apparently decides to jump on the bandwagon of Kat-critiques as he points out, "You know, this is a bit different than the simulators and the clunkers they have you fly as a recruit." I say nothing in response. He turns to Gia. "Colonel, are you seriously going to have some fresh-out-of-recruit-school troop attempt to pilot our state-of-the-art vessel?"

Gia looks uncomfortable, and I, for one, am damn glad of it. I look at each unit member and give my very best, most insincere smile.

"And it's delightful to meet each of you as well." I glance at Gia, who is rubbing her temples. I reward her with an artificially wide smile and several over-the-top eye blinks.

Her eyes widen at me, and I'm sure in her brain she is begging me to behave. I told her I can be polite and charming. And I fucking will be, but I'll also make these three eat their words.

"Golly," I say and attempt to keep the sarcasm from dripping too copiously. "I sure appreciate this opportunity."

This seems to mollify the three unit members, and Gia motions to the ground crew and the controllers that we are heading for a takeoff as we walk out to the airfield. She walks us over to a Whydah-61 Banshee, one of the newest and best models of vessels in the Force. As we board, I quickly survey the setup, looking for any variations from a standard Bosch vessel. It may be cutting-edge, but it is set up traditionally, though with more modern curves and seats that look incredibly comfortable. The helm is situated in the center front and has the usual configuration for pilot and navigator. There is a seat for each gunner near the weaponry instrumentation situated to the left and right and slightly behind the helm, and the flight engineer seat is directly opposite the helm toward the back of the vessel with its own instrumentation panel. The far back of the vessel can store product or carry passengers. It looks as though there are places to attach additional seats, which is a nice upgrade. I know there are several hidden holds in the center and along the walls for smuggling items or simply carrying extra cargo. I can barely make out where the lines are, though. Also a nice improvement. I glance up and see I am being scrutinized by the skeptics. Guess I'll play my part. I give a little smile and put on my North Country accent. "I tell y'all what, since this is an audition, how about we get to it? So, where do I sit?"

There is a very satisfying, collective groan from the three officers, and Gia looks at me and blinks once. "Take the left."

"Oh, I will." I give her a wicked smile as she slides into the navigator's seat. I sit in the pilot's chair, fastening my belts, and take a moment to appreciate its updated structure, which feels as comfortable as it looks. The rest of the unit moves to their places, and I turn to Gia. "So, Navigator-Colonel, where do you wanna go?"

"Let's just fly a loop over the forest, around the mountain, and come back here."

I lean and look out the front and side windows at the ground the vessel sits on, checking landmarks. "Right back here, then?"

Gia drops her eyebrows in a way that indicates suspicion. "Uh-huh."

I nod. "So, just a little loop? No waterworks?"

"Uh-huh. And not this time…"

"As you wish, and yeah…I will annotate later." I say this as sweetly as I can, then ask over my shoulders to the crew, "Is it okay if I play a bit of music? It helps my nerves."

I hear a delightful, disgusted exhalation from behind me. "Sure, Troop. Let's get on with this."

I turn back to the helm, smiling to myself, and hook in my playlist. I call out, "Let's get this done!" as I hit play on full volume and push the throttle, moving down the runway. The loud guitar and heavy beat drown out the exclamations from the unit as I pull the yoke back, and we are airborne. I keep my altitude low, the vessel just shy of skimming the tops of the trees. I think I hear a few curses behind me, or they may be prayers. I put on speed, gain altitude, and yell, "I know a shortcut to the mountain."

I am rapidly approaching the hillside, and again, I hear my passengers suck in air and swear. I can't blame them. I felt the same way the first time I flew it years earlier. Teddy had me up in one of his pets, practicing hammerheads, when I spied it. It really is hard to see it until you are right on top of it. I turn the vessel on its side to maneuver through a narrow crevasse, the canyon sides so close, you could almost touch them. There is a tense silence coming from the members of the unit, but my playlist queues up another of my old favorites, and I do a little "shoulder dance" as I make the far side of the canyon. When we are safely through, I begin to take on elevation quickly and move the vessel smoothly from side to side as if slipping and rolling in a fight, then I point the nose of the vessel down and dive toward the mountain, coming out in a smooth glide around the peak.

I decide to add to my casting spectacle, and I pause the music and put on my very best tour guide voice. "On your left, you'll see the caldera that was formed some four hundred million years ago after the last known eruption of Mount Tamrood." I grin and turn up the music. As another song comes on, I accelerate and run some tight, fast, aerobatic maneuvers specifically designed to roil my detractors' stomachs before going beyond the airfield, looping the vessel around, and bringing it in for a quick but smooth landing. I turn off the ignition and the music simultaneously as I look out the window.

"Dang, I missed the old spot by a good ten centimeters." I look innocently at Gia. "Bet I get points off my audition for that." I am holding onto my laughter.

Gia is staring at me. She starts to speak but then stops and looks out the windows and then back at me. Her eyebrows are all the way up, and I see a smile begin on her lips.

Then I do laugh, leaning back in my incredibly comfy pilot's seat. "Hey, you only ever flew with me in class. I'm not going to let loose with those kids. But you people, well, you're all grown up and can take it."

Behind me, a voice breaks the unit's silence. "Soo, I guess we have a pilot."

I raise two fists in victory and am rewarded with a round of applause.

I let the door slam as we exit the mess after a typically unremarkable lunch. "So, you grew up in the New Caribbean, Demery? I guess that explains your music."

Bailey laughs as I say this, and Tom, which is what Lieutenant Pikari prefers to be called, starts to mime a steel drum solo. After the rough "audition" introduction, I am really enjoying getting to know the members of my unit over the past couple of weeks. Tom is a wizard of an engineer and stands a full head or more taller than me, with close-cropped black hair and deep brown skin and eyes. He is one of the gentlest people I have ever met, but I have to work to keep up with his scores on the shooting range. He also recently got married.

Bailey's hair falls in a cascade of thin black braids, and they prefer classical music like Haydn and Chopin. I hadn't really listened to any before, so I have enjoyed learning more about the classical music and musicians of Old Earth from them. Our friendship was cemented the day I said to them, "Your name makes me think of a delicious drink." They had stopped and raised their eyebrows at me and said, "You mention that again, and I will forever after call you 'Kitten.'" Our eyes had locked, and I saw theirs sparkle, but I also knew they would make good on that threat. Then we both laughed. "Point taken." I had conceded. "No drink references."

Demery is broad-chested with deeply tanned skin and light brown hair. He is a non-com like me, and we have enjoyed discussing the joy of not having "real" officer responsibilities. He and Bailey have been gunner partners for years. He and I were both surprised to learn of the other's love of Shakespearean plays and have started exchanging books.

For Gia's part, she seems relaxed and pleased that her exceptional unit is coming together. I know she wants us to shine. Gia has her sights set on a commandership, and I am all about her getting there. While it doesn't come easily for me, I have shared some of my history and background, albeit a very tidied-up version. I have also made a marked effort to keep my swearing under control. It's easier now that I have kids to shut it off, though I have seen Gia look at me perplexed when I use words like "darn" and "frick."

We are laughing and joking as we head back toward the hangar to fly some maneuvers after lunch when a trio of young, unsmiling officers intercepts us, blocking our path. The one on the outside is almost as tall as Tom with a shock of wavy blond hair that falls over his forehead and into his blue eyes. He brushes it back as he shifts himself in front of me, crossing his arms menacingly and glowering as he looks at my face. His features are quite handsome and include an angular jaw and full lips, but he wears an expression as if he is smelling something quite repulsive as he takes me in. This really pisses me off, and I take a step back and look him up and down. "What the holy fuck is your fucking problem?" So much for curbing my language.

"You are." He growls and juts his chin toward me. Demery starts to approach, but I flick my hand up with my forefinger raised, sending a clear "hold on" message.

I tip my head and consider this pompous little prince. "Well, as it just so happens, I'm a lot of other people's problems too. I think there's a support group on Tuesdays. Maybe you should drop in."

I move to walk around him, hearing my unit chuckle, when he responds, "I know what you did." I look up at him. He has on what must be his best attempt at a thuggish stare, which I think simply makes him look a bit constipated. His two buddies are standing with their arms crossed, looking like bouncers from Ray's.

I grin on one side of my face and move a little closer to him. "Oh, honey, everybody knows what I did. That's why we call it a secret. It's a little joke. Just like you." I gently tap him on the chest in time with each of my last three words, feeling his muscles tense in surprise from my touch, and then turn and walk on.

Mr. Constipated calls after me, "This isn't over!"

I merely wave the middle finger of my right hand at him and continue my conversation with the unit.

Demery looks over at me as we walk. "Uh, Kat, you know that was an officer."

"Really?" I respond without missing a beat. "I thought it

was a little puckered asshole with legs. I didn't see that it had a shiny vest on as well. Good to know."

Demery lets out a hoot, and we all head for an afternoon in the sky.

The trio of lieutenants now shows up almost daily, glaring at me from a distance and posturing. They are so omnipresent that I begin to wonder if this is their actual assignment. I'll have to ask Miles if there is a special glowering unit tasked with trying to menace me. I don't want them to feel their efforts aren't appreciated, so by the fifth day, I begin to wave to them, calling loudly, "Hello, tightly puckered assholes—I mean, tightly puckered assholes, sirs!" I then give them a proper BPF salute that I embellish with a middle finger at the end.

After a couple of days of watching this performance escalate, Gia calls a brief meeting in our vessel before we begin morning maneuvers. She looks pointedly at me. "So it's pretty clear those looies and you are spoiling for a fight." I start to protest, but she stops me with a hand up. "I need you to bring the tension down, Kat, not rev it up."

Tom Pikari responds, "Don't worry, Colonel, we've got her back." I warm from the allegiance and friendship that I hear in his voice.

Gia seems less swept up by the emotion. "That's not my concern. I've seen her in the ring. She can handle herself. I don't want this unit to get fucked."

The guys and Bailey look a bit astonished at this language from our usually careful ranking officer. But I start to chortle. "I am such a great fucking influence on you people."

A ripple of laughter comes from them all. I spread my arms

out. "Gia, I promise you, I am not looking for a fight." She relaxes a bit. "However, if an invitation shows up on my doorstep, I won't decline." I give her a wink as I watch her eyebrows crease, and she sighs deeply.

It's Thursday afternoon, and the day's work is complete. I'm in no particular hurry to get home as my babies have been ferried off to Takai's ship for their first long weekend aboard the *Venturer*. I am vaguely disappointed that I can't go as well, but Takai didn't seem particularly interested in me coming, and my unit has a debriefing scheduled for Friday to discuss our first mission, which we ran the previous Tuesday.

The mission had gone swimmingly from my point of view: We had dropped off the Glitter with Paddy, my favorite disreputable drug runner from the FA. I had managed to negotiate a higher price due to Paddy's increased "visibility" and because I threw in what I purported to be the best whiskey money could buy. In reality, it was actually mid-grade whiskey I had repackaged, but Paddy wasn't checking beyond the label. As a bonus for me, I was able to chat privately with him about what Abernathy intel he had. When Tom and I got back to the vessel and cleared FA airspace, I explained to my unit (funny how I am thinking of them as mine) that anything above the price set by the quartermaster is to be thrown into the pot and then split up equally among the unit members.

Gia had said, "I've never heard of that rule."

I had grinned at her and said, "It's a pirate rule, savvy? No prey, no pay," and then winked my left eye.

So this Thursday I find myself with time alone. *Easy to be in charge of my life when it's just me,* I muse as I pack my things for the night before starting the short stroll home. The sun is just dropping below the horizon as I leave the base, but I leave my coat open. Even though it's February, I can feel a bit of warmth in the air that whispers of spring.

I turn onto my street as dusk gathers. The homes are large inky shadows; here and there a few windows glow yellow and orange with electric lights. The trees and hedges have their dark branches outlined against the moonless sky. I hear shuffling in the quiet, and there, under the bare boughs of my neighbor's big maple tree, are the three looies, recognizable by their collective shape. I sigh heavily. Apparently, the invitation from the Prince of Constipated Lieutenants and his goon duo is being hand-delivered tonight. I drop my bag, roll my wrists, work my fingers, steady my breathing, and then turn toward them. Not sure where on the tally sheet this is going. But it is happening.

Little Lord Constipation is coming at me. "You got off too easy," he says, raising his fist to me.

The next moment, he is holding a broken nose that gushes blood. The enforcers immediately come to his aid, and I place them neatly on the ground, one holding his middle and the other his groin.

"It's just you and me, princess," I call to the blond with the bloody nose. "C'mon, pretty boy, show me what you got."

He squares himself to deliver a blow, leaving his front open, so I squat down and deliver a punch to his liver. I watch as his hands come down belatedly, trying to protect his midsection, and gift him with an uppercut that causes his teeth to crash together. I have to imagine he did not see this panning out this way. I'm guessing he figured a couple of blows and menacing stares would be enough to put some woman in her place. Asshole. He didn't even think to guard himself defensively. Now, I'm pretty sure I've given his dashing smile some broken holes. But I'm not done because I'm pissed off. I still like hitting people, and it hasn't happened enough as of late. So, as he wavers from the uppercut, I provide a rear cross to his right eye and follow it with my lead elbow to his left temple and the corner of his eye. Both make contact, and he collapses to his knees, forehead in the chill dirt.

"There you go, pretty boy," I say in a hiss. "Not so pretty now. Maybe think twice before ganging up on someone walking home?"

I turn, pick up my bag, shake my hand, scowl, and listen to the adrenaline hum in my ears as I walk on to my little empty house.

I stand at attention the next morning on the left side, facing Miles' desk. The constipated lieutenant stands in a similar position to the right. His face has a swath of bandages covering his nose with a roll of gauze protruding from one nostril. His right eye is swollen, and the bruising is starting to take on what I feel is an excellent color. There is one butterfly bandage at the corner of his eye and another at the peak of his cheek. His lower lip is swollen and puffy from where he bit it with the uppercut. I smile in satisfaction to myself and wiggle my fingers where the slightest bit of delightful discomfort rests in my knuckles. Tally sheet: except for the scolding I am about to receive—so *good*.

Gia sits off to the side, eyebrows drawn, as Miles shakes his head with disbelief and leans back to address us, the miscreants.

"While fighting is a skill we pride ourselves on in Bosch, it is not meant for us to fight among ourselves. This brawl did not take place on base, but you are always representing the base, wherever you are. This behavior will not be tolerated."

"Trooper Wallace, Lieutenant McCloud: What do you have to say for yourselves?"

I take a moment to process the lieutenant's name: McCloud. Shit. Of *the* McClouds. The McClouds are good friends with Mama and, before his death, were with Papa. I remember meeting them during an outing with Mama and Papa. I glance over. Now the resemblance is clear. Dammit. They are one of the most influential families in the Bosch financial center of District One. I really should make amends. I look over at the blond man.

"McCloud, huh?" I give a mock pout. "I bet powerful Papa is upset his boy lost a fight. Hope he doesn't cut your allowance, Trust-Fund." The old Kat is back and burning bridges.

The looie makes a move toward me. My fist pops up fast and I give him a "just try it" look while Gia puts her hands to her face and Miles rolls his eyes and says in a slightly elevated tone, "Attention, now, both of you."

We both move back to looking straight ahead with hands behind our backs, but not before giving each other scathing glances.

"Lieutenant McCloud, what in the hell were you thinking?" Miles asks.

The lieutenant clears his throat. "I was angry to see the person responsible for our former revered Master Commander's death go unpunished. Teddy Bosch was a personal friend of my family, and I felt I needed to—"

"To what? Become a one-man vigilante? Trooper Wallace served her sentence. Are you questioning Bosch justice?"

"Uh, no, sir, Master Commander. It was just—"

"You thought you could do a better job? Well, look in the mirror, kid. It didn't turn out so well," Miles concludes with his eyebrows drawn.

A small smile curves on my face as I hear Miles' last comment.

"And you, Kat? Rather, Trooper Wallace? What made you decide to beat the hell out of this officer?" Here, Miles accentuates the word "officer."

I look at Miles and say with a straight face, "Well, there were only three of them, sir. You know I don't have a problem until there are more than five."

The corners of Miles' mouth twitch, but to his credit, he maintains his composure and continues to question me. "The other two came away simply uncomfortable. Why the beating to Lieutenant McCloud?"

"Because he was the frontman, sir, and so he got what frontmen deserve." I use this adage as it is a well-known part of Boschian lexicon, and likely will allow Miles to cut me some slack. As if planned, he shrugs and says, "Fair enough."

I really should just leave it at that, but I can't resist adding, "Also, he's a tightly puckered little asshole that needed to be brought down a few pegs."

Miles closes his eyes briefly and rubs between his brows with two fingers. Uh-oh. I know that move. I should have edited that last comment. Dammit, the *not-so-good* column gets a mark.

Miles stands to pronounce the sentence. "Both of you will be docked a week's pay." I watch as a slow smile creeps onto his face. "And to help you children learn to play well together…" He looks first at McCloud and then at me. "…Lieutenant McCloud is now reassigned to your unit. You will be flying heavy for the foreseeable future."

I cannot believe my ears. How are we supposed to accomplish anything with some privileged scion of shittiness aboard? Now I feel myself getting angry. What is Miles thinking? This won't help anything. I glance over at McCloud, and his face is tight. I hear his breath shake ever so slightly as he inhales. He is angry as well. He shouldn't be. He should be grateful he gets to be part of the top unit.

"Permission to speak, sir," I hear him say.

Miles pauses long enough before responding to make it clear he holds the power here. As if we didn't know that. "Make it brief."

"I am part of Major Warner's unit. He needs a flight engineer."

"Major Warner is a big boy. He'll figure it out. Lieutenant McCloud, you are to report to Colonel Ka'ne on Monday morning at five bells. You and Trooper Wallace can lead your unit in PT drills." Miles says this very matter-of-factly. Must be nice to be able to make such pronouncements.

There is a beat as McCloud takes this in. "Yes. Sir." It is the only response, but there is obvious anger in his tone.

"You are dismissed, McCloud. Wallace, I believe your CO has a few things to discuss with you."

I watch as McCloud turns on his heel and walks out the door. As soon as the door clicks shut, I turn to Gia. "I am so sorry, Gia. I didn't mean for the unit to get punished."

"I'd hardly call it punishment, Kat," Miles cuts in. "Will McCloud is one of the finest flight engineers we have on this base."

"But so is Tom Pikari. We don't need a second—"

"You've got one, Kat. Figure it out." Miles' tone is final.

Gia looks at me. There is no recrimination in her eyes, but she looks a bit tired. "This is your unit, Kat. I may be ranking, but you are the leader. Miles is right. You are going to have to figure out how to integrate him into the unit."

I sit down in what I consider to be my chair in front of Miles' desk and rub my forehead, taking several deep breaths.

"Okay. I'll do my part. But he better not get anyone hurt or killed."

"Excellent." Miles nods to both of us. "Now if you two will excuse me, I have a phone call to return to William McCloud Senior. I suspect it will not be pleasant."

NINE

Trust-Fund

There is the tiniest bit of light in the Eastern sky as I move across the green. I pass several units whose members are arriving as I am for early PT. As I walk over to the section of the green our unit has claimed, I can just see Gia in the dim light off to the side, involved in what looks to be a heated discussion with a tall, copper-skinned vested officer.

"Are you trying to wreck my unit since I wouldn't defect? He's my engineer." I hear a decided edge to the man's deep voice as he gestures at McCloud, who stands nearby.

"No. It has nothing to do with that. Take it up with the MC, Warner. I'm not happy about it either, but maybe if you had a better grip on your team, they wouldn't be hiding out and ambushing my people." Gia has her authoritative, *don't fuck with me* voice on, and I smile as I move toward the conversation.

"Ambush?" The voice rumbles with disbelief. "Did you see the beating your pilot put on him? He should be pressing charges, but he is being pretty tightlipped."

I come up just behind the officer. "If his lips are tight, it's because they are swollen shut from my uppercut."

He turns, startled by my sudden appearance, and I tip my head to look at him and am struck by his looks. Widow's peak and stubble-beard and deep, dark eyes—the Force has loads of good-looking men and women in it, but this guy would win a top prize. I kinda want to see his whole unit if he and McCloud are two of the members. But looks are certainly not everything. His Gia-like eyebrows pull together, and he looks down at me skeptically. "You? You're the pilot? You're the one who caused this?" I'm a bit taken aback by how incredulous he sounds.

"Hey, I didn't cause anything. I was merely defending myself." I stare at McCloud, who is scowling at me. "At first." I stare more intently. "Then I beat the shit out of the little prince." I turn my head back toward Gia and the pilot. "For shits and giggles." I beam a smile at the pilot and see his face go from annoyed to surprised to forming a tiny smile at the corners of his mouth.

He sighs and turns to McCloud. "Good luck, Will. You'll need it." He salutes Gia, looks at me with an odd expression, and leaves.

I turn around, and the rest of my unit has assembled and is grinning at the exchange. I join them, leaving Lieutenant William McCloud off to the side. Gia looks at us and motions him to move toward the group. He takes a small step nearer and then stops with plenty of space left in between.

Gia pulls her comm up and reads from it. "This is from the Master Commander to Trooper Wallace and Lieutenant McCloud, but I think we all need to know the parameters. 'You are both required to perform all assignments together for the next two weeks. You will stay together during meal and break times. There is to be no harassment or violence or you will both be suspended for one month with no pay no matter the cause of the fracas.' Is that clear?" She looks expectantly first at me and then him.

I can just hear Miles' voice saying this, and I know he is absolutely loving this shit. I nod in agreement, and I see a quick, tight nod from Lieutenant Recently-But-No-Longer-Constipated.

We look at each other. "Okay," I sigh. "Let's get this done. We can take turns. You take the first exercise."

"Fine." His voice is no longer a growl. And we start with high knees.

The exercises I pick are ones guaranteed to shake up McCloud's sore head and face, and I am rewarded with several moans of discomfort from him by the time we are done and ready to run. As I call out our kilometers for the day, the entire unit pushes past McCloud and kicks up dust onto his clothes and face as they embark on the run. I chuckle as I am clean and relatively dust-free. He stands for a moment, his face wearing a disgusted expression and his body slumped defeatedly.

"Well, what did you expect?" I look at him evenly. "Generally speaking, jumping a mother of three as she walks home from her job doesn't play well."

He draws his brows close as he brushes his vest and the rest of his uniform off. "I didn't know you had kids."

I give a derisive snort. "What you don't know about me could fill the Glitter mines, Trust-Fund."

"Back at you." He glares at me. "I don't like that name."

"Works out. I don't like you." I start my run. "Catch up," I yell over my shoulder. "Trust-Fund!"

It was a clear, warm night with a quarter-moon shining down as Takai walked slowly back from the landing pad of the *Venturer*, his experienced eyes taking in the ship and its crew and assessing for any issues that he would need to address at the next officers meeting. He had just tucked all three children into their seats for their return trip to Bosch with the Bosch pilot and the pilot's wife, and he was exhausted. The children had been with him for five days, and he had lost count of the number of snacks he had made, arguments he had to referee, and questions he had to answer. He knew it would have been too much for him if it hadn't been for First Officer Miyamoto. Hayami had appeared at his quarters the day after the children arrived with books to read, paper to fold into toy animals, an extra pair of hands to ease his load, and her lovely, quiet way of knowing just what he and the children needed. Takai smiled to himself. Hayami was a delicate flower, perhaps a unique orchid; after all, her name meant "rare beauty." He would be delighted to express his appreciation for her help. He quickened his steps. He was in his element.

TEN

Use What You Are Given

"So, first mission flying heavy today…we are off to Dobarri." Gia stood in front of her unit in the small meeting room off the main hangar, holding the device with the details of the upcoming Glitter drop. She glanced up and saw Kat roll her eyes and glare at Will McCloud. The two weeks of forced association had done nothing to improve relations between the pair. While McCloud seemed to be trying to make the best of it —she had seen him having substantive engineering conversations with Tom Pikari and pleasantly chatting with Demery and Bailey—Kat was being stubborn and intractable, barely speaking to the lieutenant and then using the "Trust-Fund" nickname when she did communicate with him. And any goodwill McCloud had for the unit evaporated when he was around Kat. She was going to have to do something to improve the situation. She looked at the unit and decided that a toss into the deep end was the only way.

"Kat, you and Lieutenant McCloud will take the lead on this one. I want you both to go in, but I want him to do the negotiating."

"Why?" Kat asked shortly, a scowl on her face.

"Do I need a reason? I am the CO in the unit." Gia furrowed her brows at her friend.

Kat sighed. "No. Fine. Let's get this shitshow started then." She brushed by Will McCloud and headed for the door. Gia smiled encouragingly at Will, who had narrowed his eyes at Kat and shook his head before looking at his new CO.

Gia gave the lieutenant a nod. "She has a tendency to hold a grudge. I expect you to be professional and respectful."

Will pulled his shoulders back. "With all due respect to you, Colonel, with the single exception of my past deplorable behavior initiating a fight, I will always be professional and respectful, but I would like the same expectations given to Wallace."

Gia's brows shot up, and then she nodded as she considered. "You make an excellent point. I will be sure to lay out the same expectations for the entire unit." She glanced over at Tom, Demery, and Bailey, who all wore sympathetic expressions. This had disaster written all over it. "Let's all move out. Professionally and respectfully."

I am in my pilot's seat waiting for the rest of the unit and Trust-Fund. I can't believe Gia is going to let him take the lead on negotiations. That is my area, and if she thinks I am going to let some little prince screw up a mission, well, I'm not. But I'll let him start at least. I am in a shitty mood. Not quite half of the mood is due to His Trust-Fundship and the fact that the rest of the unit is softening up to his dashing smile and stupid jokes. The other half-plus is because of the conversation I had with Takai this morning.

When the children had returned from their first visit to the *Venturer* and their papa two weeks earlier, they could not stop talking about the ship and the crew. It was big, it was warm, the sea smelled amazing, the food was delicious, there were actual cows on the ship, and on and on.

I had snuggled them close and heard about Chief Engineer McAndrew, who apparently "can fix anything" and "made animal sounds when we saw the farm animals," and First Officer Miyamoto, who made each child several origami animals. Grey's were carefully preserved, but the boys had crushed theirs in their hands. They looked on the verge of tears until Grey said in her sisterly way, "It's okay. She'll make more when we go back."

Now the kids are set to visit the ship again at the end of the week, and in my regular, but still filled with awkward silences, comm to Takai, I said something about coming with them, and he shut me down with an "I don't think we are ready for that yet, Kat." *We* indeed. *He* isn't ready. I mean, he is the one who pushed to get married, and now he is pulling back using all engines because I made a decision about my life and my career. I may have had serious doubts about marriage, but fuck, now that I'm in it, I'm going to make it work. He'll just have to be surprised to see me get off the vessel with the kids on Friday. This will definitely go in the good decision column.

There's a rumbling at the hatch, and the unit plus TF—I like that; I may just start calling him that—comes aboard. Gia looks worriedly at me, and I force a reasonable facsimile of a smile for her. She slides into her navigation seat, and I turn to her and say as quietly as possible to keep it between the two of us, "Sorry for my attitude. I had an argument with Takai this morning." I shrug as her expression turns sympathetic. Gia has heard all my concerns about my marriage several times over. I jerk my head toward Lieutenant Constipated, saying, "I don't get why you want him as a frontman, but I'm happy enough to shepherd him through it if he hasn't negotiated before."

"Are you going to be able to get along with him?" Her brows move almost independently of each other as she looks questioningly at me.

"Yes. I told you I can be a team player. Sometimes." I give her a grin. "And this will be one of those times. Promise."

They are frog-marching the two of us down three flights of stairs. I had figured there were lower levels but hadn't anticipated seeing them up close. The rage that had boiled over in me upstairs is receding to a slow simmer, and I no longer hear the ringing in my ears, and the red has faded from my vision. Dammit. I can't believe I lost it so completely. I can now hear TF chatting pleasantly with the guard holding his right arm. She surprisingly is letting him talk, and—wait, did she just giggle?

I don't have time to do more than be slightly irked at this as we reach a big, wooden door that a second, burly guard unlocks, revealing a very dark interior. Without any ceremony, we are each given hard shoves that cause us both to stumble off of our feet. The door is pushed shut, and I hear a lock outside click. I get up from my knees where I landed when pushed and brush my legs off, my hand going automatically to my thigh to check my knife, which I remind myself has been confiscated. I'm not leaving here without that blade, dammit. Or Teddy's pistols. I decide to familiarize myself with the environment. The floor is packed dirt, so we must be on the bottom level—a sub-sub-basement if you will. The only light is the little that filters in through the small, barred opening in the door. There are no windows. I reach out and make my way pretty much blindly to the nearest wall. It feels like stone, not brick, and as I run my hands over it…

"What are you doing?" TF's impatient voice comes through the dark from the far side of the room—well, of the cell—and judging by its proximity, the cell ain't too big.

"Exploring our surroundings so we can figure a way out of here."

I hear a derisive snort, and TF answers, "Well, let me tell you. There's one way out, and it's this door."

I turn and can just make out his form sitting with his knees bent in front of him, his back leaning on the door. "That's probably true, but I like to know what my options are."

"Hey, here's an interesting option." He sounds annoyed. "Let's have you go back in time and not rabidly insult the host about his thralls, so we don't end up in here."

I turn from the far back wall, where my hands are still exploring the walls for any chinks or flaws. "Weren't you appalled? Enslavement is wrong. Who does shit like that?" Still, probably my response goes in the *not-so-good* decision column.

I hear him scoff. "I thought you were supposed to be so experienced." He lengthens the vowels of the last two words in a mocking way. "There are thralls in at least half of the private places we drop Glitter to."

My eyebrows wrinkle and pull together at this statement. "No. I never saw any thralls in my old Glitter runs or in any of my extractions."

"How long ago was that? Because they've always been there since I've been in the Force."

By now I am back to the door as well, and I sink to sit on the floor, having found nothing of any use on the stone walls except dirt and a few loose rocks. I don't sit too close to him but near enough to continue the conversation.

"Umm…" I count off the years in my head using the kids as my milestones. "I guess, it's been eight years. But there weren't any at this unit's first mission either!" *But,* a voice says in me, *that was with Paddy, not a private home.* I am starting to have a sinking feeling.

"Eight years!" He sounds shocked. "How old are you anyway?"

I look toward him and am freshly peeved by his existence. My answer comes out in a growl. "I'm thirty-three. Which is not that old."

"Huh, no, it isn't." His voice is amicable. "I'm thirty-one. You must have started young. When did you graduate uni?"

I snort. "Never went. Hell, I never finished secondary."

"Really? But you are always talking about books and—"

I jump in, "Most of the books I have read I got off Teddy's shelves."

I hear him go quiet at Papa's name and automatically assume he is thinking the worst about me, which pisses me off anew. "I didn't steal them if that's what you're thinking, asshole."

The quiet continues for a moment. "Why do you hate me so much?" It is said in a matter-of-fact way, like something he has asked others in his life.

I let out a sound that starts as a scoff but turns into a laugh. "Let's be clear. I didn't start this relationship like this."

"You beat the shit out of me!" His voice is defensive.

"You jumped me in the dark with two of your friends. After menacing me for weeks." I am incredulous that he thinks this is my doing.

There's quiet again. Then, "Fuck."

I nod. "See, Trust-Fund? It wasn't me." I hear him growl and it makes me grin.

"I hate that name, and you know it."

"Yeah. I know it. But more importantly, you want to tell me you don't have a trust fund, oh Scion of Bosch Banking?"

I cross my arms over my chest and lean back on the chill wall.

"Well, I mean…yes, but… Fuck."

I laugh aloud now. "That's two for me! One more and I win!"

Now I hear him laugh. It's the first time I've heard it. He has a nice laugh. Deep at the start but finishing with a bit of a giggle before he speaks. "Well, okay, my turn: You assume you know all about me because I had the misfortune to be born into a rich family."

I pause for a moment and consider this. "Ah…fuck."

He laughs again and says quickly, "And you think all rich people are the same—bad."

I rub my neck and chin and blow out a breath. "Well, fuck."

"And that's two for me, and we are tied!" He sounds victorious and starts to laugh again.

I can't help but join in, and we sit and laugh for a bit. As we wind down, I turn my head and look toward him. His profile is visible in the dim light; a lock of his unruly hair is sticking out in front like a unicorn horn. I reach out and brush it back so he looks fully human. "So, what do you want me to call you instead?"

"How about Will?"

"Just Will?"

"Yeah. I have been trying to escape the McCloud name and all that comes with it for years. I don't want to be a banking scion, much to my father's dismay. He hates that I enlisted."

"But doesn't he know that you are a really good engineer?"

"No. He doesn't know that I'm a fucking brilliant engineer!"

We both laugh again, though I hear the ruefulness in his. "And speaking of brilliant, where did you learn to fly like you do?"

His question is so boyishly sincere that he makes me think of my own sweet boys, and I can't help but smile. "Teddy taught me," I say with a sad laugh. "I mean, I learned the basic skills of flying like everyone else: on the base simulators and 'clunkers' as Tom so aptly puts it, but..." I feel my eyes filling with tears and my throat get tight. "...I learned the art from Teddy. He taught me to read the wind." I let out a little sad sigh.

"You really loved him, didn't you?"

"Mmm-hmm." I nod but don't trust myself to speak beyond a murmur yet.

"But you killed him." He says it very matter-of-factly and softly.

I start to cry. "Mmm-hmm." I cover my face as the pain I have kept at bay for close to a year and a half bubbles up, and I sob. I feel him tentatively pat my shoulder, and when I continue with the crying jag, his arm goes around my shoulders, awkwardly at first and then with confidence as I lean into his broad shoulder and cry for several more minutes. He doesn't say a word.

There's a rattling at the door that wakes me, and I lift my head from where it is resting on Will's chest. I realize where I am, and I feel him come awake at the same time. We both scoot quickly away from each other, our collective warmth replaced by the damp chill of the cell.

After I finished my cry earlier, we had started talking about Teddy and how he had died, and then we talked of Will's childhood, which was spent with a series of nannies, mostly from the New Caribbean, and the overwhelming expectation thrust upon him to live up to the family name. He had started taking things apart and putting them back together even better when he was a kid, and it always made his father angry. "Such a mess. It was fine the old way." So, naturally, he went into engineering. We talked lightly of my time as a thrall, and he said that it seemed to him there were more thralls every year at many of the colonies and outposts we dealt with. The instructions were clear when he was a new trooper: Simply deal with the Glitter drop and don't get involved. This infuriated me. Miles is going to get an earful from me about that. At some point, we must have fallen asleep. Truth is, it felt nice to be warm and next to someone who didn't pull away.

Suddenly, the door opens and light pours in. The giggling woman guard who was part of our escort here is standing there, smiling at Will. She motions to him. He stands and I stand. She scowls at me. "Not you. Not yet." And she takes Will's hand and draws him out into the hall, closing the door and locking it. I stand on my tiptoes, look out of the grating, and see her wrap her arms around Will's neck and lean up. Shit. She's kissing him. I mean, really kissing him. I see her push open the door across the corridor from ours/mine, and she backs into it and pulls Will with her. I recognize the sounds of what's happening, though, heaven help me, it's been so long that I actually find myself surprised. And a bit aroused. And a little pissed off. Though I'm not sure why I feel that last way.

I take one more peek out of the grill, and then I move to the far back wall where the impassioned sounds are a bit more muffled. *What the hell is he doing? Well, I know what he's doing.* At least, I can imagine it...and I do for a few moments. I feel a flush that flows from my face down my body and lands squarely between my legs. I clap my hands over my ears and hum to myself, considering what I'm going to say to Miles about the whole thrall business. I have gone through several iterations of the conversation in my head when I hear non-passionate discussion outside my door, and then the lock is turned and the door swings open. I stand, squinting against the sudden light. Will stands there with all our weapons, wearing a sheepish smile. The guard, on the other hand, is wearing a languorous smile and looking adoringly up at Will. I step forward and grab my knife that he is proffering, strap it on, and then take my two pistols and replace them in their holsters.

"Shall we go now, lover boy?" I smile sweetly at Will.

"We shall." He seems unruffled by the events. I, on the other hand, am extremely ruffled.

The guard walks us quickly to the door and the stairs, stepping aside to let us go. I head up the stairs but hear no footsteps behind me, so I look back and see Will pull the guard to him with one arm and kiss her passionately. He has his lieutenant vest on with a white shirt partially buttoned underneath and his weapon in his other hand, and if I squint, so help me, he looks like some of the pictures of Golden Age swashbuckling pirates. I draw my breath in quickly and feel the flush start again, and so I decide to be vexed. I watch as he whispers something to her and touches her face with his palm. Then he turns and takes the stairs two at a time to catch up to me.

We move the rest of the way up the three flights of stairs in silence, and I am glad I have the climbing effort to credit for my heavier breathing. We get to the door, and Will motions me to the left, where we find a door to the outside with, wonder of wonders, two cases sitting next to it holding the markers for the Glitter. I pick them up, but before the door closes, I look at him. "Anyone else you need to fuck before we leave?"

He grins. "Nope. All set in that department." He pulls the door shut meaningfully.

I let out an exasperated snort as we start the trek back to the vessel.

Will shrugs as he moves purposefully along with me. "Hey. I just use the tools I was born with. It got us out, didn't it?"

I stop and turn to look at him. "It?" I raise my eyebrows, trying to imitate Gia. "So, the story is going to be that your 'tool' rescued us?" I gesture meaningfully at his pants.

He looks somewhat offended. "You know what I meant."

Now I give a dirty laugh. "Oh, I do, JustWill. I know so much more about you now than when this mission started."

Even in the dim light, I see him flush. There we go. "Let's get this done." I smile and tug his sleeve.

ELEVEN

WTF, Miles?

Miles jovially sets another whiskey down in front of me, neat, before returning with his whiskey, holding his signature single ice cube, to his comfortable seat on the working side of the Master Commander's desk. "So, I haven't gotten a mission report back from Gia yet for yesterday's mission with McCloud. How'd it go?"

And here is my entry. I have been blithe and convivial and have actually participated in small talk up until now.

"Well, funny you should ask." I take a draw on my drink and set it on the corner of the desk near the compass rose. "Gia decided to force McCloud and me to work together by sending us in with instructions for him to negotiate. And who should greet us to bring us to the buyer but an array of thralls, causing me to completely lose my shit, get us imprisoned for several hours, and require that Will bone one of the guards to get us out." I look up and see Miles' jaw drop ever so slightly as I push onward. "Lo and behold, upon our return to the vessel, I discovered that none of the unit members were surprised by the thralls as they said, and I quote…" I pull a paper card from my jacket pocket and read from it. 'Thralls are a part of the trade.' 'There are more thralls now than when I first graduated.' And my personal favorite, 'What's the big deal? Thralls have always been around.'" I toss and spin the card over the compass rose toward my MC who stops it in front of him with two fingers. I hear him murmur under his breath, "Goddammit, Teddy."

I stare meaningfully at him. "You can't pass the marker on this one, buddy. This is happening under your command."

He stares back at me and purses his lips. "Okay." He breathes out. "So, we are having this conversation."

I wait for him to continue.

"I told him he needed to come clean on this, but the bastard arranged his own death to get out of it." I would normally have been offended by anyone but me referring to Teddy as "the bastard," but Miles says it with such love and admiration that I let it slide.

"Come clean?" I prompt Miles to tell me what I know he wants to avoid.

He looks at me and creases his brow, then says in one breath, "Teddy made sure to only send you on missions where there would be little or no thrall involvement. He figured you would do better not seeing it, and he was not wrong. You excelled."

I hold up my hand to stop Miles from continuing. I have to process this. "And you knew this? But—"

Miles jumps in. "It was not my place to tell you. Teddy made that clear."

I flash again on the number of times some man has decided something for me for "my own good." I have lost count. I close my eyes and take three steadying breaths as I have learned to do while raising my tiny pirates.

"I. Can't. Even." I shake my head and look at the man

across the table whom I have come to trust. "So, Miles, what do you propose to do about it?"

He looks at me, and his eyes widen questioningly. "Me? What shall I do about it?"

"Well, who else?"

"I don't know, Kat. Maybe the right person for this task isn't the old guy who has been a part of 'the club' of old pirates for twenty-plus years. Maybe someone with a fresh outlook and drive to change things would be better. But, hey, that person would need to be an officer to evoke change, so, I guess that's pointless." He looks intently at me.

I stare at him. "Nice try, MC. But don't go pointing this at me. Let's see if I have this straight: Teddy and you have gaslighted me about the extent of thrall ownership for ages, and now, suddenly, you decide to throw me out into the reality that you have sat by and watched as the number of thralls has increased over the years." I am leaning forward in my chair. "Well, don't look at me to clean up your mess. I am no officer and am no fucking thrall savior. You just shift that pointed finger back at yourself. And Teddy." I stand. "Sweet New Earth, I can't believe you two." I turn and walk out, leaving my whiskey unfinished on the table. Now that is a message.

TWELVE

Mynian Mission

Back to work. Just have to run this mission, and then the kids and I will head to the *FA Venturer* late this evening, aiming to arrive mid-day on the ship. *Surprise, Takai. Let's do lunch.* I'm nervous on several levels today. First, the mission.

The mission specs are simple: Go in, deliver the product, collect the fee, and go home. But I have learned from experience that virtually no mission is that simple. The success or failure of each mission hinges on details: details known and details omitted. Because Glitter is seen as contraband in the FA countries and most of the Southern Colonies, units have to be on the lookout for local and international law enforcement officers and often for a competitor to the liaison who wants to scoop up product without going through the proper channels. On occasion, the connection decides to attempt a double-cross. This almost always ends badly for that consumer, who, if they survive, will never be able to negotiate with a Bosch representative again.

This mission is with a new customer in the colony of Mynia deep in the South-Central Continent and high up in the mountains. They are receiving their first product drop. First meetings always tend to be potentially dicey as the parties size each other up. Tom, Will, and I carry the product to the assigned meeting place and realize that it feels more like January than mid-March at this elevation. We arrive at the drop site, and I look around me and double-check the coordinates. We are standing in a concrete structure that is obviously used to store vehicles. It has no full walls, and the chill mountain air eddies through it. I am unimpressed.

"A fucking parking garage? In March? It's freezing!" I rant at the contact. "No. I'll tell you what. When you can show me a comfortable chair and a warm cup of tea next to a fireplace, then we'll consider doing business. C'mon, guys, let's head back to the vessel."

Our contact, whose name is Solaki, holds up his comm. "Please, wait. I will make a call."

I give the men a small nod and pause but continue to emphatically demonstrate I am cold and uncomfortable by wrapping my arms around myself and making audible shivering sounds.

Solaki walks away briefly and then returns, tucking his comm in a pocket. His voice is smooth. "My employer invites you to their home. All the parameters you requested are there. We will take you by vehicle."

I gaze at Solaki for a few seconds. There is no fucking way I am putting my unit into a closed vehicle controlled by someone else. Does this Solaki and his boss think I am that stupid?

I consider and respond, "We will need a vehicle that we can drive on our own. We will follow you." I make sure my voice is firm.

"Certainly."

Solaki signals to his people, and a vehicle is brought around. Tom and Will do a rapid but thorough check of it to assure there are no dangers within or without. JustWill offers to drive, and I shrug. Will and I have formed a rather pleasant detente of sorts. He volunteers for stuff, and I don't undermine him. We load the product and follow the other three vehicles about twelve kilometers to the east, where a large home sits on a vista overlooking a lake.

"Pretty fancy digs." I peer out of the vehicle window at what can only be described as a mansion.

"Looks like my grandad's place on Willow Lake up on the east side of Mt. Tamrood," Will says.

Tom and I give him a dubious look at the mention of this posh area, and he looks disgusted at us. "What? I didn't make the markers. It's not my fault."

We start to laugh, and soon Will joins in with a small "You assholes" murmured under his breath.

"Takes one to know one, kiddo," I say and playfully give his shoulder a small shove. He grins at me, but I am careful to stop myself from grinning back.

We pull up through a set of gates that seem firmly fixed open to the palatial front doors. Before we open the vehicle doors, I send our coordinates to Gia. Upon getting out, the guys move to the trunk to retrieve the product, and I survey the surroundings and the people, counting almost silently, "Three, four... Upper level has three more. Shit, that's just outside."

"What are you going on about?" Will keeps his voice low to match mine.

"Counting weapon-toters. There's a lot."

He shrugs. "It's a big place owned by a rich person. There's gonna be security."

"Your grandad has all these armed folk, does he?" I look up at him and lift my brows.

Will shakes his head. "Nope."

"Okay, then. That's lots more weapons than we have. Let's be aware in there."

We are escorted into a large, warm room. There are at least two dozen young men and young middles sitting and reclining on comfortable poufs and chatting amiably with each other. They pause, and the room becomes silent for a moment while they take us in. Then they return to their conversations and to snacking on the trays of olives and grapes and sipping glasses of wine. I see no young women. At all. Interesting.

I know Mynia is matriarchal, but I've never visited it before. I am pleased to see that one entire wall is taken up with a crackling fireplace. I laugh to myself as I see in the center of the room a dais with a very comfortable set-up of a pair of chairs and a small table complete with a teapot and two cups set on it. Parameters, indeed.

The doors at the back of the room open, and an older woman, dressed in what looks like a series of diaphanous scarves, floats in and steps gracefully onto the dais. The other people in the room become silent and attentive in her presence. I can feel my discomfort rise. *Take it easy, Kat. You told Miles and your unit you could handle this.* I am currently having serious doubts about my abilities. The woman pauses in front of me ever so briefly, then steps onto the dais. She settles in front of one of the chairs and silently motions me to the opposite one. I nod but withhold a smile and climb up and take my seat.

The woman tosses her silver-gray waves of hair and gracefully pours two cups of tea. "I am Metztli. And you are called?" Her voice is deep and pleasant.

"Katrina. You may call me Kat."

"I am so sorry to have insulted you by the choice of our first meeting place. I had not realized the exchange would be made with a woman. You do not seem old enough to be the doyenne."

I raise my eyebrows and allow myself a wry smile. "I have the respect but not the years." I take a long sip of my tea and hold the cup to warm my hands without taking my eyes from my host. I gesture with an open hand. "These people here: They are your family? Your employees? Your…" I trail off to allow Metztli to complete the sentence.

Metztli smiles. "Some are children, now grown. Some are part of my paid staff, and some are chattel."

I feel my body stiffen. *You can't change the world, Kat, that's what Miles said. At least not all at once.*

Why the hell can't I? I wonder now.

"You do not approve?"

I take a breath, and I know Will and Tom, who are privy to this conversation as they stand at the base of the dais, are holding theirs. Especially Will. Not sure he would want to employ the same method here as he did in Dobarri during our first mission. But then again, he might, I realize as I consider one of the more attractive male guards. Images form. My outside self gives my inner voice a little slap in the back of the head, and I refocus on Metztli. My voice sounds even, but I can hear a quaver of rage in it. *Settle the fuck down, Kat.* "We are not here to discuss my approval nor disapproval. We have a product you wish. We need to discuss a price." I reluctantly put a slash in the *good decision* column.

Having said this, I can see the guys relax, and this relaxes me. They set the Glitter cases down on the edge of the dais, still within their easy reach. Metztli and I haggle back and forth, and I forget my outrage as I sink into the game. I spread out in my chair a bit more with each offer countered and talk just a hair louder than Metztli. The room recedes as we parry and thrust with offers. Finally, we reach a place that makes me smile, and I nod and clap my right hand to my left shoulder, signaling a deal as I was taught to do when dealing with the people of Mynia. Metztli smiles broadly and signals Solaki to come close, which he does readily. She whispers to him. He steps out a side door into another space in the villa, and I take this opportunity to survey the room. Apart from the young men and middles—some thralls, some not, there are four paunchy guards with weapons that they likely are adept with but not deeply connected to. *There should be three cases of markers. Each of us could carry and still shoot.* I note the doors that could provide ingress to foes, guards, and other folk I do not care to see. Then, I zero in on the exit. Blinking, I refocus on Metztli and return her smile, chatting idly about the weather and the upcoming FA elections. Neither of us is invested in either subject.

Solaki returns with two assistants, carrying with them four cases to lay at my feet. I lift the first one and open it, running my hands across the markers, rifling the depth of the case. I carefully repeat this with each case. I pause after the fourth case, leaning back in my chair, and look at her. "This is heavier than we discussed. Why?"

Metztli stands and steps off the dais and smiles predatorily at Tom and Will. "Your attendants are lovely. I wish them to stay."

Oh, boy. Keep quiet, guys. I eye the guards in the room and quickly calculate the number of steps to the exit.

At that moment, Metztli runs her hands over Will's backside, and he exclaims, "Hey, now, stop that," and steps back from her.

Metztli looks unperturbed but only speaks to me. "He seems a bit truculent. Is this how you find him?"

I suppress a laugh and only grin at the word. "Well, yes, at times."

Metztli looks at Will as if she is considering her purchase

and then runs her fingers along his jaw as she purrs, "Perhaps you need a new mistress."

Oh, JustWill, be quiet, be quiet. I know this is said in my head, but I feel like I am yelling it as I stare at him.

"She is *not* my mistress. I am a free Bosch man…"

Fuck. "Will..," I attempt to cut him off.

"…just like all of these people you keep here should be free."

So, he's not wrong, but it's an awkward place to decide to make a stand. Of course, maybe I should have thought of that during the last mission. "Okay, well, we probably need to go." I stand up and toss a case at the chest of each man, taking two myself, and begin to climb off the dais.

"No!" Metztli calls with distress and signals for her guards. She grasps Will's arm, causing his marker case to drop to the ground, and tries to hustle him off toward the corner. He shakes his arm and gives her a shove, causing her to land on her ample bottom.

I see a guard take aim at Will, so I yell for him to get down. I turn and fire several times at the floor in front of the guard, shattering the tile at his feet and dropping my cases. The people in the room are yelling and scattering. The guard jumps back and is slow to level his weapon again. Just the time we require.

I hit my comm to the vessel. "Need some help here…." I fire toward another guard. I'm not looking to kill anyone, but I need to protect my people. Tom and Will now have their weapons out and are making for the door.

"Don't forget the markers," I call over the ruckus and am delighted to see the men grab three of the cases, Will with one under his arm and one in his free hand.

I nab the fourth and shove my way toward the door. I take a moment to fire high at the crystal light fixtures. They explode and drop shards everywhere, making for good cover for my unit. We reach the large door, and the men heave at it, all of us kicking and using the butts of our weapons on guards trying to bodily stop us. Then the door swings open and the three of us are outside just in time to see the vessel hovering above the front gardens with the ladder dropped.

My vessel is taking some heavy fire from the outdoor guards, but it's built to resist small weaponry. I see Gia hanging down from the hatch with a weapon in hand, firing and covering Tom as he clambers up the ladder. Will tosses one case to Gia and then starts his climb with the second. I look back to the house as I run suppressive fire from below, protecting my crew. I hear noise from the roof and watch, astonished, as a large piece of ordnance is wheeled out on the roof.

"Let's get the fuck outta here!" My voice is loud and insistent. I run a second round of suppressive fire with my semi-automatic weapon at the...Sweet New Earth. There are a lot of guards.

I scramble up the ladder. I can feel ammunition whizz past me, and I am grateful when I finally feel the hull on my belly. No time to rest, though. I yell to Demery and Bailey, "Fire on the roof!"

They are already at their stations and fire in unison.

I get myself to the helm, and Gia and I engage the engines. I pull the nose almost straight up and put on full power. I hear the boom of the ordnance firing and then the explosion, but I know we are well out of range. I level off and look down at where my vessel had been. There's a sizeable crater there now.

"Okay, then." I let out the breath I hadn't realized I was holding. "Dem, Bailey—they can't keep that artillery. Blow it to the moon!"

"Aye" and "On it" come from either side of the vessel. I

hear a few keystrokes and then a resounding crash, followed by my gunners' whoops of joy. Gunners: they do like blowing shit up.

There is busy silence for several minutes while we all attend to our jobs as we flee toward the border. Once we are out of Mynian airspace, the mood lifts for most of us, but Will McCloud is brooding, silent, and unsmiling.

"So, JustWill, still like old Grandad's place?" I hear Tom give a hoot of laughter, but Will just looks away. *What is his problem?*

I put the autopilot on and retrieve the cases of markers. I am practically giddy as I squat down to open them and survey the funds. "This is almost double the QM price!" I exclaim to the unit. "The balance goes into the pot, and now we'll divvy it up six ways."

"You shouldn't," Will finally speaks, and his voice is bitter. "I almost got you all killed out there. I completely fucked up. I don't deserve anything."

So, that's the issue. I sit back on my heels in a low squat, rocking back and forth, and smile at him. "Jeez, JustWill, we all fuck up sometimes. Think of me on our last mission." I give him a teasing, crooked grin and shrug. "And when we do, we figure out how to do it better the next time. You are part of this unit. You take your share of the pot's riches when it is there, and you help pay the pot's debts when it comes due."

Will looks at me, and I see the worried lines soften and those steel-blue eyes look right into mine. "The thrall thing feels a bit different when someone is looking at you as one."

My hand goes automatically to my brand, and I run my fingers over it. I see JustWill glance down at it, and then his eyes go back to mine, and he gives a small half-smile and tips his head to the side. There is an apology in those eyes. I am held by his gaze for a moment, then I smile back. "Yeah. It does."

"It won't happen again, Troop."

"I know. And, hell, we have our own Helen of Troy. A pretty face to take down a civilization…" I give him a teasing grin. "…even after all the rearranging of it I attempted."

Will's abashed expression breaks, and he gives me a broad grin that lights up his whole face. "I'm a fucking modern medical miracle."

THIRTEEN

The Venturer

I hustle the twins off of the vessel after it lands on the deck of the *Venturer* just before sunset. Grey is well ahead of me and making a beeline for her papa. The boys are being scrappy with one another and with me. Six hours confined with a pair of unslept three-year-olds is enough to make anyone break, so I'm impressed I didn't toss them into the Southern Sea. Small parenting wins.

I pause, collecting some of the flotsam and jetsam of the children from on board the vessel and thanking the pilot and his wife, Renzo and Kitty Berry, when I hear the boys exclaim with delight as they spy Takai. I am nervous about how Takai will respond to my surprise appearance. I'm hoping the children haven't told him I am here, but they aren't the best secret keepers. I make my way out, but Takai is already headed inside with his back to me, Grey on his shoulders and a boy in each arm.

I come up behind him and put my hands on the outside of his shoulders. "Surprise!" Time to see which column this decision goes in.

"Sweet New Earth!" I love that he says that now. Takai

almost drops Kik as he whirls around, staring at me. "Kat. You are here? But we had said… What are you…? Why are you…?"

I hear the children shriek in joy as I watch Takai's face. Maybe they do keep secrets well. I grin at him as he stammers. "I miss my husband. That's 'what, why, how,' my love." Granted the 'my love' might not land well, given that he didn't want me to come.

I watch as Takai stands frozen, his eyes shifting left and right for several seconds. I can see his brain working to decide on his response. Finally, his eyes settle on me. "And I missed you." He nods, and then I see a smile on his face, though it looks a bit forced. "You are here. That's…good. I mean, it's wonderful."

I smile coquettishly at him. "I figured I had better make my presence known to ward off the long lines of hearts you are liable to break." I am only somewhat kidding. Beautiful women do tend to flock to Takai.

Takai's head comes up and he looks at me with wide eyes. "Oh, Kat, I…"

"I'm joking, Takai. I just really wanted to see you. If you know what I mean." I try to send a look that balances lust and love. In response, I see Takai's face soften as he looks hungrily at me. The look is clouded quickly as the children pull on him, demanding his attention.

The walk from the landing pad to the cabins takes almost half a bell. I am amazed at how large the *Venturer* is. "It's like walking home from the airfield!" I exclaim as we turn up yet another section of the ship. "This ship is huge!"

"It is one of the largest sailing vessels in the FA fleet." Takai sounds proud, but he also seems distracted. Both his hands are occupied with a rotation of children, but in the brief periods in between, I see him reach for his comm only to be stymied by another small hand. I consider slipping mine into the mix.

As we walk, crew members salute and speak to Takai and he to them. He seems to know all their names. I am impressed, though not surprised. He has always been an excellent leader.

We finally arrive at the door to Takai's quarters, and the crewman who has been carrying our bags sets them at the door. I feel a small headache coming on, and I kneel to fish some medicine out of my luggage as Takai and the children barrel on into the quarters. I swallow them down sans water, pick up my bag, and head into the captain's suite.

I pause at the door. The children are on the couch talking animatedly to a beautiful young Edoan woman with raven black hair that flows well past her shoulders. She is dressed in a silk dress adorned with a print of pale pink cherry blossoms. I watch as she folds intricate animals out of paper. Clearly, this is First Officer Miyamoto. She looks quite at home. Alarm bells begin to clang in my head, and I know the medicine I took will do nothing for my headache now. The first officer looks up and sees me, her face moving from a gentle smile to a surprised expression to a panicked glance at Takai and then a calmer face back to me.

Grey hops down from the sofa and says, "Mama, this is Hayami. I told you about her. Hayami, this is my mama." I force my legs to move. It feels as if they are weighted down with stones.

I have children. I am their example. Sweet New Earth, don't let me kill in front of them. I focus on bringing air into my lungs as I approach the young woman who is holding my sons in her lap and extend my hand, forcing a smile.

"Hayami, such a lovely name. It means rare beauty,

correct? It fits. It's delightful to meet you." I make sure to maintain eye contact.

Hayami reaches up to meet my hand with hers. She gets to her feet a bit awkwardly as she must shimmy out from under the three-year-olds who are playing contentedly with her hair. Her voice is, as I should have expected, melodious. "I am the one who is delighted. You are Kat? I did not know you were to accompany the children on this visit."

Clearly. "I decided to keep it a surprise. And I see I have succeeded."

I break my eye contact with this Edoan vision and look around the room for Takai. He is standing to the side, his shoulders tense and his thumb rubbing his fingers the way he does when he is nervous. I look at him, attempting to read his face and look in his eyes, but he glances down.

Then I hear him clear his throat. "Officer Miyamoto is my first officer. She was very kind to the children when they last visited." Takai steps a bit closer to the sofa but then seems to power down.

The melodious voice tunefully chimes in. "I was looking forward to more stories from them about Bosch."

I decide to disengage. "I am going to go get cleaned up from the trip. I have the angst of two three-year-olds and the ennui of an almost seven-year-old all over me." I try to keep my voice light and humorous for the children, but I assure the eager beast inside me that she will get equal time. Later. I grab my bag and start to head for the bedroom and the bath and then realize I don't know where it is.

"Um…I need a guide."

"I'll show you." Takai jerks to life and comes to me, taking the bag and heading into the hallway. He stops at the second door on the left. "This is my—our—room. The head is just off it."

"Perfect," I nod. "I'll be out as soon as I have showered and dressed." I open the door and take my bag.

Takai hesitates, and I hold my breath hoping for...I'm not sure... An apology? Reassurance? An "I love you, Kat"? Instead, I hear the captain of the *Venturer* speak. "Just a five-minute shower, please. I gave the order this morning as we are low on fresh water until we desalinate some more."

My jaw clenches slightly. "Aye-aye, Captain." The beast growls, and I am compelled to toss it a morsel. "Oh, wait, perhaps I should use a different title. Wouldn't want you getting us mixed up." The beast gives a small, contented sound but sits awake and alert. I smile, step into the room, and close the door in my husband's face.

I lean back on the closed door. *I wonder if the first officer can wash all that hair in five minutes.* I envision taking a large pair of scissors to those lovely locks, which pleases the beast. I head to the shower, which I find is an excellent place for a five-minute cry.

Okay, I took a seven-minute shower. I respect water rationing, but Takai can just cut two minutes off his own in the morning. I reach for the incredibly fluffy towel that hangs on the hook on the back of the head door. *They do take care of their Captain.* As I pull the towel off toward me, something slithers to the floor. I stare. It's a yukata, and it shimmers in pinks and mauves like a sunrise. I reach out to pick it up. It is silk, and the fabric practically flows like honey over my hand. I lift it to my nose, not knowing why, and inhale it. Spring blossoms with a hint of citrus. It slips from my fingers to the floor again. I start to feel tears again but blink fast. I glance down at the towel I had pulled and realize who may have used it. I drop it quickly, kicking it away. I look around the head and see a stack of neatly folded hand towels. I take one from the middle and use it to dry myself. I open the door, skirting the two pieces of fabric on the floor, and step into the bedroom to get dressed.

I look at the bed, and a picture forms in my mind about who has slept, or done whatever else, in it. I feel the beast rouse in me. I reach out from as far away as possible to grab the underclothes I had pulled out and tossed next to my clean tunic and leggings and snatch them toward me. I grab my leggings and draw them over my legs and then turn to the tall bookshelf where I put my weapons. As I gently pull the holsters, they come away quickly and land in my hands empty of their weapons. I frown, confused. Where are they? I stand on tiptoe to see the shelf: There is no blade, no pair of pistols. *He took them.* I growl in concert with the beast. I consider searching the cupboards, but I have had enough unexpected discoveries today. I strap on the holsters and then pull my tunic from the bed and slip it over my head.

I step out of the room and hear the children chatting gaily with Takai. I listen for a moment but hear no melodious voice. *The children are the most important thing. They love their papa.* I take a deep breath and set my jaw. *After they are in bed.*

Turning around the corner, I focus on my little pirates. "Avast, me hearties! Let's get a snack and put on cozy pajamas!" The children giggle furiously because they love it when I use the old pirate-speak and come tumbling toward me, while out of the corner of my eye I see Takai's face drop into a frown and he rolls his eyes.

∾

Takai finally appears from the children's room with all three deeply asleep. I am sitting on a chair in the living room sipping on a glass of wine. It isn't District Seven wine, but it is pretty good. I have turned the chair so I can see the whole room. He stops at the door from the dining room and looks at me.

I break the uncomfortable silence. "Are you going to stand or are you going to sit?" He looks at a chair, and I see his eyes flick to the door that leads out. "Running is not an option. I have things to say."

His eyebrows crease, and he slowly comes and sits down. He finally speaks, and he actually tries to admonish me. "I told you not to come, Kat…."

I give a full-throated laugh that startles him. "Oh, this is not my doing." I am pleased to hear my voice strong and steady. "I said I have things to say. I have little interest in what you have to say." He starts to respond, and I hold up my hand. "This is not like the others." As I sat here waiting for him, I stripped off the covers that I had carefully placed to assure myself my husband was faithful. Now I can see beneath them all the other lovers that have been in my husband's arms. But I also know they were transitory, short-term conquests. This, though… I look at him. "You are here—playing house with your first officer—after running away from home because you didn't like where I moved us."

"Officer Miyamoto was simply here to visit the children…," Takai begins, his right hand brushing the hairline near his ear.

The volume and pitch of my voice rise somewhat. "I'm not an idiot, Takai. Do not treat me as one. I think we both know that lovely yukata in the bath is not yours."

Takai finally looks me in the face, and he has no response.

"I will not sleep here. I will stay for the weekend for the children, but you will find me alternate quarters. You will either end it with her or end it with me." Takai looks at the ground but still says nothing. "Now, where are my weapons?" His head comes up and his eyes are wide...with fear?

My jaw drops, and I stare at this man I have shared so many years and so much with. "Did you think I would attack you or her?" Now, granted my beast did toy with some rather violent images, but that isn't the same. "Me? The woman who promised to care for you through storms and sunshine, who birthed her children into your hands." I feel the angry, hurt tears begin. How could he think that of me? I'm currently unsure which cut is the most painful: his infidelity or his distrust. "You. You betray me and your family and then try to turn the tables by accusing me of being a danger?" I stare at him. I make a new column marked *Bad Decisions* and put a tally mark in for rescuing my husband from the Chinese all those years ago.

Takai looks back at me, and for the first time ever, I see what looks like regret in his eyes.

But I am unmoved. "Shame on you." I stand and move toward the bedroom to grab my bag. I tap on the console table under the mirror. "I expect all three items to be on this table before I come back." Takai sits unmoving.

When I return, Takai is standing, and my pistols—magazines in, safeties on—and my double-edge bone-handled knife are sitting on the table. I set my luggage down, and I silently check each one and place them in their proper places on my body. Picking up my bag, I look at Takai expectantly. He clears his throat.

"There are some VIP guest quarters. I will walk you..."

"No need. Just call whoever you need to, and I will find my way to them." I look at him and he slowly nods and then picks up his comm. I think of something else before I walk out the door.

I turn around, and he looks up with a small light of hope in his eyes. "Kat, you know…"

I talk over him. I don't want to hear him say he loves me. I don't even know what that means anymore. "I don't want her here with the children. It's too confusing for them. Until we know what's happening, she is not to come near them, savvy?"

Takai's face loses its hopeful expression, and I see his chin move the way it does when he is pouting. Poor baby. I turn, open the door, and walk out, closing it gently, but in my mind, I slam it behind me.

Part II

FOURTEEN

Leave Me Alone or Don't

We arrive back from the *Venturer* late on Sunday night, and the children go to sleep quickly, comforted to be in their own beds, but I can't bring myself to even go to the room I had shared so often with Takai. I sit, then lean, and then recline on the sofa, finally falling into a fitful sleep.

I can smell the salt and hear the seabirds call as I move from the dusty road to the dune where the vessel is parked. The seagrasses brush against my legs and feel sharp. I turn, and I am suddenly inside the vessel with Teddy at the helm, and I remember that I am on a mission with him. I know the plan because it is the same every time. We are getting thralls off this island. I look over at the cargo hold and the cargo door. There are so many of them, I don't know if they'll fit on the little vessel. Then Teddy holds up his hand and says, "That's all we can manage."

"But what about them?" I ask, gesturing to the unbroken line of mostly women who are trying to shove onto our vessel. One of the women reaching for the cargo door is petite and blonde and looks like a frightened rabbit.

"He'll take them." Teddy points to a man standing off to

the side in a silken jacket with an elegant necktie. Rob Aber-nathy has a loathsome smirk on his face as he looks right into my eyes. He reaches out and grasps the upper arm of the blonde woman roughly, and I am filled with rage. I will kill him this time. I pull my blade and start to rush toward him, fighting my way through the throng of thralls.

Suddenly, my dad is in front of me. He sneers at me. "You're useless. Nobody wants you. Not even him." He points, and I see Takai with his arms around his first officer. They laugh and Takai says, "Who would ever want a pirate? You don't even have a compass," before he leans down to kiss the woman in his arms. I watch as her hair shifts from black to red to blonde, always long and flowing. Somewhere behind me, I hear Sergeant Marin's voice. "You are the worst, Kat Wallace. You are the worst mama, mama, mama."

"Mama. Mama. Mama." Grey's little voice appears like a metronome from out of nowhere. "Mama. Kat. Kat Wallace. We are hungry. I have school."

My eyes pop open, and I see three beautiful faces staring at me from where I lay on the sofa. Grey is holding her brothers by their hands. I squint at them and look at my watch. Almost seven bells. Ugh. I simultaneously try to keep the dream in my mind because I want to return to killing the monster and try to push it aside, disturbed by my old insecurities. I sigh and sit up, tugging my tunic where it has wound around me.

"Breakfast. Right." I yawn, then remember what I heard and look at Grey. "Did you call me by my name?"

Grey giggles. "Yes. Kat Wallace. You are Kat Wallace." The boys start chorusing, "Kat Wallace!"

I soften and chuckle and wrap them all in a big hug. At least I have them. "Yes, that's my name. But I like being called 'Mama' by you three. Now let me get up, and then we can make cinnamon toast and strawberries." *And coffee, lots of coffee*. The dream has receded, but the feelings of rage and inadequacy still bubble in my belly. I push them down and cover them to get my children ready for the day.

I slide silently into my spot at the helm, having missed PT and the mission brief this morning. The rest of the unit is already on board.

"Sorry," I mumble. "Overslept." I glance at Gia, not wanting to make eye contact for too long. *Better to stay apart.* "Just plug in the coordinates, and you can brief me on my role when we are airborne." I see her brows drop as she looks at me with a curious expression. She doesn't say anything.

Bailey does, though. "What the hell, Kat? Spill. We want to hear about your trip to the ship and the mysterious Takai."

I pause, then rotate my seat around to see the other four members of our unit looking eagerly at me. I glance to the side and see Gia's face, a mask of controlled expectation. "Major, I have no interest in telling that story. Let's get our job done so I can go home to my children." I swivel my chair back and start to power up the engines, listening to the silence behind me.

And so the week goes, for that mission and the next. I show up to work, speak only when I have to, and leave as soon as my responsibilities are completed. Gia has tried to get me to chat during breaks or in training, as have the rest of the unit. Except for JustWill. He has given me space, though I have looked up a few times to see him studying me. When I look back at him, he says nothing, simply giving me a half-smile and a nod. I appreciate the lack of expectation.

At home, the kids and I take care of each other. I am careful not to mention any conflict to them, but they, being of my body, can sense my sadness and anger and are at times conciliatory and, because they are children, at other times are antagonistic. Mama knows something is up, but she has, as always, gently let me know she is around when I need her. I don't want to share the story. It will make it seem too real. I wonder occasionally if I could have been mistaken, but then the memory of the smell of blossoms and citrus and the silken feel of that lovely yukata reminds me that this isn't like past suspicions.

No comms from the Southern Sea come through this week, though, on Friday afternoon, an envelope is delivered from the *Venturer*. It holds a letter for Grey to share with her brothers as well as some neatly folded paper animals. I resist my urge to throw the whole lot into the fire.

We sit down in the living room, and Grey reads the simple letter from their papa aloud to her brothers, who are playing with their paper swans and horses.

Dear children,

I am so glad you visited me on my ship. It was wonderful to spend the weekend with you. I know I usually comm you, but I thought a letter would be a nice change. Grey, I would love a letter back. Kik and Mac, you can draw some pictures and include them in the envelope. I will call early next week, and then I will be in Bosch to celebrate your seventh birthday, Grey!

With love,

Papa

Excitement explodes from the children at the news that Papa will be home. Of course, he didn't say home, but Bosch. However, I don't parse the language for the children but let them enjoy their excitement and anticipation. I sit quietly, watching the three whoop and jump, and then Kik comes over to me, looking at me with his papa's eyes under a shock of black hair. He gently pats my shoulder and says solemnly, "It's okay, Mama. Papa will send you a letter too."

I force a smile and give a nod. "Papa and I will have a comm soon." He better believe we will. I gave Takai an ultimatum, and he has yet to respond. I pick up a folded rabbit from the table and turn it thoughtfully in my hands. Or maybe he has.

I hear Takai's footsteps as he comes slowly down the stairs from tucking the children in. There is an audible pause at the foot of the steps before he turns to come toward the front room, where I sit at the table waiting. We have spoken to each other but only about mundane things like dinner, the shutter that needs repair, and the agenda for the birthday party tomorrow. Somehow, he managed to evade any comms from me through the week leading up to his arrival.

Now he sits down across from me in his usual chair. "Kat," Takai begins. I am not looking at him. "Grey is on her break from school. I'd like to have all three children come back with me tomorrow evening to the ship for the week."

Well, that's a quick turn-around trip. My first impulse is to say no, but I know that's what the children want as well. So, I finally raise my head toward him, not meeting his eyes. "Okay. That sounds like a reasonable plan." He starts to scoot his chair back and stand.

"Takai…"

He sits slowly back. I finally look at him. He is still as attractive as when I met him. Maybe more so as I know the origin of the smattering of lines that have formed on his face over the last almost decade. "I asked you to make a choice." I leave the statement to hang. But it doesn't for long.

"I'm not ready to, Kat. I need more time."

I feel as if I have been struck to the ground. My mind spins. *More time?* This was meant to be an easy decision. *Choose your wife. Choose me.* But now it appears that he is actually weighing his options. I want to lash out in anger but remember how he had taken my weapons on the ship out of fear of me becoming violent. I will not give him the satisfaction of seeing me lose my temper. The beast is roaring, and I have to push it into a room and shut the door. "I see." I stand up, knowing I have to get away from his presence quickly to avoid going ballistic. "I'll get the children packed in the morning, so you can leave straight away after the party. And Takai…" I am headed for the back door and my workout shed. "Do keep me posted on your decision. And the sooner the better. I certainly don't intend to wait until your three-year assignment is completed." I step into the warm April night and take a deep breath. The heavy bag will suffer tonight.

I am standing still in the front yard as the sun sets, my back to the road, staring at my front door. I painted it a brilliant cobalt blue a few weeks ago, and I like how it makes the entry seem friendly and welcoming. But right now, I don't want to go into the house. Grey's party is over, and the little guests have all been retrieved by their parents. Takai and the children have left for the *Venturer*, and I just spent half a bell assuring Mama I was fine and that Takai and I were just going through a rough patch without going into too much detail. Eventually, I was able to convince her to go home. Now, having walked her to the gate and watched her walk to the end of the street and disappear around the corner, I am aware of it being a *not-so-good* decision. I am suddenly terrified of being alone with my thoughts.

"Hey, Trooper." A vehicle has pulled up near the gate, and I hear Gia's voice call to me. I turn. The entire unit, including JustWill, is packed into a gray, mid-sized vehicle, windows open as they all wave to me. Gia is out of the driver's seat and coming toward me.

"Gia, I don't think—"

"Girl, we don't care what you think or don't think. Grey told my girls she and the boys would be gone for the week with Takai. And we aren't about to let this opportunity go by to get you out for a drink."

"No…," I protest weakly because I think I want to go.

"C'mon." Gia pulls me toward the house. "Let's get you dressed."

I wrinkle my brow. "I am dressed," I say, indicating my grey leggings and blue tunic, which, truth be told, has a bit of cake icing on the front of it.

Gia looks me up and down and gives me a dubious smile, and that's when I notice she is wearing a snug red dress that descends in the front pretty far down. I look at her feet and see strappy sandals with a decent heel. I turn to look at the vehicle and notice the rest of them are all dressed up as well. I throw up my hands. "Fine." A cheer erupts from the unit, and Gia steers me inside to change.

When I reappear twenty minutes later, practically shoved out the door by Gia, the unit is out of the vehicle, standing and talking. The conversation is a bit raucous as it tends to be with them, but when I step off the stoop, they turn and are silent.

Gia had been disgusted by the choices of clothes I had when we went inside.

"Where's your fancy clothes, Kat?" She was digging through drawers and rifling through my closet.

"Here." I pushed past her and pulled out a tunic and legging set.

"And what's so special about these?" She had looked unimpressed.

I chuckled. "Well, for one, they're clean.

Gia shook her head. "Not a chance, Kat. What are my other options?"

So, I had sighed and looked around. "Maybe something in there?" I gestured to the box of Mimi's old things that she said she was done with. Gia began to dig through it and started to exclaim in delight.

And so here I stand, four members of my unit staring at me while the fifth is eyeing me as if I am some prized piece of art she has created. These are not the kind of clothes I am used to. I feel massively uncomfortable. The pants are leather-like and made like leggings, which is what Gia said they were, but they don't look like leggings while on. They cling to my thighs and rear, accentuating the latter pretty dramatically. The sweater, while long-sleeved, also clings and just settles on my shoulders, plunging deeply in the back and not quite as deeply in the front. Gia found Mama's pearls that she had given me and put them on me and then put her own hoop earrings in my ears. My feet are, thankfully, larger than Gia's, so I get to wear my own shoes, but I did pull out nice ones, and I am glad they are flat. The one saving grace of this outfit is that it is all in black.

Demery and Bailey come walking over first, eyes narrowed, looking me up and down. Bailey is the first to speak, shaking their head. "Sweet New Earth, Kat. You actually have a figure. How come it doesn't show in your uniform?"

"See? I told you," Gia chimes in as I feel my cheeks color. "I didn't know either. Apparently, everything she owns is a size TB: too big."

"Why the hell would you do that?" Bailey asks as Tom comes closer as well with a foolish grin.

I roll my eyes. "If you must know, it makes it easier to conceal."

Tom and Demery and Bailey all frown and Bailey asks, "Obviously, but why?"

"What is it you want to conceal?" Tom looks genuinely confused.

Gia has started laughing. "Tell them, Kat."

I'm getting annoyed. "Weapons, of course." And I hear a chorus of sudden understanding "Ahh." What did they think I meant? I glance down at my outfit and consider the options.

"Well, of course. That's important when you go out to dinner," Demery adds in his own appraisal and I can hear jest in his tone.

"Okay, this is too auspicious for Barton's. I say we hit The Roadhouse." Tom is now planning the evening.

The Roadhouse is probably the nicest restaurant around if you don't want to go all the way to the districts. It has live music and dancing on the weekends. I've never been there.

Suddenly, I realize there is one unit member yet to comment on Gia's doll-dressing of me. I look around and see JustWill still over by the fence, staring. At me. He shakes his head a little when I catch his eye, grins in a devil-may-care way, and gives me a thumbs-up. I feel another flow of color to my face, and I give an exaggerated shrug and feel a smile creep onto my lips. He starts to laugh, which sets me laughing, and before I know it, we are, all six, tucked into the gray vehicle, laughing and on our way for a night of music, dancing, and as far as I'm concerned, bourbon.

FIFTEEN

Unexpected Alliances

I'm sitting on a little hill above the airfield under a flowering tree on the Sunday afternoon after our Saturday night Roadhouse trip. We had all danced, drank, laughed, and talked until the single bells. No one asked about Takai or what was going on. It was a blissful respite from the thoughts that consumed me. Now I am back to rolling all those thoughts around in my head and trying to sort out my feelings.

Suddenly, JustWill appears next to me and flops down on the soft ground. "Here." He hands me a bunch of hyacinths and windflowers tied with a long brown piece of last season's grass and smiles. "I like windflowers. They are so lovely, but ephemeral."

I take the offered bouquet. "I planted some in Mama's yard. She says they remind her to enjoy what she has while it is here."

Will grins. "A wise woman." Then his smile drops, and his eyes study my face. "I saw you from the hangar. You looked down. I wanted to cheer you up."

I snort. "You can tell the difference between sad and hungover from that distance? That's a superpower."

He chortles. "Nothing a little water and workout won't cure." He says this out of the corner of his mouth with what amounts to a swagger in his voice.

I laugh as he has quoted every Monday-morning drill sergeant since the beginning of the Bosch Pirate Force.

"No." He shakes his head. "I know the expression you have on. It's the 'What the hell do I do about the people in my life?' expression. I wear it every time I get done talking with my dad."

I am gently touching the flowers in my hand. "Is he still after you to resign your commission?"

"Always. That'll never stop. Most recently, he has threatened to cut me out of his will. I could only hope. What about you?"

He is so casual in his question that I just answer. "Takai is having an affair with his first officer. It's not the first time this has happened either, but it's the first time it is so brazen that I can't pretend like I don't know. I told him to decide between us, but so far, he hasn't. So, I am in limbo."

There's a pause, and I prepare myself to be annoyed by the onslaught of pity and outrage on my behalf.

But my annoyance is preempted with astonishment as he says, "Why in the hell would you let him have the power to make that kind of decision about your life? It's *your* life, Kat. You decide."

I look sharply over at him. "I don't know that it's that easy."

Will runs a hand through his blond hair. It stands up on end, and I watch the tiny breeze up here move it back and forth. He shakes his head. "You are right. It isn't easy. But take it from someone who has always been told how to live his life: It's worth trying. Hell, even if you get it wrong, at least it will be your mistake, not someone else's."

I give a sad grin and consider his words. "Seems like I am in the presence of a master, then."

He snorts a laugh. "Hardly. I keep trying, but it's easy to fall back into the old patterns. I think that, along with my facial lacerations…" He rubs one of the now-healed places on his face. "…is why I was so mad about being forced to join this unit initially."

I'm confused. "What do you mean?"

"The whole bully-the-Master-Commander's-killer thing. That came from my dad. He had all kinds of things to say about 'some outsider' as he called you. I should never have listened to him."

I consider the vagaries of life and how a tally in *not-so-good* can end up shifting into the *good* column. "Maybe so. But hey, if you hadn't, you wouldn't be sitting here right now. So, silver lining."

He grins. "Definitely a silver lining." He looks at me with his steel-blue eyes, and they are soft and kind and have a sparkle of affection in them. I look back at him, and we hold our gaze for several seconds.

"Who would have figured you and I would end up friends after all that?" I finally say.

His gaze shifts, and I see his eyes flit over my face and, curiously, my body, until he looks at the ground. "Friends." He raises his eyebrows and sighs. "Yeah. Who would have figured? Not me." He looks back at me now and grins. "So, what are you going to decide, Kat Wallace?"

I rub the back of my neck and give my own sigh. "Well, if it were just me? I'd cut and run." I run my hands over the new spring grass that forms a carpet around me. "But it isn't just me. I have kids, and I have to figure out how to do what is best for them."

Will lays back on the grass, looking up at the sky. "I don't know what it's like to have kids. But if I ever do, I hope I'm as caring a parent as you are."

I lie down as well, the top of my head near the top of his as I watch the clouds scoot across the April blue sky, and a few tree blossoms gently float down on us both. I reach around and give his shoulder a soft punch. "That's one of the nicest things anyone has ever said to me."

"Really?" His voice carries surprise. "You should have nice things said to you more often then. I'll make a note."

We laugh, but I am genuinely touched by this sentiment and can't help but try to catalog the last time my husband said something nice to me. Our conversation meanders from Takai and Will McCloud Sr. to Edo and Bosch to the Force and why we enlisted. JustWill chuckles softly as I recall Teddy's talk with me in the library soon after I had arrived. It feels good to remember the old times.

"Teddy was always there for me. Even when 'being there' meant leaving me to figure it out myself." I am wistful in my remembrance.

Will is up, leaning on one elbow. He reaches over and gently picks a tree blossom from my cheek. "My dad and I always argue. Sounds like you and Teddy never did." His voice holds an equal amount of wistfulness.

At this, I hoot a laugh. "Never argue? Hardly." I roll onto my stomach and prop my head onto my hands, looking at this man who is turning out to be one of the few people I feel comfortable with. "We argued. Hell, we fought." I smile and look off at the horizon as I so often do when remembering my Bosch papa. "We had some glorious fights. I can still hear him: *Don't go off half-cocked, Kat!* Hell, I was born half-cocked, and he knew it!" I am smiling as I watch the sun start to dip below the horizon, and I realize there are tears on my cheeks as well. "And I knew I could always rely on him."

I feel Will's thumb on my cheek, catching and wiping away a tear. "And he knew he could rely on you. That's why he asked you to do what you did." He is smiling at me.

I smile back and then let out an audible breath and rub my face. "Too many feelings. Let's just focus on one. I'm hungry."

"Hunger is not a feeling." He hops to his feet and offers me a hand up, which I consider mocking but take instead.

"Is too."

"Is not."

This banter carries us down the hillside, where we decide to head to the market to get some soup as the temperature descends with the sun.

"I told Mama I would come by. Want to come?" I am not sure why I make this offer. Maybe it's because I don't want to be alone; maybe it's because I am genuinely enjoying Will McCloud's company.

We arrive at the friendly brick house, and Mama is sitting in the swing on the front porch, wrapped in a furry blanket and reading. She looks up as I call, "I brought soup!" I watch as she sets her book and blanket to the side and comes to me with a hug and a smile that tells me I am home.

Introductions are not needed as Mama remembers Will from years before. As she escorts us into the house, she gushes about how much he looks like his father until she sees how uncomfortable he is with the comparison, and then as Mama always does, she shifts the topic to something pleasant. "Tell me about your engineering, young Will."

"Nope, Mama. It's JustWill." I am getting soup bowls and spoons out, and I watch as he laughs at my comment and then shifts from uncomfortable to excited and animated. Having him over goes in the *good decision* column.

"Well, Miriam, I am currently working on a stability mechanism that stems from the one I created for vessels beyond the wing sweep to one that will aid in building stability. I think it has some great applications for use, particularly in areas that are prone to earthquakes, like Arania."

As we sit down to the meal of warm soup and crusty bread and sweet wine, he continues to describe the mechanisms he is developing, and Mama asks him encouraging questions. I am fascinated by his descriptions and insight. I realize Tom is right: when it comes to engineering, Will is something of a savant. I listen as he continues earnestly explaining his process to us as he clears the table and refreshes our wine. He is gifted. And he is turning out to be a really good friend.

We are a safe distance from the weapon fire, but I can still hear the ping and thuds as bullets hit. And I can see the brief smoke trails that mark where the skirmish is happening.

"Kat, over here." Will's voice comes through in my ear comm. "I think I see something."

I crawl through the long grass to his position, and he points down the hill to a suspiciously large mound of leaves and grasses that, on closer inspection through my field glasses, has a sizable gun muzzle sticking out of it. I grin. "Bingo! Nice recon!"

Will grins back and his face flushes with the compliment.

"Let's go dismantle it, get some pics, get out, and get paid." We are in Ruthenia on the Eastern Continent. It's a small country, not part of the League of States of the EC, but its position near the straits of the Casplack Sea makes it strategically important. Well, at least to the FA who have hired us, through an intermediary, to be sure, but I know where the markers and the mission specs are coming from. We are to go in and disassemble this large piece of ordnance that JustWill has spotted, allowing the Ruthenians renewed access to the straits and likely the FA as well.

We watch for movement and, seeing none, we look at each other and sit tight.

"There's got to be soldiers around." Will's voice is a whisper in my ear comm.

I murmur back, "It's too easy right now. You wouldn't leave this thing unguarded."

Will frowns. "This complicates things."

"Or it just makes it more exhilarating! Let's go explore!" I grin as I slip down the hill to the next rocky outcropping, seeing his eyes get big.

He slips down next to me, and we are shoulder to shoulder. "You are incorrigible." He is shaking his head but still smiling.

"But I'm also a lot of fun!" I give him a gentle nudge with my elbow.

He snorts softly. "I wouldn't want to be here with anyone else."

I look over at him, and he gives me a warm smile and a wink. I feel a flutter of pleasure at the affection I see in his face and also a niggling worry about what that look may mean.

The unit had received this assignment on Monday, so we ran a quick, fairly local, and very profitable Glitter drop and then came back to research and train for the Thursday mission. Tom and Will plotted out the easiest way to deconstruct the weapon, and Gia came up with several alternative ways in and out of the area. Demery and Bailey not only prepped the vessel for defense but wheedled the quartermaster's office for a few additional weapons and items, like these nifty ear comms, that would make the mission move more smoothly. It was decided, given my experience, I would run the infiltration and take Will along to do the work on the ordnance. So, he and I stayed late all week drilling and discussing possible scenarios, getting dinner brought in each night to our office off the hangar. At first, I was just glad to have a distraction from not having my little ones with me at home, but by the end of the week, I found myself eager just to sit and talk with Will.

"Let's move out then!" Will's voice is receding away as he slides down the hill toward the gun. My ear comm chirps, and I hear Gia giving me their position. We landed the vessel in the Casplack Sea outside of Ruthenian airspace, just off the coastline, and Will and I took a small raft to shore. Now Gia has maneuvered it to the fairly hidden cove that Bosch Intelligence had recommended. I check my map and make a note of the position for exfil.

As I click off from the comm, I hear voices below me. Shit. Is Will in trouble? I reach for one of my pistols as I peer down and see Will crouched and speaking to two men in a loud whisper as he gestures with his hands at the ordnance. He looks up the hill to me and signals me to come down.

I re-holster my weapon and do a controlled slide down the hill and come to rest next to Will, facing the men who I now see are Ruthenian. They look dubiously at me, and I return the sentiment, along with my best "Don't fuck with me" look. "What's up?" I look to Will.

"This is Artem." Will motions to the one man. "And this is Marko." He points to the other. "They want the gun." He then uses two fingers to point to our target. "Our intel said it was put in place ostensibly by the Kubans, but these two say it really was placed by the Rus who the Ruthenians have been having border skirmishes with."

"Right." I nod, looking intently at the men, trying to sense any tells on them that might indicate a trap. "That argument has been going on for centuries."

Artem turns toward me and starts to speak. He is as tall as Will and very broad through the chest. His skin is as pale as mine, something I don't encounter much in Bosch. Even blond, blue-eyed Will has colored to a deep tan, though it is only early spring. Artem has soft gray eyes and a full beard. He now speaks standard FA somewhat haltingly. "We want the gun. We want to be independent."

I grin and reply in Ruthenian, "We understand that desire. We are Bosch, and we value our independence."

Both men smile at this, but I see their smiles drop as I continue. "But our mission is to dismantle that gun. And we need to fulfill it. Can't very well take people's markers and then not do the job. Bad for business."

Marko is frowning, and the corners of his lips narrow as his brows knit downward. It is apparent in his pallid face that he is moving quickly toward anger. I don't want a fight with these people; we have some of the same values—first and foremost: independence. I quickly add to my statement, "However, Lieutenant McCloud here could show you how he dismantles it and teach you how to reinstall the parts after we finish."

At this, the smiles return, and I give an inward sigh of relief. Now to get some details. "So, what's the guard situation with the ordnance?"

Frowns return, though this time they are contemplative, and the men glance cautiously over their shoulders and return to speaking Ruthenian. Artem says, "Not good. It looks deserted, but they have tunnels and trenches around the weapon. There are usually six or more armed soldiers present at all times."

Will and I look at each other. I bite my lip. "Four against

six, plus in close quarters. I don't like those odds. What do you think?" I narrow my eyes as I contemplate this.

"Well, I can be taught. The last time I engaged an untried opponent in the dark, I got my ass handed to me, so how about we make a plan?" Will grins.

I laugh and look at the Ruthenians who are giving us perplexed looks, which is fair, given that we are grinning at each other like idiots while we discuss a potentially dangerous ingress to the ordnance. "You have been watching the weapon and the guards. What do you suggest?" I sober my face, and we all crouch down in the tall grasses. Will and I listen to the intel these men have. After several minutes of discussion, and a bit of an annoyed argument on my part and Will's, a plan is in place.

"I don't like it, Kat." Will's face reflects his concern.

"I don't much like it either, but it seems like it will work." I am stripping off my camouflage and pulling off my leggings. As I move my dagger holster from my thigh to my waist, I hear a murmured comment that has nothing to do with the mission from Artem. Marko laughs in response, and I snap, "Keep your eyes on the gun. And any more comments, and the deal is off. Understood?"

They quiet and I see Will glare at them as I use my blade to slice the sleeves off my new, finally-the-right-size uniform and create a deep plunge in the neckline, so the tops of my breasts are visible. I take the cut fabric and tie it like a scarf around my hair, creating an illusion of length.

"Here goes nothing." I take a deep breath and head toward the area our two new friends indicated was the entrance. And then I collapse in the grasses while holding my ankle and call in Ruthenian. "Ow! My ankle. I've twisted it. Help!" *Sweet New Earth, this whole damsel in distress thing better work, and Will better not throw it back at me.*

After a bit more moaning and wailing on my part, I hear scuffling at the purported entrance, and a man in Rus garb sticks his head out of the ground. He peers around like a ground squirrel scanning for hawks, and then his eyes settle on me, and he grins wolfishly. I give a cowering expression: widening my eyes, willing my cheeks to go pink, and drawing fearfully back. He scrabbles up and calls back to someone, and a second and a third man emerge. That's half. Given their faces and their bearing, I am seriously reconsidering my intent not to kill anyone on this mission. Memories of Bellcoast stir in me, and for a moment, I am transported there, and I feel the old fear. *Focus on the plan, Kat.*

In a matter of moments, Will and the two Ruthenians come up behind the three Rus, and two of them are subdued immediately. The third slips forward and comes for me, apparently planning to use me as a shield. He grabs my arms by the elbows from behind me, and I let myself be pulled back a few steps until I feel his grip loosen slightly. I am just a woman, after all, no need to use too much force. As soon as I feel his focus shift back to the men, I quickly shove my rear into his pelvis, putting him slightly off balance and allowing me to double over. As I do, my hands grasp his shins, and I pull his legs forward and up, toppling him and almost toppling me. I regain my balance, do a quick spin, and slam a heel into the downed man's groin, and number three is quickly out of commission. As I gag and tie my prize, I turn and see the Ruthenians looking stunned and Will grinning.

I grab the Rus' rifle and toss its sling over my head and shoulder as I run my hands over the weapon to familiarize myself and then cock it and look pointedly at Artem and Marko. "Don't ever underestimate the Bosch," I whisper as I rejoin the group. "Or you'll be on the ground as well." I smile sweetly at our allies, and they nod, their eyes seeming to hold more respect for me than when I was simply the female bait in the plan.

Will peers down the entrance, and I notice he, too, has taken on a Rus rifle. I point my liberated weapon down the ladder, sweeping for any soldiers in the shadowy depth. I give a thumbs-up all-clear sign, and silently, Will motions for us to follow him as he slides down the ladder, his weapon drawn and his back against the wall. The rest of us join him, and we find we are in a dimly lit tunnel. The dirt walls are damp and close. I can stand, but the men are taller than me and have to hunch over as we move through the passage. Will and I keep to the formations that we learned as recruits in order to cover each other. The Ruthenians seem to move in a similar way, but it doesn't have the same ease and efficiency to it that Will and I share.

After several minutes, we see a light ahead and hear voices speaking in Rus. Both Will and I raise our right hands up in a quick fist, and the four of us stop, leaning on either side of the walls. The tunnel opens into an open trench covered in sticks and grasses that curves off to either side. I suspect at the center of it is the gun. There are likely three or more guards present in the trench. But they are expecting their compatriots, not us.

Will looks at me, and I indicate that Marko should accompany him. He nods and with a jerk of his head to Marko, starts to move out to the left. I feel unexpected anxiety as he moves out of my sight. Marko follows him, and Artem and I start to move to the right. After we go several paces, sweeping the space with our weapons, I put a hand up. A loud bang ahead breaks the silence, and Artem and I move quickly toward it and hear the sounds of a struggle. As we come around the curve, I almost trip over a large, unconscious man on the ground as I see Will and Marko wrestling with two other sizable men. I leap into the fray. Artem is close behind me, and within a few minutes, the remaining Rus are restrained and muzzled. Will stands, his body tense, and I see blood on his face. I'm not sure if it is his or someone else's, but it disturbs me nonetheless. I see him look quickly around, and as his eyes settle on me, I can see him visibly relax, and his lips turn up in a small smile.

"Well, let's take a peek at this gun, shall we?" I breathe a sigh of relief as I hear his voice, hearty and bold. Will climbs up a short ladder into the middle-high ground the trenches surround and takes the Ruthenians with him.

I comm Gia and make arrangements to move the six Rus to a different location. Leaving them in Ruthenian hands would undoubtedly mean their death, and today's opponents may be tomorrow's customers, so best to leave them with a sense of obligation and appreciation for the Bosch. Another successful mission: I haven't had this much fun with a partner since my runs with Teddy, though this feels different.

Our six unit members are ensconced at the bar at Ray's, one of my favorite places on the planet, as we raucously celebrate a fruitful and well-paid week of missions. Ray's is a simple tavern on the edge of town. It's the bar of choice for non-coms, and I have had some great times and great fights here. Demery and I convinced the vested officers to come here instead of the more officer-friendly Barton's.

We are sitting at the smooth, shiny wooden bar on the rough stools that line it with full glasses of beer in front of us and several small empty shot glasses that had once contained bourbon pushed off to the side. Demery and Ray are talking about the upcoming Council elections, and I lose the thread of the conversation as I look around the place at the large open dance floor with its small dais for weekend musicians. The dance floor is surrounded by several high-top tables with stools, and I see a couple at one table leaning in and kissing and giggling. My thumbnail goes to my teeth as I try to recall the last time I was kissed.

Will nudges me. "Is this true?"

"What?" I startle and return to the conversation. Ray is regaling the unit with the story of a bar fight several years ago, when I had been responsible for the breakage of most of the furniture and windows in the joint. He points out that I am the reason he installed the inside shutters on the few windows in the place, assuring that the light is now always dim and diffuse.

"That shit you called furniture was ancient anyway, Ray." I grin at my bartender friend.

Ray is not tall and has a shaved head. He has muscular arms and always wears a deep gray t-shirt with the bar's logo on it: a stylized red "R" with an extended swash holding a tipped bottle that pours into the red "Y" at the end. Over the years, the shirt size has increased along with Ray's prodigious belly. He returns my grin and nods. "Aye. I was planning to replace it before the end of the year."

"So, I did you a favor, right?" I tease.

He laughs genially. "Always, Kat. You are the soul of altruism."

"You know, there's a spot on the floor at the end of the bar that never quite came clean." I gesture toward the end of the bar as a couple of unit members lean to see a dark stain on a section of the wide, wooden-plank floor.

Will leans back from perusing the area and comments, "I think there's a spot on your street stained the same way…," and he rubs his nose gingerly as if it still pains him.

I playfully pretend to punch him, and he gives an exaggerated lurch onto the bar. We all dissolve into laughter as the bourbon rounds from earlier begin to catch up to us.

"Who is up for another round?" I look around.

Tom stands up. "Not me. I am going home to my wife." He takes a last drink of his beer.

"I want to get home as well." Gia pushes her stool back. "We have tomorrow off since we got so much accomplished, and I want to get a decent night's sleep so I can enjoy the extra day."

I reach out to my fellow non-com. "Demery, you are up for beer or a bourbon, right?"

"Sorry, lass. I'm out as well. It's getting late."

We wave them goodbye, and I look at Bailey and Will. "I guess it's just us then." They nod, and I signal to Ray for three more beers with three bumps.

Not five minutes later, Bailey stands. "Where are you going?" I look at them in their denim pants and lace shirt, braids cascading over their shoulders.

"See that guy over there?" They point to an attractive dark man with a ponytail who has just sat down alone at one of the high-tops. "He's about to be my next, very best, mistake." They laugh. "Ta-ta, kids." Their eyes go from Will to me, and their eyebrows rise slightly. "Don't get into trouble, you two." Their voice is cool and light, but the meaning is clear, and I feel a flush move into my cheeks. I am at once embarrassed and a little offended. I am not my husband. I won't break my promises even if he has broken his. But I can't deny I haven't thought about it.

"And then there were two," Will intones gravely, breaking into my serious thoughts and making me laugh.

"Shouldn't you be looking for a date as well, JustWill?" I try to say this with enthusiasm that I can't seem to fully muster.

Will leans toward me from his barstool and bumps my shoulder. "I'm happy being right here."

I smile and feel a warmth deep in my heart like an ember thawing feelings I didn't even know were frozen as we sink into conversation and beer with every intent to see Ray's to closing time.

SIXTEEN

The Cave

BOSCH, APRIL 2362

"C'mon! Hurry up!" My voice comes out in a bit of a slur, and I stumble somewhat over a tree root as I call back to Will who had announced a few minutes previously "I really have to pee" and then veered off into the woods. He appears to my left unexpectedly, hitching up the waistband on his pants.

"All good now. Are we there yet?" He, too, stumbles on the uneven forest floor in the dark.

It is just a bit after two bells, and Ray has closed up and gone home.

We had stood, slightly swaying, and watched Ray lock the door on the bar and then admonish us. "Listen, Kat. If anyone breaks in and there's only bourbon and cashews missing, I'll know it was you." He had looked intently into my face. *This guy thinks I'm drunk. And he knows all the things I like.* Ray looked over at Will then. "So, vesty…" I love that Ray talks to officers this way, and I started to giggle. Both men looked at me askance, and I slapped a hand to my mouth. "You walk our girl home and then leave. No funny business." Ray's first finger waggled in Will's direction. He looked at me again as I ran my hand lovingly over the lock on the door. "Go home,

Kat, now." Then he marched off to his vehicle, slipped into it, and headed to wherever bartenders go to sleep.

Will and I soberly watched him go, then looked at each other, pointed, and in tandem said, "No funny business!" and then broke into hysterics, leaning over and howling.

That was when Will said the words that led us here. "Where can we get more bourbon?"

"The cave!" I think I may have yelled. And so here we are, staggering through the woods headed to Teddy's and my cave. We could have taken the roads, but this somehow seemed like a more direct route. It is obvious my decision tally sheet is currently not in use, covered as it is in many, many glasses of beer and bourbon.

Remarkably, we actually are in an area I find familiar, and after a few more minutes of overly loud, inebriated discussion as we stumble along, weaving between trees and catching one another as we blunder over sticks and rocks, we emerge from the woods just slightly south of the cave. I grab Will's elbow and pull him with me as he starts to veer back into the trees. We turn the corner around a rocky outcropping that we were fortunate not to crash into as it rose up under the shadows of two large hemlocks, and there it is, Papa's cave.

I stand staring at the entrance to the cave, paralyzed by the wave of unanticipated emotion it brings me. The camouflaging vines and tree branches I had put in place over a year and a half ago are askew, and some have dried and collapsed, allowing the large, front passage to be visible in the moonlight. My breath is coming fast, and I feel the tears starting. I don't feel that drunk anymore.

Will is ahead of me and pauses, looking clumsily around, finally turning and then walking back to me. He looks at my face, and I see his brow wrinkle momentarily. I see his hand start to reach out to touch my tear-wetted cheek, but it is withdrawn before making contact. "Oh, Kat." His voice carries a tenderness I have only heard in Mama's voice, and something about the way he says my name tugs at me. "Why the tears?"

I snuffle and my voice shakes a bit. "I haven't been back here since... Well, since..." I look at him and hear my voice trail off.

His face takes on a look of dawning realization. "Ah, shit. Is it okay I am here?"

The kindness and respect in the question draw me back to the now. I wipe my cheeks with the backs of my hands and shake my head a little to clear it. Then I smile at my inadvertent friend. As I look at him, my heart does a flip-flop, and I realize I have other feelings for Will that are also inadvertent. "Teddy would have been happy for you to share this with me," I hear myself say, and I realize Papa would have embraced Will in a way he never did Takai. "Let's go." I push forward, and together we start to clear the remainder of the old brush away from the cave.

I wake up, feeling a light breeze on my cheek and the warmth of the morning sun. I can hear birdsong as my brain slowly begins to come awake. My eyes flutter open, then snap shut against the bright sun. I put my hands up to my face, shade my eyes, and then try again, squinting and trying to get my bearings. I am on the dirt, but there's something under me. I reach down and feel for what it is and lift the sleeve of a man's shirt. It's black and it's an officer's sleeve. *Uh-oh.* I drop the sleeve quickly and reach with both hands to my body. Clothes are still on. *Good.* I look to my left and see the entrance to the cave, fully cleared. I look to my right, and about half a meter away I see an empty Fire Hill bourbon bottle, one of Papa's favorites, and just beyond, the bare back of a softly snoring Will McCloud. I let my eyes linger for a moment, then glance down and breathe a sigh of relief as I see his pants are on. Apparently, I can still make good decisions even when fully toasted. My head is throbbing as I struggle to remember what happened after we got to the cave. I roll onto my hands and knees and then slowly get up. Water. I need water, badly.

There's a spring in the cave that has created a small, deep, very cold pool. I make my way to it, turning on the electric lights that I helped Teddy install. I had intended to just take a drink, but I feel grimy and gritty from a night sleeping rough, so I kick off my shoes and shed my pants, sweater, and under-clothes and gasp as I slip into the chill of the clear spring pool and feel my head clear immediately.

I am swimming the short distance back and forth to keep my blood moving when I hear a voice.

"Why is it you can look so beautiful swimming in that cold water? Women are amazing. My body would fold in on itself if I got in there."

I pivot and tread in the clear water. Will is standing there at the edge of the pool, still bare-chested, smiling at me. I grin and oddly don't feel self-conscious. "We women are life-givers. A little cold water can't stop us." I playfully splash toward Will, and he jumps back with an exclamation. I laugh. "It only hurts for a moment, JustWill, then it is amazing."

He shakes his head as he lays down on his belly and takes a long drink from the pool. "I'll find out later. Let me go get the towels. I think I remember where you showed me they were stowed last night." He turns to walk away, and as he moves out of sight, I hear him ask, "Have you read the letter yet?" And the night's events flood back.

≈

We had quickly cleared the brush from the cave, and then I fumbled around the edges of the deeply dark interior to find the electric lights. Once on, I made a beeline for where I was sure Teddy would have stashed his bourbon. It was pretty deep into the cave, three chambers to the back-right. We had always called it Teddy's Grotto. I hadn't been able to bring myself to go in there when I was working on my Teddy-in-the-Sky venture. I turned the light on, a smile spread over my face, and then I heard Will exclaim. Yes, against the walls there were crates upon crates of Teddy's favorite bourbons, all imported from the interior of the Central Continent and "made the old-fashioned way" as Teddy liked to say. I'm not sure there is any other way to make bourbon, and that was an ongoing argument between Papa and me. I even became partial to Edoan whiskey while I lived there, something Papa grudgingly also enjoyed but never to the same extent he loved his Old Fire Hill bourbon.

Perhaps even better than the cache of liquor, though, in the center of the grotto was a small, sleek vessel that years ago I had dubbed the *Deuce Coupe* after listening to some Old Days music from the far west part of the Central Continent that now lies under several dozen meters of seawater after the earthquake of 2290 and the subsequent flooding. The *Coupe* is made for two. It originally wasn't made to haul cargo. I made a few modifications, though, and now, behind some barely visible panels, it can store a fair amount of booty. There are also two fold-down seats for passengers. I had worked on it industriously before I had left Bosch and given birth to Grey.

We both went to the vessel and climbed up and into it, Will commenting on all the things that make a flight engineer's heart sing. I was grinning proudly as I made my way to the helm. Then I stopped. On the helm was a broad, white envelope with my name in Teddy's familiar hand. I picked it up and stood for several moments with it in my hand, alternately staring and squinting as the script wavered under my vision until Will came up very close to me and asked in my ear, "Aren't you going to open it?"

"I'll wait until morning. I can't see straight right now." He grunted in agreement, then I tucked it into my tunic pocket, and we went to raid the bourbon.

I grab one of the towels Will has stacked on the rocks near the pool and shake it, pleasantly surprised the cedar chest has kept the mice at bay. I quickly dry myself before feeling my tunic pocket. I hear the reassuring crunch of paper. It's still there. I breathe a sigh of relief. I start to think about the *Coupe* and its location as I dress. The *Coupe* is the vessel I flew on my aborted revenge flight two Septembers ago, and I know I parked it in the airfield outside when I returned. How did it get in here? No answers come to mind, so I focus on the letter. I need more light. I make my way to the mouth of the cave and see a now-shirted Will tending a small fire and smell…. Is that coffee?

"Where did you find coffee?" I come and stand close to the fire as the early April morning is chilly.

Will looks up at me and smiles, his eyes lingering on my face. "There was a cupboard marked 'Emergency Supplies' I found coming back with the towels. And inside, among other things, were two tins of Guyana coffee."

I laugh. "That fits. Teddy loved his coffee." Will hands me a steaming cup of the nectar of the goddess, and I gratefully accept. Our hands touch as I take the offering, and we pause for a second, looking at each other. Then I pull the cup to my lips and take a slurp so as not to burn my tongue. Will's smile doesn't waver as he turns to refill his own cup.

We sit down in a patch of sunshine, and I draw the envelope out of my pocket and break the seal. Will leans back on his hands and cocks his head to the side. His hair is askew, and I can see a few twigs and leaves in it. There is darker-blond stubble on his face. "Will you read it out loud?"

I look at his boyishly handsome face, and I'm glad to have someone to share this moment with. "Sure. But I warn you, I'm a crier."

He gives a small, gentle laugh. "I think I already know this about you, Kat Wallace."

I grin and feel that warmth inside of me that I had felt at Ray's glow brighter. I draw out and unfold the letter, and a smaller piece of paper and several photos slip to the ground. Will gathers them up and nods at me to go ahead and read.

May 12, 2360

Kat,

I am so very sorry.

I was, like many in New Earth, convinced for years that trafficking was a necessary part of the economy. The thralls I saw were generally hearty and well cared for, and I chose to believe that they were likely better off in the care of their owner than scraping out a living in the impoverished lands they had been born in. I really didn't fully understand the horrors of enslavement until I read your testimony from Abernathy's trial.

I pause and glance at Will's face. He is looking at me, and his face has taken on a horrified expression. "I don't suppose you haven't read…," I begin.

He interrupts me. "Kat, that trial was what? Seven years ago? But it made a big splash. I was working in my dad's office after uni, and everyone read the transcripts, and we were all appalled." He continues to gaze at me, but there's no pity in his eyes. He reaches over and runs a finger a few centimeters over my scar. "It was you." He removes his finger, but I can still feel its warmth there. He keeps going, a small smile appearing on his face. "Of course, it was. Who else would have been strong enough to survive that and then Bosch enough to seek revenge?" I watch as his chin comes up and his eyes shine. "It would have to be Kat. Kat Wallace. Well done, Kat."

I swallow hard at the compliment and the admiration and smile back. I take a breath and return to reading the letter.

I am ashamed as I consider the number of times I put you off from raiding Bellcoast. Lives were lost, including your friend, Carisa's, and that weighs on my conscience. So, I ran a small reconnaissance mission to New Detroit. Having done business with Abernathy before, I figured gathering some details might be helpful to you as you seek to bring a close to that dog.

I see a space, and then there is writing in a different colored ink.

August 25, 2360—It's not to be, Kat. I'm sorry I can't give this to you, but Kenichi is right. It is too dangerous. Your family's safety is more important than my plans for you and more important than your wish to end Abernathy. You'll likely never read this. But know everything I did, I did out of love for you.

"There's no closing. He didn't finish the letter. What fell out?"

Will is rifling through the items. "There are photos and…a map." He looks up at me incredulously. "Let's get a table out here. Then we can look at them more closely."

◠

"He was inside of Abernathy's New Detroit house? I can't believe it. He could have been killed." I am shuffling through the half-dozen photos of the doors and windows of a large, sumptuously appointed office. One of the photos has Abernathy's back in it, and I can't bear to look at that one. I toss them onto the table that Will drug out from the small work area just inside the cave entrance and stand up, rolling my neck and pacing.

"I'm going to walk the airfield. Clear my head." Will glances up from studying the photos, nods, and thankfully hears the "by myself" that went unsaid.

I sort through what I've seen and read as I walk among the covered vessels. Surprisingly, Teddy's pets, as he liked to call them, are pretty well kept. The forest undergrowth should have overtaken them. Odd. I see the space where I had left the *Coupe*, and it clearly has been empty for some time as the grasses are no longer compacted, and wildflowers are blooming in the fading footprint. Then I walk over to the spot where the *Skyhawk*, Teddy's favorite and the vessel I took him up in on his final flight, had always been parked. I am somehow freshly offended that its mooring has almost disappeared under a year and a half of nature's repossession, though I can't help but smile as I look at the wee saplings that are reclaiming this space as their own. "Oh, Papa," I sigh. "You leave me a map of the outside of a house with directions and some pictures of a library. What am I supposed to do with that?"

I hear him answer in my mind. "It gives you some details, girl. And the devil is in the details."

"Papa, storming into a house in the wealthiest area of New Detroit, guns blazing, is pretty foolhardy."

"Aye, it is. Unless you have a good plan and good people."

A good plan. I can come up with a good plan, and I even

have allies. I grin and turn to head back to the cave. Time to make some *good decisions*.

As I get close to the entrance, I hear voices. Someone else is here. I check my weapons, though I don't pull any as the voices sound conversational. I come around the bend in the trail and sitting at the table with Will is my brother, Peter.

"Peter?" My voice is tremulous and questioning. He stands and turns toward me, and he is smiling. I pick up the pace of my walk until I am practically running. I throw myself into him and feel his arms go tightly around me. "I'm sorry, I'm sorry, I'm sorry." I am sobbing, and I feel his chest heave as well as he catches his breath, face in my hair.

He pushes me back from him and looks into my face and I see tears on his cheeks. "Kat, you did what he asked you to do. I'm sorry it's taken me this long to let go of the hurt that he didn't ask me." His voice breaks a bit as he says this.

I look sorrowfully at this man who means so much to me. "Oh, Peter, he loved you and Paul and Mimi too much to ask you to be a part of his death."

Peter wipes his face and smiles at me. "He loved us all. And he chose the right person for the job. Just like he always did."

I glance over, and Will is looking at us with an expression of pleasure and something else. "You met my brother?" I say unnecessarily.

"I did. He came up not long after you went for a walk. Guess who stashed your little vessel in the cave?" He grins and gestures toward Peter with his thumb.

I look back at Peter, who shrugs. "I had been left instructions about the cave and the airfield and the *Coupe*. That letter, though, I found in Papa's study. I figured he'd want you to have it, so I put it with the *Coupe*. I mean, he knew the law was lifetime banishment, but the old man wanted things in place anyway, likely because he had some afterlife plan to bring you back here."

I give a short laugh as I consider the likelihood of Papa taking charge of the afterlife. "It only happened because of you and Paul and Mimi getting Steve Dalton."

Peter looks a bit confused and shakes his head. "No, Kat. We had nothing to do with that, though I wish we had. It was all Mama. When the council called the recess, and we walked out of the tribunal, she turned to us and said in that crisp, business-like way she has: 'Well, we aren't losing both of them,' and she turned and walked off. The next thing we knew, Steve Dalton appeared, looking like a scolded schoolboy, saying, 'I just spoke with Miriam.'"

I consider this shift in what I had assumed was the story and chuckle. "Fuckin' forces of nature, those two."

Peter slings an arm casually over my shoulder as he had so many times before, and the familiarity catches in my throat. "That they are."

Will looks at the two of us. "I'd say the apples don't fall far from the tree."

I hear Peter hoot a laugh. "Hardly on my part. I'm just a simple gunner turned weapons engineer." Then he nudges me but looks at Will. "This one, though. She is destined for greatness and destined to lead. That's why Papa brought her home the first time and Mama did the second time."

Now it's my turn to laugh. "Okay, I'll cop to being great at three things: flying, Glitter negotiations, and extractions. But leadership is not for me. Put that monkey on someone else's back." I catch Peter and Will looking at each other as they grin and roll their eyes. "Seriously. Never going to happen."

Will is chuckling as he says, "Of course not, Kat." He motions me over to the table where he has been surveying the pictures with a small magnifier. "Now come look at these pictures and see what you think. Do you know who this woman is?"

I slowly move over next to him, wrinkling my brow. "Woman? I didn't see any woman in them."

"Right here." He taps on the table. The magnifier is on the upper left-hand corner of a photo. It is the one with Abernathy's back in it. He stands at an open door, taking a tray from a petite, blonde woman. My breath catches.

"Sweet New Earth." My thoughts are a jumble. I look again and gasp, then I look up into Will's questioning face, then at Peter as he comes around the table.

"Sweet New Earth," I repeat. I step back, my breath speeding up and my hands going to rest on top of my head. The world is spinning very fast, but I'm unsure if it is moving forward or backward. My eyes are wide, but I'm seeing a booth in a dusty marketplace on Bellcoast, not my familiar Bosch woods.

"Kat, what is it? Who is she?" Will's voice breaks into the buzzing in my brain.

"It's Carisa. She's alive."

SEVENTEEN

The Really Good Plan

BOSCH, MAY 2362

"Whoa! Whoa! Whoa! Slow down, Kat." Miles holds his hands up and stands from behind his desk. "You want to do what? Where? And what does Teddy have to do with it?"

I am pacing the width of the MC's office like one of those leopards I saw at an animal display in Truvale...back and forth, back and forth. My brain is already planning the mission as I explain it again to Miles.

"Teddy infiltrated Abernathy's home in the spring before he died. He was getting intel for me. And he took pictures. But he didn't give me the intel. He decided it was too much of a risk—well, he and Kenichi did. I'm gonna have to have a word with Kenichi about that. Such a Teddy move, deciding what is best for everyone." I let out a sigh and shake my head. Miles is looking at me intently as he listens. "Anyway, the photos. Carisa is in one of them. That means she didn't die in Bell-coast, and she may be alive in New Detroit. I want to find out if she is still there, and if she is, I want to go and get her." I know this is the *right decision*. It's another column entirely.

"Stop there." Miles points to me. "Let's expand on what you want to do."

I turn toward him and stop my pacing to listen, but my legs are bouncing, and I am rubbing my hands together. "What's your point, Miles?"

"My point, Kat, is that you want to go to Eternia—the heart of the Federal Alliance. The Federal Alliance, which I might remind you, has the largest and strongest military force on the planet."

"China would disagree," I say automatically.

Miles tips his head and stares at me for a moment. "You really want to wander off into that debate or stick to the issue at hand?"

I sigh. "Go on."

"Largest and strongest. And you want to go into one of their major cities and invade a home, not of some regular person but of a recently elected…?"

"Re-elected," I correct him.

"Fine. Re-elected senator of said Federal Alliance and then kidnap a person from his home?"

I consider the expanded plan Miles has described. "Well, he likely will see it as stealing property, not kidnapping a person, but that's splitting hairs. So, yes. That's the plan."

Miles sits down at his desk and pushes on his eyes with the heels of both hands before placing his palms on the desk and leaning toward me. "And you don't see a problem with any of that?"

I move to the front of the desk, put my hands down, and lean in. "Not for me. The political fallout is your problem. I just want to get Carisa out safely." I tip my head and give him a grin.

Miles begins to laugh softly. "Someday, Kat. Someday it'll be your problem."

"Not in this lifetime, my friend. I'm just a simple Glitter runner." I put on my best mischievous smile and bat my eyes.

Miles smiles back. "Is that all you are? We shall see." He sits up and leans back in his high-back chair. "Sit down."

I sit.

"I can have Bosch Intelligence try to find out if Carisa is alive and there, but that'll take some time…," he begins.

I interrupt him. "No need. I have my own sources in New Detroit. I already have them on it and should have word in a day or two."

Miles looks at me and purses his lips. "Fine." Then he draws in a breath. "Bosch cannot sanction this mission. It would go against all the agreements we have made with the FA. If we did, they would retaliate."

I wave my hands dismissively. "Oh, what would they do?"

He holds up his little finger. "One, they would cease to look the other way when we deliver Glitter." His ring finger pops up. "Two, they would no longer look to us for extractions and infiltrations." Up comes the middle finger. "And three, they may just decide a proportional response would be called for. Which means attack on Bosch."

I pause, look off to the side, and squirm slightly in my chair. "Miles, I need to do this." I turn my gaze back to him.

Miles looks straight into my eyes. "Yes, you do. But you need to go in one of Teddy's vessels, not an official BPF one. I am sure you can get the gear you need without attracting much attention. And we never had this conversation." His dark eyebrows go up, making his face look even leaner, asking for assent.

I pop up from my seat, quickly go around the desk, and lean over and give this good man a quick hug. "You are the best, Miles! You won't regret this! And I was never here."

Miles smiles, and it reminds me of the indulgent smiles Teddy would give me. "Stay safe and stay alive, Kat. And get your friend out of harm's way."

I am standing at the table we had carried out of the cave, sorting through some of the possible gear for my Carisa mission. I want to get this done before the kids return tonight. An entire week without them has been alternately agonizing and exhilarating. I cannot wait to see them and smell them and kiss their sweet faces and hear them call me "Mama". I've talked with them on the comm, but it isn't the same. I need to have them home to feel complete. Still, I haven't gotten this much done at work in over seven years, so that is a plus. And it has been a delight spending time, both work and social, with the unit. And Will.

Will. His face appears in my mind, with its tousled hair sticking up at odd angles and steel-blue eyes and full lips. *What am I going to do about you, Will? How have I moved from despising you to thinking about you constantly? But thinking about you makes me happy—a feeling that has been missing for the past couple of years.* That's the thing. Will makes me happy in a way I haven't been for a very long time.

I'm alone, so I let myself imagine what it would be like to actually be with Will. The image and sounds of him with the guard in Dobarri come to my mind, and I close my eyes for a moment and sink into the fantasy of it being me in that small room with him, not our jailer. My breath comes a little faster, and then I shake my head. I better not continue down that path. *You are married, Kat, no matter what kind of shitshow your marriage has become.* I sneak behind my proper self's back and close my eyes once more and imagine Will's strong hand reaching to caress me. I feel a pleasant tightness in my middle that flows to my heart and between my legs. *Okay. Enough.* Damn. It has just been so long. At this point, when I think of Takai, all I can see is an ongoing cycle of betrayal and lies like a wheel. But it is still our marriage. Our family. Our life. My life. And I am going to take control of that part of my life when I see him tonight.

The crack of a stick pulls me from my contemplation, and I look toward the sound.

Will and Gia are coming toward me, and Demery, Bailey, and Tom are not far behind. I look curiously at them as they approach. Will is smiling at me in that devil-may-care way he does that makes my heart flutter a bit.

Gia smiles as well and lifts her hand in greeting. "Whatcha doing, Trooper?"

I exchange a glance with Will that tells me he has told the unit about Carisa. Probably a good move. "I'm not acting as a trooper, Colonel." I smile at Gia as I use her rank. "I am simply a private Bosch citizen puttering about."

Tom lifts a compact rifle—the Rus KORD 9R70 that I took during the Ruthenian mission—and studies it. "Interesting. I usually think of puttering as sorting the junk drawer or pulling weeds, not gathering small arms." He grins as he sets the weapon down.

I grin in response. "To each their own. You putter in the junk drawer. I'm planning a visit to New Detroit."

"Strike that. *We* are planning a visit to New Detroit." Bailey, who is not typically one to make such pronouncements, tosses their braids back as they move their finger in a circle encompassing my unit.

"You guys, this is not sanctioned. I don't want to drag you all along on something that may be disavowed if we get caught."

"Too bad. We are going. Now, what's the plan?" Gia pulls a chair over and picks up the photos of Abernathy's place I have out and flips through them, pausing to squint at the one with Carisa.

I narrow my eyes, look around, and start to compose my argument against such a foolhardy move but am struck mute when Will casually flings an arm over my shoulder and hugs me slightly toward him.

"We are a unit, Kat. We work together. And you have family coming home." He pauses and smiles wickedly at me. "You need us."

I poke him in the ribs, and I look up at him and we both laugh, mine colored with the discomfort he knows I have with needing help. I pause but don't shift because I like the feel of his arm on me. "Fine. *We* are going to New Detroit."

I am watching the horizon for the vessel that is bringing my family back home as I talk on the comm. "So, is she there or not, Paddy? It's kinda important I know if there's someone to actually rescue before I go storming the gates of the Abernathy estate."

A small crackle comes through the comm as he answers, "I am still working on it, Kat. That place is like a fortress. None of my people will take the assignment. He scares the shit out of them. So, I'm going in myself tomorrow under the guise of delivering Glitter. Usually, we just leave it at the gate and pick up the markers a few hours later, but I've made arrangements to take it to the house for a drop with his assistant."

The vessel has appeared and is curving around to land, and I am half-listening to Paddy as I think about holding my babies again, and how I will let Takai know that there will be no more cheating if he expects to (wants to?) stay married to me. "Okay, then. Sounds good. I'll expect to hear from you tomorrow." I click off the comm. I need this intel. That picture was taken two years ago. If Carisa is still alive, I can't imagine what she has endured. No, actually I can. I just don't want to.

The vessel is on the ground, and I am headed out as the flight crew assembles. "Hey, Fred!" Fred Driscoll, or Master Sergeant Driscoll as indicated by the fully red belt on his uniform, waves to me as he directs the crew to their places, where they assist the pilot with parking, check the tires, and prep the vessel for cleaning and recharging. Two roll airstairs to the door, and as it opens, I see Kitty Berry appear, holding the boys' hands. They holler as they see me—"Mama, Mama!" —and I sprint up the steps, scooping my two three-year-old sons, who seem to have become giants after a week away, into my arms, kissing them until they squeal. Takai must still be with Grey onboard. I peer and see Grey's happy face as she throws her arms around my waist. "Mama! I missed you!"

"I missed you, baby!"

"Wha' 'bout us?" Kik demands

I laugh. "I super-duper missed you too! The world was far too quiet and tidy without you two around!" They both laugh. "Where's your papa?"

They are still laughing. "You are silly, Mama. Papa is on his ship."

Kitty Berry looks at me as they say this. "He said he needed to stay on board."

I pause for a moment, taking in this news before nodding and forcing a smile. "Got it. Thanks so much, Kitty. You and Renzo surely go above and beyond for us."

I turn and head down the stairs with the children. So, Takai didn't come back with the kids as planned. I try to keep my face curved in excited happiness, but inside I am a jumble of emotions. So much for getting to state my terms. He has decided to avoid seeing me. He has chosen Hayami. My heart crumbles a bit, and my smile falters as the children are speaking non-stop about their week. I consciously recall the latest conversation I had with Will as he encouraged me to take control of this part of my life.

"You know what is best for you and for your kids, Kat. You've been patient long enough. Set your terms and take command of your life."

My smile returns, and it feels a bit stronger. Fine. I think of Will. I have options as well. My mind meanders.

A little voice insistently pulls me back to the now. "What?"

"I'm hungry!" Mac is tugging on my arm as we maneuver past the mess. They love eating at the mess.

Kik joins in on the call. "Me too!"

I look at my daughter. "How about you, Grey? You up for a mess night?"

"Yes, please, Mama!" Her sweet face blossoms into a big smile.

"Fine. Mess it is." I give the boys each a pat on their bottoms as I drop their hands and say, "Go on!" The three of them yell with excitement and run ahead to get whatever unidentifiable food is being served today. I guess this is what life will be now. The four of us. And maybe, someday, a good friend who makes me feel whole.

Takai Shima sat looking out the window of the airship that carried him away from his ship. As the airship took on elevation, the *Venturer* got smaller and smaller. He pictured Hayami as he had left her, curled up in his bed, her dark hair spread across the white pillowcase, the sheet carelessly pushed down around her waist, exposing the creamy, soft, perfect skin of her shoulders and the firm, small globes of her breasts with their delicate pink nipples blossoming like two miniature rosebuds. He smiled at the delightful image.

He had known from the moment they were introduced that he wanted to add her to his bouquet. She was lovely and young and delicate and vital, but the initial attraction, though very much still present, had given way to what he had thought was an excited and spirited infatuation. Now, though, he knew he had come to love her. They had so much in common. They both were ambitious and driven, though she was happy to refocus her drive to help him move forward as a diplomat. Her family was much like his: traditional and influential. She said they would be an asset to his career. They both embraced The Way and abhorred violence of any kind. She showed the children such gentle ways to play—no rough games of fighting and wrestling. Here he felt a twinge of remorse as he had promised Kat to keep the children from her. But they had asked after Hayami, and Grey even went looking for her and invited her to dinner. It was a sign.

He had not returned with the children as he had initially agreed to as he wanted to spend some time alone with his new lovely blossom, making plans. His parents would embrace her as the proper wife, and she would easily captivate them and all the village society and beyond with her grace and charm and modesty, as she had him.

Now he had to go to Bosch and tell Kat he was leaving her. He knew it would be hard for her. She depended on him so much. Kat had little experience with relationships when they had met almost a decade earlier, and he had been very patient with her, but she had pushed that patience to the breaking point with her need to return to a life of piracy. So, she would have to focus on her Bosch family for support. He had decided the children would stay mostly with her. It seemed only fair, although he would insist on certain rules to curb their Bosch behavior, and there would be ample visiting both on the ship and in Edo when he and Hayami returned there. He did love his children with a fierceness he had never known he could feel, but they were quite a handful. He certainly depended on Hayami to ease his burden when they visited.

Kat would be fine alone, the way she was when he had first met her. He smiled when he thought of how vibrant and alive and attractive she had been then. Now when he pictured her, he could only see her as the respected mother of his children, complete with her soiled clothes; uncombed, short hair; and perpetual tired expression, or as the person who unilaterally blew up his comfortable life in Edo. Yes, he was making the best choice. He settled back in his large, plush seat to nap until the airship landed in Bosch.

The May evening was warm and pleasant as Takai made his way from the base to the little white house Kat had returned them to. As he walked, he breathed in the scent of balsam and heliotrope and listened to the sounds of birds chattering good night in the trees as the sun was dropping low. Bosch did have some lovely natural beauty. A few pale-pink clouds mounded on the horizon, and Takai knew to expect a rainstorm tonight, but it was still distant. He could not yet detect any pre-rain scent. He had intentionally timed his arrival for after the children were asleep so his and Kat's conversation would be uninterrupted.

He arrived at the gate and looked at the drive with a tip of his head and a question on his face. There were two unknown vehicles in the drive, one fairly large and gray, and the other a very small, sporty, red vehicle. He lifted his head and frowned as he heard a few strains of music wafting from behind the house, along with the occasional laugh. He let himself in the gaudy blue front door. *What had possessed Kat to choose that color?* The house itself was quiet, but he could hear the music more loudly, along with voices as the windows were slightly open. He narrowed his eyes. Miriam usually would be headed home by now. It must be Peter, Paul, and Mimi and their families, though he didn't see any signs of extra children around the living room and dining table.

He moved into the darkening kitchen and peered out onto the back porch. It was not her family. It was her unit. Takai sighed and looked around the kitchen for empty bottles. There was often quite a bit of drinking and raucous celebrating when the Bosch completed a mission. But he saw only two bottles of wine, one still mostly full. He looked back outside. Someone had placed a firepit there, and a crackling fire blazed with six people sitting around it, talking as music played from an unseen speaker. He could have heard the conversation, but he was suddenly laser-focused on one person: his wife.

Kat sat with one knee up and one leg down. She wore clothes Takai had never seen on her: a pair of blue, short pants that only cleared halfway down her thighs and a simple striped knit shirt that fit her closely. He could only recall her wearing such fitted things when they had gone to Truvale for the first time and then only for a formal dinner, not sitting outside on a weeknight with guests. Her feet were bare; he saw her sandals casually kicked off on the ground. His eyes then moved to her face, and he inhaled audibly.

His pupils dilated as he took in what he saw: A confident and beautiful woman with a glowing smile and an easy laugh was speaking as if she was holding court, and the people around her seemed to glow not in the firelight but in the reflected illumination of this woman. He was completely and utterly entranced. Then he heard the person sitting nearest his wife say something, and he saw Kat turn to respond. He watched her face soften as it turned toward the man he had heard speak. Takai glanced over and was surprised to see a very handsome young man who gazed reverentially at Kat. As she turned to him, she reached out and gently laid her fingertips on his arm as they spoke quietly together and then laughed.

Takai forgot everything he had considered on the airship. Every anger and frustration with Kat and her Bosch ways evaporated. Even the thought of his bouquet and the most recent flower he had added seemed to vanish. He only knew that he would not allow this pirate man to woo his wife away from him. He turned and took a swig from the bottle of wine on the counter to curb the jealousy that was growing inside him. Then he ran his hands through his hair, smoothing it, wiped any remnants of wine from his upper lip, opened the back door, and stepped out onto the small deck.

"Kat, I'm home."

"What the hell, Takai? You just appear out of nowhere after, what, three weeks of almost no communication?" I am annoyed over what oddly feels like a sudden intrusion into my life.

The unit and I decided not to train for the Carisa mission on base since it was not a BPF-approved mission. I hadn't shared with them Miles' tacit approval, nor his statement of denial of any knowledge. So today, we had trained here: in my home. Then we extended it as Gia and Demery fixed dinner for the kids, and Tom and Will chased them about the yard. Bailey and I had sat, each nursing a beer, and watched them.

"You like having children, don't you?" They looked at me with a gentle smile.

I had laughed. "I do. Most of the time. There are moments when I'd like to fly away, but those aren't often, and the sweet ones keep me here. And it's like any adventure—you just want to stay and see what mess comes next!"

Bailey laughed their warm laugh. "I don't know if I ever actually want kids but watching this makes the idea of it attractive." They look pointedly at me. "Almost as attractive as that blond fellow there who has remembered how to smile over the past few months."

"Well…" I am conscious that I am furiously blushing. "He does add…" I laugh and I hear a schoolgirl in it. "…to the…uh…landscape."

Bailey had looked at me and grinned. "You are quite the poet, Kat. Though I don't expect it was your eloquence that made him love you."

It had taken me several moments to get over hearing this said aloud. I had known that he cared from the way he looked at me and listened to me, always urging me to be true to myself. And I knew how I felt. But to hear someone else say it…

I heard Bailey laugh as I looked away. "Girl, it's been written on both of your faces for weeks. A person would have to be blind not to see it."

I had shifted uncomfortably, and they had grabbed my hand. "You deserve to be happy, Kat." I squeezed back as I considered this. Did I?

The evening had progressed quite pleasantly until Takai dropped out of the sky, making his pronouncement. Then the ebullience was quickly scuttled, and everyone headed home. Will and I looked long at each other as he was leaving, and he gave me an inconspicuous double-beat of his right hand to his chest: the Bosch signal to be strong. I had nodded in response.

Takai had not said much after he arrived, but he came very close to me and sat on the arm of the outdoor couch, one hand on my shoulder. He was polite but cool as my unit left, and now he stands in the doorway of the living room looking at me as I turn from bidding the last person goodbye. He smiles a smile I haven't seen in years, even as I bark at him.

"I told you I needed time, Kat." He approaches me and reaches out to where I stand with my arms wrapped over my middle, hands holding opposite elbows. His hands run lightly along my bare arms. The day had been quite warm as we had worked, so I had changed into these new hand-me-downs of Mimi's. Now I am feeling the need for a sweater. I'm not sure if it is because of the chill of the evening or the uninvited touch. He smiles warmly at me, again with a look that has been absent since I don't know when. I think on this for a moment, and then it finally occurs to me: he hasn't really looked at me since before Teddy died.

"So, you've had time." I decide to jump in. "Well, let me tell you. I've had time as well." My voice elevates. "You run away from home and start a relationship—not just your regular, random fucks—but a relationship…" I watch as my curse word hits him, and he looks as shocked now as he did the first day I met him. I hold myself from going down the hall of happy memories. "And then you show up here unannounced with a 'Honey, I'm home!'" He doesn't watch Old Days shows the way I used to before the kids, but I have shown him enough that he surely gets my point.

"I am home, Kat. Well, I have to finish my captaincy, but you are my wife. I want to come home. To you." His eyes are sparkling, and there is a hunger there that has been absent since before the boys were born.

I look at this man I have first built a life with and now am considering constructing a life without. I lift my chin. "Well, now I need time. You stay here. The children will be thrilled. I'm going to sleep at Mama's. We can talk tomorrow." I grab a sweater from the closet nearest the door and slip it on, then turn the knob.

As I walk in the dim of the May night, listening to crickets and peepers, I realize that there will be no more conversation, no more back and forth, no more negotiating about these issues between Takai and me. No, I simply have to decide which path to take in my life. It is my choice and I will make the decision.

EIGHTEEN

Breaking Up Is Hard to Do

BOSCH, MAY 2362

Mama was happy to see me even though she looked as though I had roused her from bed. She made us both a cup of tea, and I sat leaning onto her as she listened, gently murmuring support, as I spilled the story of my marriage and my Will.

"You have always joked about Takai being a ladies' man, but I didn't realize…" Mama's tone is disapproving.

"I guess I pretended not to know. I don't know. The kids were little, and we were so busy, and I was plopped in Edo. It was just easier to assume all was well." I shrug and take a sip of the wine I have graduated to after my tea.

Mama strokes my hair gently as she admonishes me kindly. "I imagine it doesn't seem easier now."

"No. It doesn't. At least I've learned that."

I hear Mama give a small laugh. "You know, Kat. I was engaged to someone else when I met Papa."

I sit up and pivot on the couch so I can see her face. "Really? Tell me what happened!"

She smiles and looks off into the distance. As she gazes and remembers, softly smiling, I think I can see her as a young woman loved by two men. "There's not much to tell, dear. You know how the story went. I chose Teddy." Her face brightens as she says his name. "My point is, there is not just one love for any of us." Here, she looks back at my face and takes my hands in hers. "There is who we choose to be *the one*. But we have to continue to want to choose that every day, even when the storm rises."

"So, you think I should stay with Takai?" I need to know what to do.

One warm hand cups my cheek. "No, sweet Kat, I cannot choose for you. It is up to you."

I give a rueful laugh. "Rats." I stand, still holding her hand. "Go to bed, Mama. I have thinking to do."

Paddy Owens struggled slightly as the two large men bodily escorted him up the marble stairs of the palatial mansion. They hustled him down a long hallway lined with sconces and what Paddy knew to be original artwork, elegantly framed. One of Paddy's more lucrative side hustles was in forgery. So, he knew his art. He could see several of the paintings were from current-day artists, but he also saw some from the Old Earth days. Even under the current circumstances, Paddy could appreciate what a treasure trove this building was. Just one of those paintings could set him up for several months. He looked up and saw Casey, the assistant to the home's owner, standing near a large wooden door about three-quarters of the way along the right side of the hall.

Casey smiled insincerely, opening the door. "Mr. Owens, Senator-Elect Abernathy will see you now."

The damned assistant had lured Paddy into the house with promises of additional markers for the personalized delivery, and Paddy had felt safe enough, given this man's small and delicate frame. Such a nub move. The little guy had disappeared, and the two goons on either side of him had appeared, and so, here he was.

Paddy felt himself shoved into a sumptuous room through the wide wooden doorway. He stumbled, put his hand onto an exquisite desk made of some type of hardwood Paddy couldn't identify to keep from falling, and heard the door close behind him, but he heard no locking sound.

He looked up from where he had caught himself and saw a handsome man sitting at the desk studiously writing in a notebook. His hair was a dark blond with sandy highlights and perhaps a bit of gray at the edges. The man also looked up from his notebook and blinked as if Paddy's appearance was of utmost surprise.

"Well, Mr. Owens. To what do I owe the pleasure of your visit?" The man stood and put on a pleasant smile.

"Well, sir, I…" Paddy stumbled over his words.

The blond man interrupted him. "Dear me, where are my manners? Allow me to introduce myself. I'm Senator Abernathy."

Paddy nodded, noting the man's premature use of his full title, and regrouped. He stood a bit straighter and picked up a small, carved box from the console table to his right. He casually regarded the knick-knack before setting it back. "Good to meet you, Senator. The pleasure's all mine. Not sure why I was practically carried up here. I'd have been happy to walk on my own."

"Yes, Casey can be a bit overenthusiastic. But he would do anything for me. That, Mr. Owens, is the key to a strong business: loyal employees. Do you find that to be true in your Glitter dealings?" Senator-Elect Abernathy stood and poured two drinks, companionably handing one to Paddy and motioning for him to sit in one of the high-back chairs in the sitting area.

Careful, Paddy. This fox is trying to trap you. "Absolutely, Senator." Paddy sat, taking in the room with its wall of floor-to-ceiling multipaned windows finishing in a graceful arch. He took a small sip of the drink he had been given and found it to be sweet but with an alcoholic burn. Paddy did not drink much as he wanted to keep his head, a statement he made quite literally, ever since a rival Glitter gang had attempted to push into his territory last winter. They had decapitated one of his employees and sent Paddy the head. Paddy had responded in kind, five-fold. The gang had wisely gone in search of easier territory. "Loyalty and commitment to the job."

The senator smiled and nodded. "Casey tells me you've been asking a considerable number of questions about my comings and goings and about my household. This is concerning given my status as a past and soon-to-be-seated senator. Politics can be a messy business, and we must know who is on our side and who is not." Here, the man caught Paddy in his gaze. Paddy was good at reading people. Usually, when he looked into a business associate's eyes, he could read the underlying feelings and motivations, whether it was over-confidence, fear, or artifice. This man, though...his eyes were strange, empty almost. He could sense no emotions from them as if Abernathy was simply reading lines from a play with little commitment to the part.

Paddy figured honesty was appropriate here. At least in small doses. "I was approached by a customer who wanted some information about you. They pay well, and I'm a busi-nessman."

Senator-Elect Abernathy smiled and sipped his own drink. "A reasonable answer. But let me counter. I can pay more to hear who this customer is and what he wants."

"No, sir. I maintain confidentiality in my work." Paddy shook his head.

"Good man. That is an admirable tenet and an excellent quality. So, you are willing to take the information to your grave then?" The senator leaned back in his chair and looked impassively at Paddy as he said this.

Paddy could almost hear the snap of the trap on his leg. He shifted uncomfortably. "Well, I could—for a good price, mind you—give you a rough idea of what my customer's interest is."

"There will be markers for you, most definitely. And you may live to spend them if I like what I hear. But foremost, I need a name, Mr. Owens."

Paddy sighed. *Sorry, Kat. It's you or me, and I pick me.* "Kat Wallace of Bosch."

The man's eyes fixed on Paddy's, and now they were not empty. There was a rage and menace in them that Paddy found deeply alarming. "That is perhaps the best news I have had in a long time." Senator-Elect Robert Abernathy stood and walked over to the chair where Paddy sat. Paddy was almost certain these were his last moments. Then the tall, handsome man smiled a vulpine smile and reached a hand toward Paddy. "Let us shake hands. We are now partners in a small venture. A venture that will gain each of us what we truly desire."

The way this man said "desire" caused the hair on Paddy's neck to stand up. But he stood and took his hand nonetheless, shaking it. *Have to do what I have to do.*

I hear the clock on the green chime seven bells. Will and I sit in the small office room we use on base, a meter or more between us, both our faces masks of misery. I came knocking on his door just after sunrise, and we had silently gone to get coffee and then walked to the office. I hadn't slept last night after talking with Mama. I had wrestled with how to balance what I wanted and what was best through the dark bells, and this morning as the sun came up, I knew what I had to do, and I knew this was the first step.

"But tell me what you feel!" Will looks beseechingly at me. "You know I love you." The words he has now said several times both buoy my heart and stick in the pit of my stomach. I gaze at him, committing to memory each curve of his handsome face. I remember when I first decided to not hate him, but his combination of blond good looks and steel-blue eyes unsettled me because of my memories of Abernathy. But now I have seen those eyes radiate kindness and tenderness and love, and his unruly hair makes me laugh, though I am not one to talk. I run my hand over my own messy curls. So, there is another Will gift: I no longer think of Rob "The Asshole" Abernathy when I see a blond, blue-eyed man. My eyes drop to the floor. I can't look at him as I do what I must.

"I feel…" I think wildly around my feelings. "Oh, Will, I feel all the things." My body is now turned away from his as if I don't dare get too close. Which I don't.

"Knock that shit off, Kat." His voice is angry, and it draws my gaze back toward him.

"What?" Although I know what. I wrap my arms across my chest.

"Always the glib one-liner with you. Distract and divert. Then you don't actually have to be vulnerable." His body looks tense as if he knows a blow is about to be delivered.

I feel the tears start to well and my throat get tight. I swallow hard, close my eyes, and lean my head back. When I open them a moment later, I turn my whole body toward Will, and both of my hands come up to my head and gently squeeze.

I extend my arms and hands out as if I am trying to hold the entirety of my feelings. "Well, yeah. Glib is easy." My hands press briefly to my face, and then I look at him. "God, Will, until you came around, I didn't think I had the kinds of feelings you are talking about anymore. I thought they were all beaten out of me in Bellcoast. I mean, I do love Takai in the way I could years ago because he never asks me to show him too much of what's inside. Glib seems to work with us." I look at my Will's gentle face with his now-sad eyes as he patiently listens. "But you…" I smile at him, and that smile comes from deep within me. "You have opened me up and shone a bit of sunlight in those dark places in my soul. You've made me feel things I thought were gone." I see his mouth curve softly upward.

I wipe my eyes of the tears that are flowing unchecked and continue, knowing what I am about to say will hurt us both. "But New Earth help me, if I am going to be open and vulnerable with someone, I need to attempt it…" I gasp a little. "… with my husband first. No matter what he has done."

I watch Will's face pull in on itself, and he pauses. "Are you making this choice for yourself or for the kids?"

He knows me so well. I grimace slightly. "At this point, I can't really separate one from the other."

He nods and looks at me tenderly. He knows, as I do, that this, whatever "this" has been, is over. My eyes go back to fix on the whorl in the wood of the floor and I blink rapidly.

"Yeah, I expect you are right." There is a long pause as I hear him take some breaths against the tears that are threatening him. "I guess I should see if I can get reassigned to my old unit."

I nod in agreement without looking up. "I guess so."

Suddenly, I see his feet appear in my sightline. He is so quiet when he moves; I hadn't even heard him stand. I look up at him from where I sit. His hands come to my face and gently stroke it, wiping the newest batch of tears away, then cradles it, holding my chin. Time pauses for me. We haven't touched much. There was that night we huddled together for warmth in the Dobarri cell when we barely could tolerate each other. We have touched hands and helped each other up and over obstacles during missions, like in Ruthenia. The drunken night on the way to the cave, we grabbed arms for balance a few times as we staggered through the woods. And the few times, very recently, when Will has thrown his arm over my shoulders. It was done as a friendly, buddy type of gesture, but both of us could feel the underlying tension, the tightly bound passion. Now that I feel his hands with their rough calluses touch me so softly, I want to go back to the first time he reached for me and every time after and melt into his arms.

My body starts to move instinctively toward him, and then time restarts and I remember we are saying goodbye. I open my eyes, though I can't recall closing them, and look again into his steel-blue ones. They are so gentle, and I see the un-spilled tears glisten in them. "Kat Wallace. Let me repeat, I love you." I take a quick breath in as he continues, "And I will love you as long as I draw breath and likely after. And you don't have to say it, but I know you love me too. And you know…" He gives me his old what-the-hell grin. "…that's enough." He leans down and softly kisses my forehead, then puts a finger to my lips as I start to reply. Then Lieutenant William McCloud, tightly puckered asshole, Trust-Fund, engineering savant, turned JustWill, turned my Will, turns and walks out of my life.

NINETEEN

Negotiation

Step two of taking charge of my life: I walk back to my little white house with its brilliant blue door that makes me smile every time I see it. I time my arrival for after the children are at school and preschool. I stand at the door, take three breaths, and turn the knob.

I hear Takai moving about in his study, so I go to the kitchen and brew another cup of coffee for me and a cup of tea for him. I carry them both to the study door, setting my coffee down on the side table momentarily as I turn the handle and see Takai look around as I come in. He closes a sturdy wooden box and places it back in its place on the bookcase. He faces me and smiles. "You're home."

I pick up my coffee and wordlessly walk to him and hand him his tea.

"Thank you." His voice holds the old warmth, and his eyes look at me like when we first met. But I am not that person any longer, and I will need more than warm smiles and appreciative looks to be brought home.

"Let's sit down, Takai. I have things to say."

He smiles and sits in one of the burgundy upholstered

175

chairs, and I sit across from him. I take a deep sip of my coffee and set it on the small table that sits between the chairs. I put my Glitter negotiation face on. *No personal feelings yet, Kat.*

"So, you said last night you want to come home to your wife. Is that still what you wish?" I keep my face carefully neutral.

Takai keeps his smile, but his eyes narrow slightly, and his brow comes together as he tries to figure out my angle. "Yes, Kat. You are my wife. And I am home." He relaxes back in his chair.

"Not quite so fast, Takai." I put a hand up. "We cannot return to how things were. I will not. I have some specifications that I need to have met."

He gives a laugh. "Do you? Okay. Let's hear them."

"First…" I hear Teddy in my ear when he was teaching me negotiation. *Always lay out the parameters that you won't budge on first.* "I will no longer ignore nor accept your constant infidelity. So, if you want this marriage to last, that will be inviolable."

I watch his face, but he has taken on the mask of negotiation as well.

I continue. "Second, Bosch is my home. We agreed to split time between Bosch and Edo years ago, and up to this point, we have only lived in Edo. The next several years are to be spent predominantly in Bosch. This is true for me and for the children. And for you, once your captaincy is complete."

Takai rubs his smoothly shaved chin with his hands. "Anything more?"

"One more thing. I want you to stop denigrating the work I do. Full stop, but especially in front of the children. I am not playing at 'soldier games,' Takai. I am part of the Bosch Pirate Force, a strong and well-respected force across New Earth, and I want the children to respect my work and know that you do as well—even if you only give lip service to it. Those are my parameters."

Takai nods, and there are a few seconds of quiet between us. "All right, Kat, but I have some additions myself."

My first impulse is to scoff at this statement, but I reconsider. *Well, it is a negotiation.* I nod. "Go on."

"I will still be traveling. If not on the *Venturer*, then with my diplomatic work. And I will encounter women I must talk with." The line from *Much Ado About Nothing*—"Talk with a man out at a window!"—comes to my mind as he says this, and I raise my eyebrows as he continues. "And you cannot assume I am being unfaithful when that occurs."

I sigh and tip my head. "Honestly, Takai, the burden of proof is on you. My eyes are open now, and I recognize that your old libertine ways have stayed constant throughout our relationship. But they will change now if you want to stay in this marriage. Savvy?" I give him my final-offer face.

He nods assent. "My parents will never come to Bosch. I wish for the children to spend several weeks with them in the summers. I will accompany them, and you of course are welcome as well."

I cringe at this, but it is a reasonable request. "Done."

He looks pointedly at me now. "I agree to your third point as well. I shall provide respectful support to your work. However, I want there to be no weapons worn in the family home. We can construct a safe place for them to be stored when you arrive home."

I think back to not having my blade in Edo when I was attacked. I never told Takai about that little escapade in the foothills as I hadn't wanted him to worry. I don't like the idea of not having my blade and pistols on, but it is also a reasonable request. I nod. "I agree. Anything else?" I begin to stand, assuming we have concluded the business.

"Yes, Kat." His voice holds a tone I haven't heard before, and I look at him. His face is a bit darkened as if he is angry. "The young man here last night… Will McCloud?"

"What about him?" My body is quite still, and I am working to keep my voice steady and disinterested.

"I don't want you working with him, and I don't want him in our home." Takai raises one eyebrow as if he is daring me to contest this.

I control the anger I feel at this request. "That situation has already been managed. But Takai, this is my home. It remains up to you to behave in a way that will return it to our home." At this, I pick up my coffee cup and sweep out of the room. I head upstairs to sleep, and then I have to return a call from Paddy and get my intel on the Carisa mission. Taking charge of my life is proving to be exhausting.

TWENTY

Execution

We are at the cave and the old airstrip, preparing ourselves and our vessel to head to New Detroit. We are on a time constraint. The closer Abernathy comes to taking his Senate seat, slated for early September, the more his protection will increase. Paddy has assured me that this week there are no FA guards, and Abernathy's family is out. Additionally, he has verified that Carisa is alive and still in New Detroit. I've paid well for this intel, and I trust Paddy. Well, as much as I trust any Glitter contact. No one in the unit has said anything about Will being absent, and I appreciate it. I head back into the cave to get some non-Bosch protective gear. We will not go in wearing Bosch uniforms, and we won't even carry Bosch firearms. I go to the weapons cabinet to retrieve my Rus KORD 9R70 and then I reach out and pick up the one Will had liberated.

"Hey. That's mine." I spin at the sound of the voice, see Will standing a few meters away, and my heart leaps and then drops.

I try to frown, but my lips keep their upward curve. "What are you doing here, Will?"

"Kat. I need to finish this mission."

I start to interrupt him, but he pushes on. "Listen, we found the envelope and letter and pictures together. I found Carisa in the pictures. I've been in since the start. I need to see it through."

I inhale deeply. "I don't know, Will."

He walks toward me and takes the KORD, letting his hand linger on mine for the briefest moment. "C'mon, Kat." He grins, and his eyes look lovingly at me. "Last mission together. We've had some great ones. Let's finish with a bang!"

I can't resist the idea of a little more stolen time together, so I relax and give a laugh. "Okay. But this has to be the last mission we do together. We both have to move on." I see him close his eyes briefly as I say this. "Are you back with Warner's unit?"

He smiles at me, but there is a sadness in it. "I am. But it's temporary. I'm going to draw on my trust fund and start the business. I can't be on base anymore. I'll get distracted." He points at me and raises his eyebrows.

I feel as though he has run his hands along my body with that gesture. My breath is shaky. "Good for you. Good for Bosch. Bad for the BPF." I gaze hungrily at his face. Then we both break the gaze, and I shake my head to clear it, reminding myself of what I am trying to achieve, so far, with little success, at home. A recent memory pops into my head.

I have been somewhat disconsolate the last few days. Takai is still in Bosch, and two nights ago, as I lay awake on my side staring at the wall, imagining things I should just let go of, I felt him settle himself onto his side of our bed upstairs. I was surprised. He had slept the first two nights in his study on the small sofa. We hadn't shared a bed since Grey's birthday back in April, and that was simply sleeping. I tensed because I was not ready for anything more yet.

He had turned to me, cleared his throat, and in an even voice said, "I think we should talk about Will McCloud."

I stared more intently at the wall, realizing that Takai believed I had a real affair with Will. And maybe I had. Not in the physical sense, but I had shared so much of my heart with him that maybe it counted. Then I remembered the yukata and all the letters and messages from various women over the years, and I hardened. "Only if you'd like to include your first officer in the discussion as well," I said, keeping my body very still but sending as much venom as possible into my response. "In fact, let's start there, and then we can branch out to all the others."

Takai went very quiet at my statement. Without a sound, he turned off the light. I felt him roll away from me to his side, where I knew he could gaze at the wall opposite me.

This was the state of our marriage, and I wasn't sure how to fix it. How to fix me. I return to the present and am delighted that Will is in it.

I hand him some of the gear I collected, and we each sling our rifles over our bodies and head out of the cave.

"It'll be six going in and seven coming back," I announce to the rest of the unit who obviously were waiting for this confirmation. When I make it, there is much laughter and back-slapping. Bailey shakes Will's arm and welcomes him, then comes to me.

"You gonna be okay?" they ask quietly as they reach out and touch my elbow.

I am touched by their concern and give a small grunt. "We shall see. But we will have a good mission. I've been waiting for this for a long time."

I turn to the unit with a final reminder before take-off: "Remember: No one shoots Abernathy. After we get Carisa out, I get to deal with him on my own."

Five thumbs go up, and we are ready to go.

~

"Casey, bring Anne upstairs, please." Rob Abernathy's voice was calm and collected.

There was a scrambling sound from Casey's end of the comm. "But, sir, we really should be leaving for the safehouse. The intruders are very likely…" Rob heard a window shatter. "Sir, that was a gunshot! And close by!" Casey's voice was moving quickly into the upper reaches of panic. The tone made Rob smile.

He responded in his same calm voice. "All the more reason to bring her upstairs, Casey. You know my rooms are well-protected. I'll expect you immediately." Rob Abernathy poured a small measure of wine into his glass. "Oh, and Casey…"

"Y-y-yes, sir?" His assistant did not do flustered well.

"Be sure you hurry. I'll be locking the doors in five minutes." Rob smiled as he listened to Casey drop his comm and call for Anne. He pulled his side desk drawer open and took out the small lockbox. He put in the code and unlocked it, surveying the marker cards and important papers kept within. Then he opened his center desk drawer and drew out the long braid of hair he had entwined with a green ribbon. He briefly held it to his nose and inhaled, then he meticulously coiled it and, carelessly tossing three marker cards aside to make room, dropped it into the lockbox and fastened the lid, setting the unobtrusive box on the corner of his desk nearest to the display case of his many and varied awards.

Reaching into the desk drawer a second time, he drew out his pistol, checked it, turned off the safety, and tucked it carefully in the special concealed vest pocket he had his tailor create. He had no intention of killing her yet, but he had no intention of dying either. As he straightened his jacket, he heard the doorknob to his office turn, and Casey burst in breathlessly, dragging a petite, blonde woman by the arm into the room. She didn't look upset, just resigned, even blank. Casey pushed her to the floor, then turned and slammed the heavy wooden door shut.

"They've made the front entrance, sir. We really need to go! They'll be here any minute!" Casey panted as he turned the old-fashioned key in the metal lock. He narrowed his eyes as he considered the key.

Rob Abernathy appeared at his side, took the key from him, and said in a soothing voice, "Why, Casey. We will go. Once I have taken care of my business. Why don't you go sit over there?" Rob motioned to a deep, comfortable upholstered chair that had a lovely antimacassar covering, the back of which his wife had embroidered several roses. He gave Casey a small push, and the man quietly went to the chair and sat down, elbows on his knees and head in his hands, trying to slow his breathing.

"Now, Anne, come here."

The woman stood from the floor, where she had landed like a cast-off rag doll when Casey shoved her. She came close to Rob, looking straight ahead, but then leaned her head onto his chest.

Rob frowned at this familiarity. "Stop it, Anne. I don't like that."

The blonde head popped up, and she murmured two words flatly, "I'm sorry."

He grasped her by the arm and walked with her to stand in front of the desk. He opened the bottom drawer of his desk caddy, and he could feel Anne's body go tense as he withdrew his knife. He stroked her hair with his other hand. "Now,

Anne…" His voice was cajoling. "I don't want to use this, but there are some bad people coming, and I need it to protect us both. I won't use it on you unless you make me."

She shook her head vigorously from side to side, the blonde locks flipping toward his face, which tried his patience. "No. No. I'll be good. I promise." Anne's eyes were wide.

"Enough," Rob snapped. "Now turn around and stand still." He didn't like that she tried his patience, and so he squeezed her upper arm hard with his fingers denting into the soft flesh, bruising it, until he heard her give a small moan. "Quiet," he ordered as he listened for someone in the hallway. She quieted, though he kept the pressure on. He discreetly set the knife on his desk.

After several tense moments, during which he wondered if the information the Glitter dealer had fed him was inaccurate, he was mollified to hear scraping at the lock. He had known she would come. And he knew the bait to bring her back to him was cowering in his grip even now. He moved Anne's petite form in front of him.

The lock clicked, and the heavy door was pushed open. A rifle barrel came into view. *Interesting and quite…intriguing.* "Mary, dear? Is that you?"

A helmeted head peered around the corner, and he saw her face. It had been years, but it was just as he remembered with the blue-green eyes that sparked fire and the soft curves of her cheeks and jaw. The smile wasn't there, but he would soon pull it from her. As he recalled, a bit of Glitter had made that happen in the past. How ironic. The pirate soldier garb would have to go, but perhaps some other type of pirate costume might be enjoyable. The woman pivoted into the room, pointing her rifle at him. "Let her go, Abernathy." His Mary spat out the order as though she fancied herself in charge.

"Why, of course, Mary." He released Anne's arm, and she stood in place.

"Carisa." Mary's voice was urgent. "Carisa, it's me, Kat. C'mon. We are here to get you out. Where are the other thralls?"

Rob Abernathy frowned slightly at the word "we" and Mary's interest in the other thralls. The Glitter dealer had made it sound as though she was only interested in Anne, though the other thralls had been sent away to serve his family as part of the plan. "Mary, she is happy with me. She doesn't want to leave." He gently put a lock of hair behind Anne/Carisa's ear and said soothingly, "Do you, darling? Do you want to stay with me or go with Mary?" He gestured slightly between him and Mary.

Carisa looked fearfully at the woman in the battle garb brandishing a rifle and sank into Rob. "Stay here."

"No!" the pirate woman yelled. "No, Carisa. He hurts you. He hurt me. But you can get away like I did."

Rob was pleased she remembered her pain. It would make it easier to access all those feelings later. He didn't ever actually feel any emotions himself, so he enjoyed watching the grand array of sentiment in his underlings, especially the housemaids. Especially Mary. However, most went dead in spirit long before he took their lives, much as Anne had. That was why he so wanted Mary back; she had never broken.

He glanced over and saw Casey, wide-eyed, staring at the woman and the rifle. He motioned for him to come over to the desk. He saw the barrel of the rifle shift. "Now, Mary. It's just Casey. You remember him." She said nothing, but the dark look she gave his assistant was answer enough. "Come here, Casey. Stand here with me where Mary can see us."

Casey cautiously stepped over, holding his shaking hands

out from his body. The rifle barrel followed him, but that was all.

"So, Mary, surely you aren't planning to shoot three unarmed people, are you?"

She took a deep breath. "I just want Carisa. Send her over to me."

Both Rob and the woman holding a gun on him looked briefly at the door as another rifle barrel appeared. "You good, Kat?" A man's voice called from the hallway.

"I'm good, Will. I found everything we were looking for right here."

A tall, well-built young man dressed similarly to Mary stepped into the room. He looked at the three stationed against the desk and grinned. "Nice work, Troop."

Rob watched as his Mary's face blossomed into a smile in response to this man's voice. He heard her voice, warm and rich, answer him. "Thanks, Will. For once, things are going according to plan." He saw them exchange a glance and saw both of their faces soften ever so slightly. He felt his rage rise. He had seen that look between people before, and it caused the reptilian part of his brain to alarm. It was the look people who were in love shared. And while he did not feel that type of connection, he knew he would not allow it to exist between his Mary and this intruder. The senator felt his jaw tighten, and he shifted to settle the discomfort he felt. No. It would not do. *She will look at me that way. Only me.*

Abernathy glanced from Casey to Anne to Mary to this... what was it? Will? And he decided he could be patient. He would take control of her. But another time. For now, she simply needed a lesson regarding proper behavior and to be reminded who controlled her world. His left hand went silently back for his knife. He had planned to kill Anne in front of Mary for old times' sake. But now...

"Mary." Rob said her name as he pulled Anne in front of him and put the knife to her throat. Firm enough to command submission but not so firm as to draw blood. "You have been living with the pirates. You must understand negotiation." He saw both rifles point to him and then drop slightly floorward for fear of hitting their rescuee.

"What do you have in mind, Abernathy?" Her eyes narrowed, but there was no hesitation in her voice. She had become bold and strong, and he wanted to be the one to break that strength. Rob swallowed his disappointment that he would be unable to keep her today. But he knew that time would come.

"You came here to take something of mine. Something quite...precious." His voice was warm as he stroked Anne's cheek, and she leaned into him. He looked at Mary, and his voice went hard and flat. "You can have her. But I must have something precious of yours in return."

Mary's eyes held a suspicious look, and her face looked unconvinced, but the barrel of her rifle dropped a bit further as she gave a short, humorless laugh. "You are cornered in this office, Rob. You aren't really in any position to negotiate terms."

"You could be right." He tensed his body in readiness. "Or perhaps not." In one fluid move, as Rob Abernathy dropped the knife and pushed Anne toward Mary, he withdrew his pistol from his vest and aimed and shot at the no-longer-smiling young rival. He missed his head, but from the blood spray he saw, he guessed he had hit the man's neck. He pivoted, pulling Casey to shield his back as Rob pushed a button under the front edge of his desk and grabbed the lock-box. He heard the report of the rifle, along with the scream. He wasn't sure if it came from Anne, or Mary, or Casey, but he was not waiting to find out. The display case had slipped open, and he jumped and slid down the tunnel that appeared. He could hear the scraping as the display case slid back. The Glitter dealer would be waiting at the bottom as he had personally assured Rob of safe transport. He would be well paid. And Rob smiled to himself as he descended. He would no longer have to go looking for her. Just like today, the next time, she would come to him.

Time slows. As I hear first Abernathy's shot and then my own, I leap toward Will as he spins and collapses on the floor a moment later. I hear my voice call his name. Blood is spurting from his neck. *Put pressure on it*, the Edoan physicians call in my head. I pull a kerchief and press it to the wound. "Hang on, Will." I am urgent in my statement. I press my ear comm. "I need help. Will is down."

"Kat." His voice is a whisper, and he blinks his eyes twice; each time they are slower to open. "You...okay?" I can't believe he is thinking of me at this point.

"Shhhh, love," I admonish him. "Save your strength." I look wildly around. There is a body crumpled by the desk, and Carisa stands where she was shoved, looking helpless. "Go get help, Carisa." She just stares at me.

I feel Will's body give a small shake, and I lean back to him, getting close to his ear. "Stay with me, Will. Please. I can't..." My lips are on his ear, and I am watching his eyes; they shift toward me and are taking on a faraway look. *No, please, no.*

He turns his head ever so slightly toward me, causing another pump of blood to flow between my fingers as they fumble to keep the pressure. He whispers, and it is so quiet, I have to put my ear to his lips. "Last...mission, love. Kiss... me...goodbye." My heart crumbles, and I hear footsteps come into the room and then stop. As I come close, I smell his smell of leather and cypress now overlaid with the heavy, coppery scent of blood; then, without hesitation, I press my lips to his and he…he tastes like warm sugar cookies: sweet and rich and like coming home. I feel them kiss me back for a brief moment until they start to grow cool. A moment later, the kiss stops as Will goes limp, his life simply slipping away from me. I run my hands across his still-warm face and press my ear to his unmoving chest and hear nothing. My hands are covered in his blood. Someone starts to scream his name, and from a distance, I realize it is me screaming as I kneel beside this man I love surrounded by his life's blood, knowing his death is my fault. My worst decision.

Part III

TWENTY-ONE

Picking Up the Pieces

BOSCH, MAY 2362

"Kat." I feel someone shake my shoulder, and I try to drag myself up from the depths of sleep. "Love, wake up. I'll take you home." My brain is addled for some reason, and I am trying to place the voice and orient myself. "C'mon, Kat, I'll help you stand." I squint and see Takai. A blink, and I realize I am in Miles' office curled up on the small sofa nearest the bar. The events of the day and my conversation with Miles in the afternoon return to me in one swift motion.

"Good lord, Kat." Miles had stood as I came in, still covered in Will's blood. Betsy appeared with a blanket and wrapped it around me. I hadn't even known I was cold.

It had occurred to me that I was standing in Miles' office reporting yet again that I had killed someone. *Someone else you loved*, comes the whisper. "Will is dead." The words sounded foreign to me, and I heard Miles say a soft, "Oh, no."

"We brought his body back." I closed my eyes and saw in my mind the image of the cold clay that had been Will. We had carefully cleaned him and wrapped him in a ship's sail tied with red twine as was the Bosch tradition, then carefully placed him on the floor of the vessel near his station, well-secured. All Bosch vessels carry the sails and twine for this purpose. I had never before broken the seal on the compartment holding them.

"He's at the old airfield. Along with the body of Abernathy's assistant." Now, I see the assistant's body pushed into the corner of the vessel, an old blanket over its face. Demery had insisted that it couldn't be left behind. "This will already blow up an investigation. No sense leaving clues." He and Bailey had rolled up the rug that Will's blood had soaked into and taken it on board to burn in the incinerator here. Gia had splashed peroxide over the remaining stains as I sat and held Will's head to my breast.

"And..." Here I gave a laugh that had no humor. "Carisa is on board: alive." When I left the vessel, she was silent, Gia at her side, sitting with her knees under her chin, just staring, her blonde hair streaked slightly with a bit of the omnipresent blood that seemed to define this mission. I looked at my mentor. "The mission was successful, Miles. But Will..."

I turned to the bar and shrugged off the blanket. I picked up a bottle and pulled the stopper. Not bothering with a glass, I lifted it to my lips and drank greedily. I heard Miles call to me and come to take it, but I pushed him away and continued to drink. I registered as the liquor rolled down my throat that it was not my first drink of the day. I recalled I had grabbed a bottle at the cave as I ordered my unit to sit tight until I or someone returned, and I drank it as I walked to base. I only vaguely recall the walk.

Miles had tried to talk to me, to make sense of the events, but I quickly passed out on the sofa. Or was it the floor? Somehow, I ended up on the sofa, and now, here is Takai.

He speaks quietly in my ear as he maneuvers me to our seldom-used vehicle. "Just a bit farther." He knows how sensitive I get to sound when I am hungover. I'm not sure I have graduated from blackout drunk yet, but I appreciate the quiet, nonetheless. He starts the engine and pulls away, and within moments, I call, "I'm going to be sick." The vehicle stops, and I open the passenger door, lean out, and vomit. I feel Takai next to me. He wipes my face with a cool cloth as he murmurs, "I've got you." I wonder vaguely where the water came from, then I see him lift his own water bottle to my lips and encourage me to rinse my mouth. He straps me back in the seat and then takes his place as the driver, and we restart. It's a very short drive home, but he has to stop twice more for me to empty my stomach. Each time, he patiently wipes my face and provides me with water.

"We are home, Kat." He gives my shoulder a little shake, and I rouse from my stupor in my seat. Leaning heavily on Takai, I make my way to the bathroom where my husband strips my ruined clothes off as I passively stand. He gently showers me, soaping my hair and my body. He softly scrubs the blood off my skin with a cloth and then uses the nail brush to clean my useless hands. Hands that couldn't save him.

All through these ablutions, Takai is careful, solicitous, and tender. "I love you, Kat. I'm right here." He even helps me brush my teeth, and then he leads me to our bed and tucks me in. He slips in next to me and draws my head onto his shoulder. I have kept the tears in until now. Now I start to cry, and he rocks me like he has rocked each of our babies when they were small. He doesn't ask me any questions; he doesn't say it will be okay. He just holds me, softly kissing my head and saying, "I'm here, Kat. I'm here, love," until I fall into a dreamless sleep.

$\sim$

I set a cup of deep black tea with just a hint of milk in front of Miles and look at him over the desk. For the past ten days, I've spent my non-mission time on base here. I show up to the hangar three mornings a week to fly out, negotiate, drop Glitter, get markers, and fly back in. I then immediately leave. I know my unit is dismayed by my shunning, but it's the only way. Instead of spending time with them, I sit and watch Miles clean up some of the mess I created. Sometimes we talk about whatever project or agenda he currently is dealing with, and he is careful not to ask anything about me or Will or my unit. I figured him putting up with that, with me, is worth an occasional nicety like a well-brewed cup of tea.

Miles looks up, his lean, brown face placid as he lifts the cup. "Thanks for the tea." He takes a long sip. "That will get me through to the end of the day. Now, what will this cost me?" He smiles warmly.

"I didn't make it as a bribe, Miles." I move my face to what amounts to a smile. I don't actually smile the regular way anymore.

When I awoke after Takai brought me home that first night, I had stretched and opened my eyes, content just to be awake until the memory of Will's death grabbed me by my throat. I had rolled over, and the pain of loss stabbed into me over and over. I couldn't see or hear the living world, only the sound of weapon fire, and Will's gray, lifeless face filled my senses. And the blood. I finally forced my body up as a wave of nausea took me, and I ran to the toilet and retched.

I sat on the floor of the bathroom barely breathing as I rocked back and forth. The world had been rent into two parts: the time before Will was killed, and now. I didn't know how to live in the now. So, I made a decision that was neither good nor bad, just necessary. I took a sizeable slab of what amounted to emotional wet clay and packed it firmly around my heart, sealing it with slip and letting it dry hard and rigid. I have quietly folded my tally sheet and pocketed it. Now I can move through the days.

My clay heart has its advantages. I don't even really feel sad. So, no crying. And I don't feel anger. So, no hitting. Remorse, tricky bastard that it is, escaped my heart just before the clay hardened and took refuge in my head, where it continues to whisper at me: *You let him come. You dropped your defense. You should have seen. You should have anticipated. You let Will bleed.*

There are some disadvantages, though Remorse assures me I deserve them. I can't seem to feel friendship any longer. Nor can I find a reason to hope. Nor can I feel content. And happiness is a phantasm.

The only time I allow feelings is with Grey and Kik and Mac. I have left a tiny tunnel in the clay for them. For them, I will smile and even laugh a bit at their antics. It feels like a fresh spring rain. But I find even this is becoming a problem. My clay dissolves in that sort of rain, and I feel other emotions, sensing a weak spot, seep in toward the small portal. I have to quickly close this little gap and bolster it with thicker slips and slabs of clay each time. It is the only way to keep all the encroaching emotions contained.

Miles smiles a real smile at me. "But I know that look. You have something in mind. Out with it." He flicks his fingers toward his palms as he says this.

Nodding, I present my plan. "I want to run some extractions. I can take my own vessel and pick up some missions that I know are backlogged for you."

Miles' eyes are soft as he considers this. He has not refused anything I have asked for since the funeral.

Will's funeral: It was very traditional. The land in Bosch is too precious for burial gardens like the Old Days cemeteries I still see on the mainlands, so the Bosch have a land ceremony, and then the undertaker and the immediate family travel to the District Four port city of Saltend and take a small ship out from Saltend Harbor to a sacred space for a sea burial. There is a wall of names in the district near the port that commemorates the final voyage for all our dead. I was at the land ceremony but felt little as I had shored up my clay heart beforehand. I stood with my unit and just got through it. The only face I remember seeing was that of Will McCloud, Senior. He looked angry and betrayed and beaten. That made perfect sense to me.

Now, Miles is considering yet another of my requests. He wrinkles his brow slightly and bites his lower lip, all signs that he is worrying about me and my choices. "You're already running thrice-a-weeks with Colonel Ka'ne. Seems a bit ambitious."

"I need to keep busy, Miles. Thrice-a-weeks leave me with too many open days. When I'm working, I can forget. Please?" I am not used to pleading my case. "You know I can do the jobs right."

Miles nods, but he is still biting his lower lip. "All right. I'm sending the extraction roster your way now." He scrolls and hits a button on his Obi. "But…" He leans across his desk and taps his finger on the burnished wood of it close to me. "…I don't want you taking any foolish chances, understood?"

I create what I hope passes for a reassuring smile. "Definitely not. Just trying to keep busy and be useful." I am actually seeking the adrenaline rush that surges on a solo mission when I just make it out with the rescued soul or the intelligence data. I suspect Miles knows this is my motivation as well.

I thank my Master Commander, step out of his office, and immediately call up the list. There are some intriguing options and lucrative ones as well. *Might as well boost my portfolio at the same time.* I select one and make a couple of comms with plans to request details from the Bosch Intelligence division this afternoon. I'll be in the air in the morning, home with the cargo secured and dropped off before the kids are out of school. How perfect is that?

As I walk from base, I begin a conversation with Will. This is the other thing, besides the clay, that has kept me functioning. I chat with Will several times a day. He asks about the mission, and I give him the specs.

"Seems a solid choice. Be sure you keep your vessel in tiptop shape if you are running solo. I can talk with you, but given that I'm dead, I can't fix a broken aileron."

"Excuses, excuses…" I laugh in my head, and there, the laughter feels real.

I can see the house, but I'm yet not ready to be home. It is getting dusky, and I slip next to the neighbor's arrowwood hedge to watch my family frolic in the warm evening. The children are playing some kind of tag in the yard, and as I see how Grey slows her pace, just a bit, to be tagged by Mac, I feel something in that secret tunnel my heart has just for the children nudge a chunk of clay out of the way, and I smile.

Mama sits on an outdoor chair she has brought around from the back, reading a book with a small book light and responding to Kik several times as he calls, "Watch me, Mama M." Carisa sits in a chair next to her. Gia and Bailey had settled her into Mama's care, just as we had agreed to before. Before the mission. Before Will died. I scrutinize Carisa as she sits passively in the dimming evening. She is clean and fed; her hair is pulled back with a clip, but she remains silent except for a few thrall responses: *yes, ma'am; no, ma'am; I'm sorry;* and the like. I know caring for Carisa is taking much of Mama's focus and energy, and I decide to ask Mimi for help with after-school care. Of course, it is a stroke of good fortune for me that Mama is too distracted by Carisa's needs to notice that I have a clay heart. Remorse perks up. *Hell of a trade you made.*

Mama had spoken to me a few days after Carisa arrived. "She is very damaged, Kat. I can provide her safety and her body's needs, but I want you to take her over to the base for therapy."

I had snorted and rolled my eyes, and Mama locked me in place with her stern gaze. "I know the Bosch think they can swagger over their emotions, Kat Wallace, but take it from me, they can't. Carisa needs someone to talk with about her trauma."

I nodded in agreement because, well, Mama. But I had serious doubts about how paying someone to listen to two-word phrases was going to make any difference.

Takai stayed only two days after Will's death. He had to return to the *Venturer* as he originally planned to be gone only a couple of days. Those "couple of days" had expanded to almost a week.

He was very gentle with me, even after I sobered up, and he offered me condolences, which bounced off the hardened clay in my chest. He never mentioned the part of our bargain where he had asked me not to work with Will, and I appreciated that. Because if only I had stuck to the agreement, maybe Will... I feel a crack in the clay and rush to repair it.

Takai was different. Kinder with me than he had been for months but also a bit more closed off. Or perhaps I am the one closed off. But he seems to still love me, and I am grateful for that. We made love for the first time in months the night before he left, and we have spoken almost daily about the children, our workdays, the house, our families, the basic fundamentals of a life shared. Each time we have said goodbye, he says, "I love you, Kat." I realize I am supposed to say "I love you, too" in response, but unfortunately, I only have a clouded memory of love. It is buried under layers and layers of thick, dry clay. But I will say it—next time. Maybe if I say it enough, I will feel it without having to feel everything else.

Takai has made changes to meet the parameters I had asked for, though it seems that conversation was a lifetime ago. Remorse cackles; *Will's lifetime*. Takai tells me he has reassigned his entire crew, bringing on new officers. He says it is not unusual on the big ships, but I suspect otherwise. He even told me that while I'm welcome to visit the *Venturer*, he understands if I choose not to, given the upset I had experienced there. I appreciate his openness and kindness. I am slowly beginning to trust him again. Perhaps this marriage may work after all.

"Hey, Kat. Can we talk?" Tom Pikari comes up behind me as I am scrolling through some information from Bosch Intelligence in one of the spare offices in the hangar.

I turn off the screen. I'm working on a solo mission and don't want my unit to know. I sigh, frustrated by both the interruption in my work and the disruption of the distance between myself and my unit members I am trying to intentionally create. "Sure, Tom. What's up?"

"So..." He pauses as if he is unsure how to continue. "Before...well, before the New Detroit mission..." I hear a roaring in my ears, and I shake my head slightly. Tom studies my face and continues. "Well, Will and I had talked about opening a business together. Those stability mechanisms he created—they could be a game-changer in some parts of the world."

I'm good with this topic. No emotions needed. "Right. He mentioned that was the plan."

"I want to go ahead with it. I was planning to go to his family and ask for the seed money to get started. I know Miriam knows them pretty well, and I was hoping she could put in a good word for me." I realize now that Tom is actually nervous as he presents this. "I was going to call it McCloud Mechanics."

Now I am engaged. "No." Tom looks taken back at the vehemence of my response. "No." I reel my intensity back. "Don't call it that. Call it Will Mechanics, or something. And he wouldn't want you to go begging to his family."

Tom shakes his head. "I know. He was going to take a draw on his money, but…. Well, that can't happen now. So, I don't have much choice."

I am quickly making calculations in my head. I have put markers aside in Bosch banks and internationally for the past dozen years. A good amount I have invested, often in young entrepreneurs, initially based on Teddy's recommendations and later my own assessments. These investments have generally paid handsomely, and my portfolio is, if I do say so myself, quite large. Teddy also left me a decent share of his markers after he died.

After you killed him, says Remorse, branching out.

Stop it, I hiss back. He left me the ones he had stashed in the New Caribbean banks since all my Bosch markers were confiscated at the time of my banishment and handed over to Mama. So, I have plenty and then some.

"Tom." I reach out and put my hand on his arm. "Open the business. Don't name it McCloud. Take 10 percent of the profits after the third year and put them toward engineering scholarships for escaped thralls, and I will fund the start-up until it starts to reliably turn a profit, which it will."

Tom looks like he is waiting for the punchline to a bad joke. "You can't be serious, Kat. Where would you come up with that kind of markers?"

I form a reassuring smile. "I am totally serious. Pull together the incorporation papers and give me a number. And don't undersell it. I promise you—the kids and I aren't going to starve."

Tom narrows his eyes at me, but I see a smile start on his face. I nod and give him what feels to me like a smile back. "Okay, then." His voice is excited, and his face now has a full-fledged grin on it. "Okay. Will Mechanics it is. I'll get papers pulled together and to you in the next couple of days. Thank you, Kat!" He leans over, gives me a kiss on the cheek, and then turns and hurries out of the office. I watch him leave through the window on the door and see him stop outside the office to say something to Bailey and Demery, who obviously have been waiting for him. I see all three faces light up, and Tom receives elbow grips and slaps on the back before he hurries out of the hangar, a spring in his step.

I go to turn my device back on, and Will pops out of his ever-present place in the edges of my mind, looks at me, and then out of the window at the unit. I see his face spread into a huge grin. *Here it comes.* "So, you've been holding out on me."

"No. Not exactly."

He cackles with laughter. "Yes, you have. That whole time you were calling me 'Trust-Fund' and complaining about the rich: You were rich too!"

"I am not," I snap but Will's face in my mind remains unconcerned.

"You are too, my love. But, hey, thanks for backing the business. You really made Tom's day."

The smile on my face feels a bit more real, and I feel a tiny bit of sunshine sneak in through a crack in the clay and warm a small part of my heart.

TWENTY-TWO

Therapy

BOSCH, MAY 2362

Carisa steps into the small office on the far left of the waiting room willingly after I make a big show of searching and clearing it. Nannette is her therapist and seems nice enough. I don't think "nice" is really going to help Carisa, though.

I turn to settle in until her session—if that's what it is called —is over. I look around the waiting room. It's currently empty. That fits. It's Bosch. The walls are a soft lavender color, and several blue, upholstered chairs are in the center of the room arranged back-to-back. Apparently, people who see therapists don't like to look at each other in the waiting room. There's a reception window where I helped Carisa check in, and there are four office doors that have the therapists' names on them, followed by an alphabet of letters. I only give the names a passing glance as I am just here to walk Carisa home afterward.

I stroll idly around the room. The walls have framed posters on them, each offering an encouraging aphorism: *It's okay to ask for help*, *Your feelings are valid*, and *Your voice is valued here*. There's also a colorful wheel of emotions; my eyebrows go up, and I nudge Will in my head and point it out. He gives

205

a guffaw. These are not my people. There is carpet in here; it's a dingy mauve color, and I cringe a bit. When I was growing up in the North Country, I thought carpet was the height of elegance. A few years in Edo quickly disabused me of that notion. Now I just imagine years of shoe dirt and skin flakes.

I sit in one of the blue chairs and look for any reading material. There is none. After a few minutes, a woman comes in dressed in an orange knit summer dress with a beige linen jacket. I feel the slightest bit of amusement that I can recognize the fabric: Gia's fashion tutelage is starting to make inroads into my brain. The woman has some jewelry on, but it's understated, a gold chain and a watch. She walks to the reception window and murmurs a bit to the woman who sits on the other side. I am watching her over my shoulder as there is precious little else to do. She comes and sits in a chair opposite my side two chairs away. I peer at her over my left shoulder and see her check her watch.

I decide to make small talk to move the time along, so I turn my body toward her and rest my left elbow on the back of my chair. "You waiting for someone as well?"

She turns to me, and her face is relaxed and pleasant. Her hair is dark but straight, and she has it pulled back and held with a clip in the shape of a seabird. She must be in her forties, I guess, but her deep brown eyes, which are open and friendly, don't really have many lines around them. She smiles. "I am." She turns toward me and extends her right arm to me, palm up in greeting. "I'm Ruth."

I reciprocate and we grasp our forearms briefly. I put on my imitation smile. "I'm Kat." I shrug. "I don't know that this is going to help my friend. No offense if it's working for yours."

Ruth's face doesn't waver. "It certainly doesn't work overnight. It can take years."

I make a sound that approximates a laugh for me. "I'm too

impatient for that. But Carisa, my friend…" I gesture at the door she is behind. "…is really hurting."

"You sound concerned. Is she a good friend?"

I consider the question. "Yes, but no. I knew her a long time ago." I roll my arm over and rub at my brand without thinking.

Ruth tips her head and looks at me. "It sounds like you associate your friend with your…" She points to my forearm. "Well, that one is not a tattoo, is it? Not in the traditional sense."

I shake my head, and before I know it, I am telling my Bell-coast tale to this virtual stranger. I don't intentionally leave out any parts, but I do abbreviate some events. I am just talking about my escape and how I should have gone back for Carisa when Nanette's door opens.

"Trooper Wallace? Carisa will be ready in five minutes. We just have to schedule her next visit."

I nod and look at Ruth. "Your friend should be out soon then as well." I shrug a bit. "Hey, thanks for listening." I am a bit chagrined, thinking about how I monopolized the conversation. "I don't typically talk that much, but you are easy to talk with."

Ruth gives me a warm smile. "Let's make a plan to talk more then." She reaches into her jacket pocket and removes a pale blue card. I take it and glance at it, recognizing the name as the one on the door to the right side of the entry.

"You said you were waiting for someone." I feel a bit duped.

Now she shrugs. "My seventeen-bell appointment didn't show."

I give an exasperated sigh. "So, you just 'sneak-therapied' me?" I shake her card slightly. "Aren't you people all about the ethics?"

"I hardly see anything unethical about a chat in a waiting room. I'm not charging you." Then she gives a small laugh. "But I will next week. How's Tuesday? You and Carisa can come together."

This is very un-Bosch, but it did feel good to talk with Ruth. "Fine. I'll try it once."

"Kat," Ruth says in a kind voice. "You already tried it. Coming the second time? Well, that's when the work starts."

I wrinkle my brow. *How can talking be work*? Nanette and Carisa appear next to me, and Ruth addresses her colleague. "When is Carisa's appointment?"

"Tuesday at seventeen bells."

"That works for me. What about you, Kat?"

I frown and glance at Will, who takes up the shrug, saying, "Why not, Kat? Can't hurt. May help."

I nod and reply out loud to both Will and Ruth, "Yeah. I guess. We'll see. But I don't want anyone to know I am here."

Ruth makes a sign as if she is locking her lips. "See you Tuesday?"

I give her a noncommittal shrug as I take Carisa's hand and head out the door.

TWENTY-THREE

Adrenaline Junkie

BOSCH & PARIDA, JULY 2362

Paddy Owens looked at the comm in his hand as he prepared to dial a number he had not put in since April. He tapped his hip and leg rapidly with the fingertips of the hand not holding the comm and paced back and forth on the balcony of his new condominium in the elite Firebreak subdivision of Old Toronto. The sweat trickling down his neck, though, was not just attributable to the July heat. It wasn't his fault things had gone bad in New Detroit. He had no choice but to tip Abernathy off to Kat's plan. But he didn't expect some BPF trooper to get killed. No, he had agreed to get Abernathy away from New Detroit and to the safehouse Abernathy had in the Appalachian Mountains.

Yes, he knew Abernathy had planned to capture Kat, but figured that was unlikely. He knew Kat could handle herself, and besides, he was a businessman, and this was a well-paid gig. It also assured he didn't get knifed by the crazy senator. He rationalized that, ordinarily, Kat wouldn't have held it against him, but from what he understood, the kid who Abernathy shot was a good friend of hers—a *real* good friend. Now

Paddy felt the shadow of a target on his back that would become clear and solid if his involvement ever leaked out to Kat. He had to do something to protect himself. He pushed the comm to send the call and listened to the distant buzz on the far end.

"Hey, Paddy. What's up?" Kat's voice came through the comm, and while it sounded strong, it was oddly flat.

"I...uh...hear you are looking for some off-book work." Paddy's fingertips continued drumming on his thigh.

He heard her snort what seemed to be half-laugh and half-growl. "Only if it pays real, real well."

"This one does, though it's a bit hairy. Though I expect you might manage." He paused his tapping while waiting for the response.

Kat answered quickly, without hesitation. "Why don't you let me decide about the risk. Let's hear the job details and the pay."

Paddy smiled to himself and felt his body relax. This would work out: an impossible task in a foreign country far from him, and the target on his back would disappear forever.

I run through the basic information Paddy told me about this mission—well, this job, since it really isn't a BPF mission. A couple of FA uni kids had gotten arrested for Glitter possession in Parida, a southern colony known for its strict drug laws. They had been quickly tried and were due to be executed by firing squad. I need to go in, get them, and fly them back to FA territory. The families are offering upwards of a quarter-million markers for their darlings' "safe return." Paddy wanted a 5-percent finder's fee, but I don't give away markers. Well, not to Paddy, so I offered him 3 percent. We dickered for some time and finally came to a number that was mutually agreeable: 3 percent. He promised to send additional details over within the next bell.

I had told him what Teddy had always told me. "That's great, Paddy. Because nothing fucks up a mission like lack of attention to details."

I am sitting on my back deck nursing my fourth beer. The children are on the *Venturer* for yet another extended visit. I encouraged Takai to keep them there recently and have dropped my daily comms to him and them to weekly. Not having them near creates a deep, empty crevasse in me, but I'm attempting to mortar in that space with the same emotional clay that encases my heart. Safer that way.

I get a buzz on my comm and jump, expecting the job specs, but it is a calendar reminder that I have the first board meeting ever for W-Mech: the company Tom founded with Will's designs, tonight. I intended to be a wholly silent investor, but Tom has told me clearly that I am part of the board. So, I will show up and try to be useful.

Over the past several weeks, I have focused exclusively on solo extractions and have run through Miles' approved list and done a fine job on all the missions. But as the list has grown thin, I am now seeking missions that are, shall I say, approved-adjacent. Ones where the margin of error is narrow. The pay is far better for these, and that much more adrenaline pumps during the whole mission when the outcome sits on the edge of a knife. A few of the jobs I have muscled my way through, coming away with a fair share of bruises and minor flesh wounds. Takai was appalled at the residual marks when he saw me post-shower one day, and I had to distract him from pressing too much about my side-work. Fortunately, being naked and still wet from the shower provided me with a head start in the diversion. I get that he worries, but the rush when I succeed at those jobs is so sweet. Almost like feeling things.

Details: two kids, twenty and nineteen. The twenty-year-old is named Arruda Bishop, and the nineteen-year-old is Phillip Raines. I look at their photos. They are definitely not drug runners but foolish trekkers who had "forgotten" they had a small bag of Glitter in their backpacks. They are due to be executed Saturday morning. I figure to arrive just a bit earlier than their scheduled seven-bells (Parida time) execution and pick them up as they are being moved from cell to arena. An arena… These Paridians sure must take their public punishments seriously. I do some additional investigation into that to determine potential crowd size and find that these foreign executions are so common—here I cringe and look at their fresh faces in the pics again—that few Paridians get up early for them. It's the lunch and dinner ones that have the draw. Cross Parida off my places to vacation.

My own children are slated to come home on Friday night. This creates an extra little crimp. Takai required a bit of fast-talking and roundabout explaining as to why I was planning a "Glitter drop" the morning after he and the kids arrived. He was "only going to be home for the weekend, after all, Kat." I promised him three things: I was going to make a tidy profit, it would be an early morning run, and I'd be back before the boys started clamoring for a second breakfast. All completely true. I did omit some of the parts he might find objectionable, but this job really felt delightfully edgy, and I wanted that adrenaline hit.

I stock and prep the *Coupe* early Friday afternoon so I can be fully present when the kids and Takai arrive. As I do, Will and I chat about the W-Mech board meeting the other night. Beyond all the regular discussion about budgets, market strategy, and quarterly projections, it was exciting to hear about product development.

"I am really glad Tom is doing this. I hope it makes him a fortune." Will is sitting on the helm of the *Coupe* as I roll my dual-fuel motorbike in, plug it in, and strap it down.

I give a chuckle. "I hope it makes me a fortune."

"Oh, you'd be fine either way, but Tom has been stretched thin for a long time. He deserves a break."

"Will, you are way nicer than I am." I shake my head at his kindness.

He gets up and comes close to me, and I try to actually smell that leather and cypress, but it hovers just out of reach. "You think? Interesting that you see it that way, my love."

The alarm on my watch goes off, and I glance down. "Gotta get to the base." I actually hear my voice say this as Will evaporates for the time being.

My watch vibrates, and my eyes pop open. Four bells. I sigh. Still getting up and having to fucking function at fucking ridiculous hours. A small part of my brain tries to convince me that I could sleep for a bit longer, but Parida is about an hour's flight, and I'll need time to cover the *Coupe* and get to the arena. I slip out of bed in the dark, leaving Takai deeply asleep, and pull on my extraction gear. My flight suit and sling bag are in the vessel. I definitely don't kiss the kids because of late, this has become a dangerous hour for them. One hint of a parent being awake, and they will pop out of bed and be ready for the day, running the adults to exhaustion. So, I silently move past their rooms, opt out of making coffee to avoid the noise, and head on foot to the cave.

I keep the *Coupe* below the radar limits as I arrive in Paridian airspace. I accessed maps and photos of Parida's capital city and the surrounding area from the BI, Bosch Intelligence. With these, I had pinpointed a small lake about six kilometers from the arena with an onshore clearing big enough for the *Coupe* and small enough to provide cover. There's a road of some sort as well. I bring the *Coupe* in smoothly and silently on the lake. The lake is low, and the shoreline far wider than the pictures, and I am, for a moment, perplexed until my non-caffeinated brain remembers that this is the dry season here. This area and far beyond it had once been a tropical jungle in the Old Days, but now is more temperate, yet still given to a dry and wet season. I maneuver the vessel up to shore and into the clearing.

As I open my gearbox…

"Costume box," Will intones. "It's where you keep your dress-up clothes."

I feel a full-on grin inside my head at this comment. Will loves…loved…loves? Well, he teases me that I am playing dress-up as I select from the various camouflage garb so I can dress based on the season and my locale. "I like to be properly prepared." I stick my tongue out at him. I hear his warm laugh as I select my *costume* and slip it on. I have chosen a close-fitting jumpsuit in which I can run and climb. It is in the most fashionable green and brown camouflage color. Then I fasten on my leather helmet and turn to go to unplug my bike.

"Hey!" Will's voice is sharp.

I roll my eyes like a spoiled teen, turn, and shrug, hands turned upward. "What?"

He nods toward my head, eyes reproving as he stares at my neck. I sigh, then unbuckle my neck strap, reach under the brim, and pull down the leather neck guards from where most troopers usually keep them—neatly tucked away. From just inside their helmets. I fasten the neck strap again and look at Will.

I begin shaking and feel a flash of hot, then cold, then a wave of nausea. I can feel the clay inside my chest vibrate, and suddenly several cracks appear, and a rush of feelings starts to push on weak places. Will's face is so clear, I feel I can touch it, but I have to focus inward and reinforce the clay to keep my emotions in check. In place. Away. I take a few deep breaths. Then I look up. Will's face is still there, though fuzzier and more distant somehow. "Better?" I ask, gesturing at my head and neck.

"Better." He smiles at me and gives me a Bosch salute and a wink but still wavers as if he is see-through. I pull my goggles down.

I roll the motorbike down the ramp, lock and cover the *Coupe*, and head down a quiet dirt road under a cloudless sky with a golden sun just rolling up over the hillsides. Its warmth feels innocent, but it promises to bring on intense heat later in the day. I skirt the woods, and after a few kilometers, it gives way to the countryside with its occasional farmsteads. I see a farm couple come out of one and move along well-worn paths toward their daily tasks. Getting closer to the arena, I pass a row of white, stucco homes with red roofs and red window frames. Each home has a small flower garden in front and a thriving vegetable garden in back. I picture the families of these homes snuggled under quilts made in whatever the traditional way one makes quilts in Parida, content in the knowledge all they love is safe. A plethora of birdsong that started in the woods in its typical pre-dawn frenzy has continued, shifting in volume, tone, and tenor where the trees are fewer. Now I hear a rooster crow first from one side of the red-roofed road and then the other as I pass along the lane. Parida: truly a beautiful, picturesque, and pastoral scene. Except the public executions. As I come around a small bend, the arena is in my view, its gate open, inviting, and most importantly, unguarded.

I shut off the motorbike's engine several meters away and coast to a stop. I stash my bike near the arena, poised for a quick getaway, seat extender on. It is half-past five bells. According to Paddy's intel, the execution is scheduled for seven bells. I am feeling confident. My plan is to put myself above where the Paridian sentries will walk the kids from their cells, drop the guards, and run the kids out of the open and unguarded gate to the bike and then to the vessel. Fast as fire. I'll be back, while not by second breakfast, certainly by elevenses. This phrase makes me think of Papa and his love of the Old Days Tolkien books. I have to shake my head hard and fast to stop that memory as I can feel it chip at the block of newly dried clay I carry in my chest. I pause and refocus.

I toss my ladder hook to catch the top edge of the arena at its lowest point. It only gives a slight clang, but I hear scuffling from the far side that I plan to check out once I have summited. As I climb higher, I hear voices that increase in volume as I get closer to the edge. *What the fuck?* I peer over the coping stones into the center of the arena. Off to the left, farthest from the now apparently closed (*fuck*) gate, there are two poles securely sunk in the floor of the arena, each with a young person strapped to them (*double-fuck*). Off to the right, a sizeable firing squad is massing (*am I on triple-fuck?*). Off to the sides are other Paridians and their gear and perhaps victims-to-be, but my focus is on my cargo and the guys with guns.

Clearly the execution is not scheduled for seven bells but for six. Fucking Paddy and his fucking carelessness. He isn't getting even 3 percent now—that is certain. I run through my options: I could just bag it and go home. I take a quick glance at the nearest pole. A young woman fitting Arruda Bishop's description is lashed to it. She wears a blindfold, but it is clear she is crying and shaking. The kid on the pole next to her has to be Phillip Raines, and he, too, is crying, and I see his mouth quiver. So, no fucks left to give. They are not going to die today. I feel adrenaline surge through me. It clears my head and prepares my body. It is an amazing feeling, and I know it will carry me through my task. I turn and slide down my ladder, disengaging it and stuffing it into my bag. I glance at my watch: 0550. Hope the Paridians run timely executions.

I skirt the arena, arriving at my bike, and pull out my Bosch-issue automatic weapon. Dale would love this cowboy shit. A small crack appears as I imagine his face and his "Save it for the bad guys" refrain. Who are the bad guys again? I am starting to relate heavily to Butch and Sundance. I give the gate a pull, but it is locked. O-five-fifty-five bells. I pause a millisecond. I have the tools for this as well. Another adrenaline surge. My breath increases and my heart speeds up, seemingly unaware of its encasement.

I hustle back to the bike and from my black sling bag pull out my explosives set that holds detonators, primers, fuses, and detonating cords. Then from a separate pocket, I pull a tiny, hard-sided case containing a small amount of moldable explosive. I rig the explosive to both the hinges and the lock on the heavy, wooden gate of the arena. I hum a tuneless song as I rig the detonator, then return and mount the bike. O-five-fifty-eight bells. I turn the ignition on and pull out my blade from its place holstered on my thigh; I am glad one side is serrated. I keep the bone handle of the blade in my steering hand, then hit the detonator and wait only the barest of a moment to see the gate drop.

I flip to gas, accelerate, and kick up dirt from the road, which, along with the dust and debris from the explosion, provides me with a film of cover. In addition, the Paridian guards seem confused as to the turn of events. Apparently, they do well shooting people tied to poles but are less well-versed in an actual fight. I run a suppressive stream in their direction from the automatic and maneuver my bike to the poles.

The bone-handled eight-inch blade Teddy gave me years ago flashes once, then twice. "I'm cutting you loose." The ropes drop to the ground. Far away, I hear yelling and the report of small arms.

I give a jerk of my head and scoot back. "Get on the bike. One of you needs to steer."

Phillip gets in front of me and puts Arruda (I sure as hell hope that's who this is) in front of him. Though he looks pale and wide-eyed, he wraps his fingers firmly around the handlebars. A puff of dirt, and then another appears near my wheels.

"Hit the throttle." He looks confused, so I move his right hand. "Now head south, through the gate! And keep your heads down." I am shouting now as the sound of weapon fire rises. I pull one of my pistols to use along with the automatic and turn as close to ninety degrees as possible first to the left, then the right while holding tight to the bike with my thighs and running suppressive fire. I have no interest in killing any of these people, though I'll wing a few if it comes to that.

As we come to the gate opening, I pocket my pistol fast and take over the handlebars, wrapping my arms around these two waifs and swerving, initially over the larger pieces of gate debris and then to avoid a pair of guards who appear in front of us with their weapons trained. I kick out a teep with my left leg and shove one into the other, upending them both. We then start our sprint toward the vessel as I hear a ping off the bike.

"When we get to the vessel and I tell you to, you both jump off and lie flat." I am now yelling to be heard over the noise of the bike in full gasoline-burning throttle. I hate using it, but it does give me a decided advantage. "Do not get up until I tell you it's safe."

They nod wordlessly. They must be exhausted and terrified; I can feel them tremble in my arms as I steer the bike.

I glance back as we pass the red roofs and see a vehicle in pursuit along with sporadic muzzle flashes. I put on speed, and as we reach the edge of the woods, I call for the kids to duck their heads low and keep their arms and legs in close as I cut left into the underbrush and make for the trees that will provide some cover and that, if I am seeing the map in my head correctly, will cut off a kilometer from our journey. I can avoid the largest logs, but the low, dry branches scratch all three of our faces, and I can feel my teeth rattle as I bump over rocks and humps of earth. I spy the *Coupe*'s hiding place and hit the cargo hatch remote I have built into the bike. "We are coming to the vessel…uh, the airship." *I'll explain that whole nomenclature later.* "Get ready."

I drive the bike in and call, "Jump." And my two prizes tumble to the deck, rolling with their arms about each other until they hit a wall. There they lie, pressed to the floor. *Good job, kids.*

I cut the ignition and let the bike drop as I hit the remote a second time and hear the cargo door rise. I slip into my seat at the helm and head for water, accelerating across the lake. I lift off. As I turn the *Deuce Coupe* for home, I see a group of Paridian soldiers pull up in some off-road vehicle and run the distance to the water's edge to begin shooting at me and my little *Coupe*. I could have flown on, but I can't resist aiming my little vessel gun at their little transport, blowing the vehicle to pieces and watching them scatter and shake their fists at me.

"Sorry, boys," I call, though they can't hear me. "It'll be a bit of a walk home!" I hear Will start to laugh, and I think I can even hear Teddy giving a hoot and a clap. I aim the *Coupe* high, go full throttle, and head straight for Bosch. The FA or their parents can come fetch them from there.

TWENTY-FOUR

The Comedown

BOSCH, JULY 2362

Miles has attempted to comm me three times starting half a bell into the flight. He must have gotten wind of this mission, somehow. But how? It's a private affair. *I wonder if Paddy ratted me out. When I see him....* I send Miles a short message as I slip into Bosch territory: "Good morning. Retrieved FA kids from Parida. All is well. Bringing them to your office."

I look over to the area where I hung some cargo netting. The two have sunk into a deep sleep, arms around each other and through the netting. I gave them a bit of food and plenty of water after clearing Paridian airspace, and we chatted a bit. Enough for me to know I had actually rescued the people I had gone in for.

"Hey. Wakey-wakey, kids. Another country you can check off your trekking list." I make my voice loud enough to penetrate their slumber but keep my tone kind.

I land on base and get one of Fred's new crew to drive us to Bosch Hall. I walk my FA trekkers to Miles' office. It's been weeks since I was last here. A medical team is waiting for them. I take one look at Miles' face and know he is waiting for me.

Arruda and Phillip stop and turn as the medical team starts to escort them out the door, and then they rush back to where I stand, covered head to toe in dust and dirt. They each give me an enormous hug. "Thank you, Kat. We'll never forget you. Can't believe what you did."

I nod sheepishly. "I was just doing my job." I glance at Miles and consider telling them they should definitely forget both me and what I did.

Miles nods pleasantly to the medical team, and he and I watch them go wordlessly. I turn to say something, and his hand comes up fast to stay my comment. He stands at the main office door and watches until the team and the couple are safely down the hallway, looks at Betsy, and tips his head ever so slightly toward the hall, causing her to stand and actually leave her post, shutting the outer door behind her. He then quietly walks over to the big wooden door of his office, motions me back in, and closes the door silently. I hear him take a deep breath in as he turns to me and lets out a stream of invectives and curses that comes close to shocking me.

It continues for some time, and as I wait for him to wind down, I feel my adrenaline pulse. I spread my hands and give what I feel is a genial smile. "So, I get it. You're mad."

Miles has gone silent again and glares at me.

"Jeez, Miles, they are kids. Did you want me to just let them die?"

Miles goes so long without answering that I wonder if I really spoke and am about to repeat myself when he hands me a question posed between clenched teeth: "Did you know that the Paridians record and broadcast their executions?"

"What?"

"You are familiar with the technology, correct?" His words are clipped as he pulls out the seldom-used remote, punches a button, and a large and very updated Obi screen rises from a console table.

I nod wordlessly as he pushes another button, and the entire event is replayed on the large screen. I watch the drama unfold. My eyes are wide, and my hands come to rest sometimes on top of my head, sometimes on my cheeks, and occasionally covering my mouth, which seems to hang loosely open. I start out jumping at each rifle report that wasn't from mine, but soon there are too many. I gasp a little. How many near misses is that? It wasn't a few shots in the dirt but dozens. The guards are surprisingly well-disciplined and trained. Well, they are a firing squad after all. I watch as they fire, reload, fire, reload, fire. How the hell did any of us not get hit by the amount of ammo fire flying?

I glance to my left and see Will standing there. He grins and takes his two thumbs and gestures to his chest. I breathe a sigh of relief. Of course, it had to be that: Will helped. Otherwise, it would have been pure dumb luck, and I don't rely on that. I look at him again, and he shakes his head. Maybe it was just luck: really, really dumb luck.

Miles lets the Obi run as the bike disappears out the gate. The final frame has the two guards I knocked over standing and firing after us. He turns it off and looks at me, his hands in the traditional *What the hell were you thinking?* pose. His face is still irate, but I can also see pain and worry.

I take a moment and try to look contrite. "Okay, Miles. Yes, that broadcast makes the mission look a bit reckless and foolhardy, but I had a good plan. Really, I did. I just… I just didn't have all the details and then had to improvise…"

Miles breathes out heavily, and there is a clear edge to his voice. "There will be no more of…*this*." He gestures at the now-empty screen. "You *will* clear every mission of yours from now on with me. *Personally*. In advance. Is that understood?"

I can practically see heat radiating from this usually calm man, so I give him the answer I must. "Yes, sir."

Miles waves his hand in dismissal, and I remember when Teddy was angry with me and made that same gesture. A medium-sized piece of clay falls before I can grab it, and I feel tears for the first time in weeks sting my eyes and nose. Miles turns away and walks over to look out his balcony window. I head to the door and look back over my shoulder. It's rough to see him so overwrought, but I sure as hell won't apologize. I step into the front office, and Betsy is back at her desk. She gives me an encouraging little smile and a thumbs-up.

I wend my way down the hall to the stairs and out of Bosch Hall, wondering how I will go about getting paid for this bit of drama. Sure as hell won't be using Paddy as my intermediary.

I clear the base gate nearest my street and can feel the adrenaline still coursing through me. Watching the video—appalling as it was with all that ammo in play—was a bit exhilarating, and it boosted my rush. And my brain has nothing but good things to say about the mission. Sure, Miles was angry, but I managed the extraction successfully. By a narrow margin, to be sure, but what did that matter? Successful is successful. Even Remorse kicks in a compliment, softened as it is by all the brain chemicals. *Hey, no one died this time.*

I am awash in my own triumph and walking with an ever-increasing swagger on the road home when I look and see Takai walking purposefully toward me. He is not looking up at me, though; his eyes seem to be fixed on a point in the road just ahead of him.

"Hey!" I wave and pick up my pace to close the distance between us. I know he will be delighted that I am home and on time! But what is he doing out here on the road? Maybe making a grocery run? Who has the kids?

He stops at my voice and looks up. He stares, and I can't fathom his expression, though perhaps it's the distance. I stop moving toward him. He puts his hands in prayer position in front of his mouth for a moment and closes his eyes. That's weird even for my husband. He drops them to his side and hurries until he stands in front of me. I am about to lean in to give him a kiss but am met with: "A firing squad?! Seriously, Kat?"

I put both hands up in front of me to block the intensity of this outburst. "Don't blow this out of proportion." *How the fuck does information move this fast in Bosch?* My stomach takes on a sinking feeling as I realize that the video probably—must have —made the news.

"Blow it out... I... Proportion? Good god, Kat."

"Hey, it all worked out." I am trying to sound both reassuring and nonchalant as I reach to touch his chest and arm.

Takai takes a step back from me, and his face is incredulous. "This has gone too far, Kat. You have gone too far." His voice is loud, and I have never heard it filled with so much anger. His eyes narrow as he continues. "I will not sit by and have our children wonder if today is the day that Mama won't ever come home again. You have shown over the past weeks that you have little concern for them, me, or our family, or even your precious Bosch family. You clearly have a death wish to join your lover, that Will person, so just get on with it. I'll take the children back with me. Permanently." He turns on his heel and begins the walk back up the road to the house without looking back.

His words are ringing in my ears. How can he say I don't care? That's ridiculous. I feel a crack in the clay, and a wave of anger comes out. What an awful thing for him to say. I see Remorse sitting in the balcony with popcorn, grinning, as I realize I haven't seen Mama in two weeks. I stopped taking

Carisa to therapy after the second, far more uncomfortable visit. I saw Tom at the board meeting but didn't chat, and I have begged off regular missions with the unit for at least a month. I haven't even spoken to them. I no longer go and sit in Miles' office for hours. Takai and I haven't made love since mid-May, and my babies—Sweet New Earth, I have been avoiding my own children.

The adrenaline high evaporates. My breath comes faster and faster. Am I really trying…? My heart is beating sideways against the thick clay, and cracks and fissures form. As it beats more frantically, small pieces begin to shake loose. Fear pours out. Do I want to die? My breath is speeding up but getting shallow. I start to gasp. My chest is tight. Maybe? From some-where within, an image of Will's limp, blood-covered form in my arms appears. I cast wildly about to see him standing and smiling as he has been with me the past few weeks, but there is only this still, gray version. Large chunks of thick, dry clay fall, crashing in the pit of my stomach. My eyes fill with tears as grief and sadness break through. My chest begins to heave. *No*, I think with ferocity. *I love my children, and despite everything that has happened, I love Takai.* The final hunks of clay crumble, and all the feelings come rolling out, shouting for attention in my brain. I squeeze my ears to quiet them and drop to my knees in the dirt of the road. "Stop it! Slow down. Get in line." I find I can yell even though I can't breathe. I try again to take a deep breath but can't get it past all the clay debris. I can't seem to get oxygen. Feelings are all jumbled in me. Anger steps in front. Fuck Takai. He will not take my kids. Fuck Miles. I was brilliant getting the FA kids out. Remorse throws out a question: *Did you get Will out?*

I start to rock. I can't breathe. I try more gasps. I am dying. I am going to die kneeling here on this road and never see my babies again. What have I done? My stomach turns, and I scramble to the grassy edge of the road to vomit. Once and then twice. I am shaken to realize it's the same spot as the first time Takai pulled over that awful day. I gag and drop my forehead to the dusty grass. I don't want to die yet. But then I see Teddy, still and quiet on the *Skyhawk*, and then he explodes into a million pieces. I see Will's bloodless face next to mine. I see the dark girls and Old Dorothy, and somewhere in the distant back, I see a young, bearded man holding a chubby infant. *All your fault.* Remorse is now standing with Guilt, and they are staring at me and pointing. Anger joins them. *Fuck them? Fuck you.* Remorse squats down and looks at me, and its eyes remind me of Rob Abernathy's. *If you go back to the house, how do you know they won't be next?* At this, I hear a sob escape my lips. I collapse on my side as if I am some animal hit and thrown to the road's edge to die. I need to die. So, I wait. I lie, breathless, waiting for it to take me with a tiny glimmer of hope. The pain will be gone then.

But instead, I hear Teddy yell, "Get up, Kat! On your feet!" It is a voice I automatically respond to, and I roll onto my hands and knees, but I can't make myself rise. Then I hear a softer voice in my ear. Will's voice. "Here, you told me about this": An image appears of my children all snuggled together on the sofa on Grey's birthday, their faces glowing as her cake is brought in. She wears a huge smile and has her arms protectively around Kik on her left and Mac on her right as they point joyously to the cake. Those faces I made. Love trickles into me, and I feel a tiny breath reach my lungs.

I wipe my mouth with the back of my hand and sit back on my knees. I look down the road toward home, where Takai had angrily strode away, and then the opposite way toward base. I hear Teddy again. "C'mon, Troop. You need to decide to move."

I take a practice breath. It fills my lungs, and I drink in the fresh air gratefully. I take three slow, deep breaths that still quaver at the end. I open and close my hands in fists, rolling the knuckles and cracking them, then stretching the fingers. I begin to rub the backs of my hands alternately, first one, then the other, as I take three more breaths with less shakiness. I have to fight my way out of this. My heart is bruised and raw now that it is free from the clay, but it is still beating, a little stronger with each breath. Another deep inhale and exhale, this one steady. I move my hands to the top of my head, still kneeling on the side of the road.

"Take another inhalation, Kat." It's just me talking now. I feel the air pull into my lungs reassuringly. *Remorse isn't wrong. It was my poor decisions that brought me to this place.* I nod. *It has to be my decision to move myself forward and back into life.* I look again in the direction of home and then back toward base. I drop my head to catch another breath, press my lips together, make a decision, and then I stand.

Part IV

TWENTY-FIVE

The Road Back

Betsy comms Miles and tells him that I am back. After a few moments, she holds her hand to the comm and whispers, "He wants to know if you are coming back to argue."

I shake my head, and Betsy gives me a tender smile. I find my mouth is curving slightly up, and it feels a little like a real smile. I think I have become Pinocchio, for fuck's sake.

"No, sir. She says no arguing," Betsy passes on the message.

Betsy listens, clicks off, then rummages through her bag at her feet. Standing up, she comes around to me with a soft cloth in her hand. She gently wipes my chin and puts a soft hand on my cheek. "Better now. Go on in, sweetie."

"Thanks, Betsy. You're the best." And I know my smile is real now because I feel all the affection—the love—I have for this woman in me. *I'm a real boy!*

I quietly push the door open. Miles sits at his desk pretending to push papers about. July sunlight powers in through the windows, and a tiny breeze eddies from the open balcony doors ruffling the papers. He glances up at me, and I see no warmth in his look. "What do you want, Trooper?"

"I'm sorry, Miles. I screwed up. I've been screwing up ever since…" I take a gasp and squeeze my eyes tight, then open them and steady my breath. "…I got Will killed."

Miles' face softens, and the old warmth is now in his eyes as he regards me. "Kat, we have been through this. It was not your fault. Sometimes missions go sideways." He regards me and smiles. "And anyway, Kat. You were screwing up well before that."

I start to laugh at this and then start to cry. And my MC stands and comes around his desk and wraps me in a hug, letting me move between hysterical laughter and weeping sobs.

I finally push away, wiping at his soggy shoulder where I have drained my face, and look at him. "So, I'm a mess."

He nods and wears a genial smile. "It happens…to all of us at some point to some degree. You just like to do things bigger and messier than most." He looks down and peers at his snot-and-tear-smeared vest and grins.

He is not wrong. I shake my head. "I have so much to lose. And I feel like I may lose it all."

Miles claps me on both of my shoulders, then walks back around to the business side of his desk and opens the central drawer. He keeps it far tidier than Teddy ever did. "Nonsense, Kat. You won't allow it to be lost. I know you. You'll do what it takes to be sure that doesn't happen." He pulls out a pale blue card that I instantly recognize and holds it out to me between his first and second finger. "You, uh, dropped this…a few weeks ago."

I stare at the card I had disgustedly thrown away when I had dropped off Carisa with Betsy after my second visit with Ruth. Ruth had asked me what I wanted to talk about, and I had said "Nothing." So, she had patiently asked about where I was born, about my marriage and family, about any feelings I wanted to talk about. I told her my feelings were all under control, and the rest wasn't anyone else's business. Then I sat and gave short, single-word answers and shrugs until she eventually sighed and said, "Time is up for today. We can start fresh next week." Next week never happened. Now, I slowly reach out for it.

Miles holds it firmly, not relinquishing it, and for a moment, we are connected by this card. "Kat." His voice and face are earnest. "This can help. It helped me. It helped Teddy."

My eyebrows draw together, and I am about to ask if I heard correctly, but he continues, "Anyone who takes on the mantle of leadership needs someone to talk to, whether in sunshine or a storm."

"But I'm no—"

Miles gently cuts off this familiar refrain. "Kat, officer or not, like it or not: You are a leader."

I consider this and shrug noncommittally. He releases the card to my keeping. I hold it up to him and place it securely in my heart pocket behind the pictures I carry there: the one Papa gave me of the two of us and the family picture we took the night before Teddy's last flight.

I head for the door but remember an issue. I turn. "That video, Miles… My kids…"

He gives me a reassuring smile. "No need to worry. I've made some comms. It's already taken care of. It's gone. It will never be seen again."

I breathe a sigh of relief and head to my next gauntlet.

I open the cobalt blue door and kick off my filthy boots. The house is quiet. I imagine the kids are in the backyard. I want to run and scoop them up, but then I realize I am still in a camo jumpsuit, covered in dirt. *A shower. First a shower.* I move toward the stairs, cutting through the kitchen, and there is Mama, rinsing a plate. She looks up at me. I see her face is etched with worry.

"Oh, Kat…"

I smile at her. "I need a shower before I see the babies." I come close to her, reach for her hand, and bring it up to kiss it. Some of the worry smooths away. "I'm sorry I worried you and Takai. I'm back to being me…. Well, I'm on the road back."

She smiles and starts to respond, but I hear the children laughing. Then I hear another laugh that I don't recognize and yet remember. I tip my head questioningly.

"Come look." Mama leads me to the window. Takai sits on the stone patio in one of the white cane chairs, holding Mac on his lap while reading him a book. Beyond him, in the grass, Kik, Grey, and a petite blonde woman are rolling and laughing. I gasp, "Carisa!" I turn and look at the beloved woman at my side. "Oh, Mama. Nice work."

"No, dear. I can't take the credit. Carisa has been working hard with Nanette. And slowly, she is healing."

I feel the universe nudge me, and I roll my eyes. *Subtlety is not your strong suit, is it?* I respond, giving the universe a firm shove back and hearing it chuckle. "I'm going to shower. I'll be right back." I give this marvelous woman a quick kiss and head upstairs. I am sure Carisa and Nanette have been working, but I also know that Mama has provided the love and space for that healing.

Now showered and dressed in a cool sundress I found in the Mimi box, I step to the back porch.

"Mama!" I am set upon by children, who jump on me and talk at me, pull me, and ask me to watch them, kiss them, read to them, listen to them, sing to them. I am in paradise. I kiss and hug them individually and then together. I let myself feel the pull of their love, and I pour mine out to mix with theirs. Carisa has stepped away to give us space, but I turn to her and offer my arm in greeting. "I am so glad you are here. I am so glad to see you smile."

Carisa's eyes shine. "Thank you." She grasps my arm, then wraps her arms around me in a hug. "For not forgetting about me. And for bringing me here."

After several more minutes of play and cuddles, Mama calls the children in for a snack. *Hey, I did make it by elevenses!* Carisa walks hand-in-hand with the boys while Grey chats with her about making a flower necklace. I pull a chair next to Takai and sit down, both of us looking straight ahead.

I lay my hand out, palm up. "I'm sorry, Takai. I have indeed been bereft and distant. But I love you." And I as say this, I realize I am not faking this phrase. "And I love our children—our family." I now turn to look at his face. He turns his head to look at me, and I hold his eyes. "I have no desire to die. We have just restarted us. I would be a fool to endanger that." I feel him lay his hand in mine. "I am not yet better. But I know that I will be." I give a small grin. "I have a plan."

I hear him chuckle and am warmed by it. "Of course, you do, Kat Wallace. I never really doubted you did." He squeezes my hand, and I lean over the two broad chair arms that separate us and give him a kiss and am rewarded by a warm response. Then we settle into our seats and chat amiably about the day and what each of us plans for our week both on-ship and in Bosch.

∾

I am up early and go for a long run before heading to the PT sector assigned to my unit. As I approach, seeing them stretch and jump and sprawl, all my defenses are on. *Get away, Kat. They know what happened. Turn around!* Then in my head, sitting happily in a comfortable chair, beer in hand, Will is clear. "Get going, Kat. It's your unit. You need each other."

I snort. "What about you? You don't look ready to work."

He grins and shrugs. "One of the advantages of being dead, love, is I no longer have to work out. But you do."

I smile a mournful smile and nod, moving toward these people with whom I share the trauma and tragedy of losing Will.

I slip up behind Tom, who always likes to hang to the back, and say my usual, "Let's get this done!" Four heads turn to me, and I am rewarded by four faces lighting up with smiles. We grasp arms and elbows and throw around the usual "Good to have you back!" and "I've missed you guys." Eventually, we finish our PT and head for a short group run. I notice they aren't taking the path we used to run before.

We finish and head to the hangar to grab a cup of coffee before starting the business of the day.

We companionably stand together, sipping the cups of caffeine as I lean on the wall. "So, what's on the agenda? Glitter drop? Extraction?" My extended absence has left me out of the loop.

My friends all look at each other and then at me. I see their bodies tense ever so slightly. "Neither." Gia shakes her head and gives a little sigh. "We all really should have stepped back from what we had been doing after Will." I see four faces give barely perceptible frowns at the memory of the shared loss. I am sure mine has the same expression. "That was what we had been counseled but chose to ignore." She gives a one-handed shrug. "After you went missing, we figured we had to change things up."

I chuckle at the "went missing" comment. "Yeah. I'm back now, though. So, what are we doing?"

Demery now picks up the chuckle. "Oh, you'll love this...." And the comment garners a bit of laughter from the rest.

I drop my eyebrows and narrow my eyes, looking quizzically at my friends. "I'm intrigued...."

Bailey finally comes out with it. "We are training recently graduated troopers who want to pursue the glitter/extraction path."

My head lolls to the side and bumps the wall. "No. Seriously?"

"It actually is pretty fun, Kat. The kids are so enthusiastic!" Tom gestures strongly, almost spilling his coffee.

I set my half-consumed cup on the coffee cart. "Yeah, but I just got done with being a recruit." I snap my index fingers across each other in an "X." "Times two." Then I look at the faces of this unit, all people whom I have come to love. "But hey, I'm up for anything. You know that." I give them a reassuring smile and am rewarded with seeing all four visibly relax. I can't blame them for being a bit on guard. I had bounced between lashing out and stony silence for the couple of weeks after the funeral I actually came to work, and then I simply stopped showing up. "So, show me what you want me to do. I can be taught!" I make a tally mark in my renewed list under *good decisions*.

TWENTY-SIX

Green

TABONNE, EARLY AUGUST 2362

"Trooper... Trooper..." I am wracking my brain for his name. "Uhhh..." I shut my eyes briefly, and it comes to me. "Marquez!" *Got it.* In my defense, this class has a Marquez, a Moore, a Moreno, and a Macado, all men, all about the same height and same young, muscular build with short, dark hair and brown skin. Bailey and I have just been calling them the "four Ms" in our conversations and toyed with the idea of simply assigning them numbers. Gia said we couldn't, though. She, naturally, has all their names memorized. But she isn't here right now. The kid looks at me with a slight tilt to his head.

"Macado." He blinks at me.

I look blankly at him. "That's what I said. Kinda." *Shit. Sorry, kid. I would have remembered number four.* "What are you doing?"

We are on the island of Tabonne, a temperate island only a short flight from Bosch. The mayor of the island, whom the people of Tabonne refer to as the Maire, has graciously been willing to help us with the negotiation training. She sends several of her people out to push for terms, and our little green babies see if they can get more than the QM price. However,

238

Trooper Macado is outside of the building where the Glitter negotiations are taking place, leaning over the split-rail fence that surrounds the central building and speaking to a young woman all dressed in brown. She has gone quite quiet and still now as I come up and inquire of the young trooper.

Macado stands a little taller as he responds. "Ma'am..." Not used to that title. "This young woman is being kept here against her will. Enslaved."

I feel my shoulders grow tight. I know that some people on Tabonne keep thralls, but I have had to accept that I can't fix every fucker on the planet.

"We need to get inside, and you have negotiations to complete, Macado." I am trying not to look at the young woman, because...well, because I hate this, and I am trying to keep my temper in check.

"But Instructor Wallace..."

Gia has not let on to these kids that I barely outrank them, so no "Trooper Wallace"; instead, I'm "Instructor Wallace."

"My family has always been clear to me on this: Never accept evil. Enslavement of people is evil. How can you just turn your back?"

I close my eyes and hear my own voice going off at Incredibly-Average-Vargas on my first Glitter run—the one that almost got me court-martialed. "What's your name?"

His brown eyes narrow, and I can tell he is offended, but he responds politely with the barest hint of a sigh, "Macado, ma'am."

"No, no. I've got that. What's your given name?" I try to keep from grinning at what I know is his exasperation. Maybe this is what it will be like to have teenagers. Sweet New Earth. I can barely imagine.

He frowns at me before answering. "Josh, ma'am. But what does that have to do with...?"

"So, Josh. What do you propose we do? Round up all the enslaved here and shoot our way out? Are we going to leave your classmates behind or just us complicit-with-evil instructors? What if there are too many to bring aboard? Who do we choose? What if some are too afraid to leave or are otherwise tied to Tabonne? Will we be doing this on other islands as well? Because guess what? The thrall trade is rampant on New Earth." I open my hands and arms to receive the answer.

He looks at me, and the proud and determined look in his eyes fades to one of questioning, bordering on despair. "I… uh… I don't know, ma'am. I just know it's wrong."

My hand goes to my arm, and I think about the repercussions of my next moves and words. I turn it over for him to see my brand. "It is wrong."

He stares at my arm for almost a full minute, and then his eyes move to my face. "But if you…"

I sigh, looking back at the central building where the generous Maire works and possibly lives, and I make a decision. "You know what, Josh? Fuck it. Let's go talk to her owner." And with that, I climb the split-rail fence, then walk over and introduce myself to the young woman who has moved away from us somewhat but is still stealing glances as she hoes at some suckers along the fence line. "I'm Kat Wallace. What's your name—your real name?"

She pauses and looks suspiciously at me, glancing at Trooper Josh Macado. I roll my left forearm over so she sees my brand, and I look at her meaningfully. "Sofia." Her voice is soft and quiet.

"Well, Sofia, I want to talk to your enslaver." She looks confused at the word. "Your owner." I explain, "Let's see what we can do to get you out of here." I turn to young Josh. "You coming, kid?"

Josh blinks a couple of times, and then with a "Yes, ma'am" climbs the fence and joins me.

As we walk across the field being tended by three other workers, probably thralls, I ask Sofia her owner/enslaver's name.

"Madam Monique." She doesn't say this with any fear, but neither is there any affection.

"Listen and learn, kid," I say to Josh as Sofia walks us to a mid-sized wooden house painted gray. Overgrown flowering bushes are on either side of the door. And as we get closer, I see the paint is peeling and the gutters are loose. Interesting. Sofia refuses to come up to the door, so Josh and I go up, and I knock.

An older woman, tiny in stature, and maybe five years older than Mama, answers. She only opens the door partway and looks at us suspiciously. "Hello, what do you want?" She says this first in Tabonnese and then in standard FA.

I put on my best kind and not-dangerous face and reply using her native tongue. "I'd like to speak to Madame Monique. It's about one of her workers."

"I'm Madame Monique. Who are you?" The door opens a tiny bit more, but her face retains its suspicious expression. She is wearing a dark blue dress with long sleeves and a neckline that covers her collarbone. She has a simple strand of multicolored beads around her neck and a gold band on her ring finger as her only jewelry.

"My name is Kat Wallace. This is Josh Macado. We are from Bosch, and I have a financial proposal for you that could be quite lucrative." I give her a reassuring smile.

The door opens now, and the suspicious expression gives way to one of maybe interest, and I'm guessing also hope. "May we come in and talk?"

"Oh, certainly. Would you like tea?" Now she is really reminding me of Mama.

For the negotiation I am planning, I decide to think of her as a Mama-contemporary and not a sadistic enslaver. "That would be lovely, thank you."

We step inside and are invited into a small sitting room with two chairs and a sofa as the older woman slips into another room. The quiet lies heavily. Clearly, we are the only ones here, and it feels like we are the only ones to have disturbed this quiet in some time. There's a faintly sour, musty scent present, which I am guessing stems from the shelves on either side of the silent fireplace. I step over to look at the shelves more closely. They are half-filled with enough old books to pique my interest, and I know Teddy would have been picking them up and considering which one to borrow, or buy, or steal. The rest of the shelves hold figurines, mementos, and framed photos of children likely long-grown. There is an old map and one yellowed wedding photo.

"Is this you, Madam Monique?" As the older woman returns to the room, I take the tray that holds an actual teapot and three cups as well as a plate of cookies from her as I gesture at the young woman in a lacey dress in the photo.

She looks at the photo, and I see her eyes grow a bit distant. "Yes, that is me and my darling, Leonce, on our wedding day."

I smile as I place the tray on the center table and watch as Monique begins to pour and distribute the cups with a clearly practiced hand. "How long were you married?"

I hear her give a small, girlish giggle. "Oh, we married quite young. I was only twenty. And he was so handsome." She gives a little sigh, running her hands through her short white curls, and looks back at the photo. "Like this young man." She nods with an indulgent smile toward Josh Macado as she hands him his teacup.

I see Josh flush with the compliment and murmur a "Thank you, ma'am" as he takes the cup. He is quite polite and good at following directions as these are the first words I have heard from him.

Madame Monique continues on a subject that she clearly adores. "We were married for forty-five years." Her face is glowing as she says this, and then it darkens slightly. "Until Leonce died five years ago."

I feel a pang of connection with this woman and steady my breath. "I am so sorry for your loss. But I am glad for your forty-five years together." I am sincere in my condolences. I step over to take my cup from her.

She nods to my own ringed hand. "You'll see. You likely have many happy years to come."

I glance at the photo. I want my marriage to work, and I am willing to put forth the effort. There just better not be any extra people in it. Anymore. "Well, that's the hope."

I sit down and take a sip of the strong tea. My hands feel the threadbare upholstery on the arm of the chair. The right side is distinctly a different shade from the left from what I am guessing to be years of sun exposure from the large window in the room. There is dust on the shelves, except for around the photos, and a few stray leaves and grass on the floor that must have been tracked in. We three sit for a moment enjoying the tea.

"So, you two are pirates of Bosch? Neither of you seem too fierce." She smiles at her own jest. "You seem quite kind, in fact." I see her take a deep breath. "So, what is this offer?" Madame Monique's eyes have once again taken on that hopeful look.

I decide to be direct. "You have thralls, and we wish to purchase them."

Now I see her face pull in on itself as she frowns. "I don't like keeping thralls. Leonce and I never did. Our crops were peanuts and beets and carrots as well as strawberries. We worked the farm ourselves and did quite well." I can hear the hint of pride in her voice as she says this. "When my Leonce died after being ill for almost a year, we had no markers to hire anyone. I tried to keep up, but as you can tell, it is hard enough for me to keep up with the house." She gestures to the floor and points to a corner where there is a small cobweb. "Luc and Roxanne, our children, wanted me to sell the farm after their père died and still want me to. But this is where I live. I raised those children here. My sweat and my blood are in this land. Leonce is buried in the family plot, and I want to be buried next to him. None of us could afford to pay wages year-round, so the children bought a family of thralls to tend the farm for the past several years. I can't manage without them." There is definite regret and sorrow as she says this last part.

I glance at Josh, and he looks stricken. *Not exactly an evil-doer, is she, kid?* I don't let on that I am almost just as surprised as he likely is.

I ponder for a moment. Tabonne is known for its rich soil, and it is not nearly as rocky as most of Bosch, District Seven excluded. "What if you could sell the farm to someone who would hire workers to maintain it, and you, and your children if they wish, could stay on in perpetuity?"

Josh's brows come together as I say this, and Madame Monique laughs softly. "Well, that would be a dream come true. But I know of no one with that kind of markers, nor with the willingness to take a chance on an old woman and an even older farm."

I stand up, taking my still warm tea with me, and look out the window. "How many acres?"

"Six."

"Six?" Now my eyebrows go up. "I'm guessing that the family of thralls has been able to maintain maybe two of those." I see Madame's head bob affirmatively. "That means four acres have been lying fallow for five-plus years and are rich and ready to produce. It really doesn't require taking a chance, given that. So, that simply leaves finding someone with the markers." I am calculating land prices and wages as well as the profit potential from the farm if crops were rotated and the land loved. I turn my sling bag around and fish inside, pulling out a pad of paper and a pencil. I write a number on the pad and hand it to Madame Monique. She gasps ever so slightly.

"This would include you surrendering all rights to the family who has been enslaved. They will have the right to stay on as paid workers if they choose or would be free to leave."

"Are you the one offering to buy my farm, Ms. Wallace?" The old woman's voice sounds stronger than I have heard it before.

"Yes, ma'am. I come from farming folk myself, and I believe I have a good eye for land."

"But this offer..." She holds the pad of paper up. "...the Bosch must do quite well with their Glitter." I sense a hint of distaste in her voice. Not everyone thinks of Glitter as just a pleasant pastime.

"I have been investing my pay for some time. I have enough put away to make the offer. And I could never have a farm this productive on Bosch." A little flattery goes a long way.

Her head comes up as does her smile. "Leonce and I once had the most productive farm in Tabonne." She looks back at the paper. "With this amount of markers, I could hire someone to fix up the house."

I hold up a finger and waggle it. "No, ma'am. That won't

be necessary. Whether you accept my offer or not, young Trooper Macado and his friends will be coming to do any necessary work on the house over the next few weeks." I turn my head to look at my young charge. "Isn't that right, Josh?"

I watch his handsome face break into a smile, and I hear Will laugh aloud in my head as Josh practically jumps from his seat. "Yes, ma'am! Absolutely, ma'am!"

I watch as Madame Monique's face grows ten years younger as worry lifts. "Oh, my. Please. I accept." She stands and comes to me, offering her hand and arm to seal the deal. "We can go tell the farm family immediately. Thank you."

I take her arm and elbow and nod. "Done, then. I'll have the markers delivered to you or to your bank as you wish. Josh, perhaps you'd like to go with Madame Monique and let Sofia and her family know the news." I suspect, given his moony looks at Sofia, he will encourage the family to stay on.

TWENTY-SEVEN

What's Next

BOSCH, THE END OF AUGUST 2362

"Still doesn't seem like a sustainable plan if you ask me." Tom leans back in his almost-black wooden seat at Barton's, sipping on a glass of beer.

I lift my crystal glass filled with a not-too-sweet bourbon cocktail in it toward him. Barton's is a whole lot fancier than Ray's. Just a few broken glasses here would cost me more than all the furniture at Ray's. "To be clear, I didn't." I grin at him.

There is a ripple of laughter at the table, and both Tom and my voices are included.

Bailey looks at me and tips their head. "Seriously, Kat. You can't single-handedly buy every thrall on New Earth and set them free. One, not even you have that kind of markers, and two, people will just buy more thralls from the traders."

I sigh. "I know. It's the damn traders. The whole fucking trafficking system. But I couldn't do nothing." I go quiet for a moment. "I wonder how many thrall owners are like Monique. Forced to participate in an evil system because of the cost of wages or because they feel like it's the only option." I rub my mouth and chin, settling my thumbnail between my front teeth as I think. I see Bailey look at me and raise their eyebrows.

Gia shrugs. "That I don't know. But I think Trooper Macado might immigrate there. He has spent the better part of each week the past three weeks, and apparently on his weekends, working on the house and the farm in Tabonne. In fact, he has asked if the work he is doing could be his assignment. He says he has a 'personal interest' there."

"Awww. He and Sofia are in love, huh?" I chuckle. "Saw that coming."

Gia pauses and I see her eyes flit around the table. She has been a bit withdrawn the last week, and I wonder if we are about to find out why. She pulls a breath in. "So, I am going to run for the open commander position in September." She looks a little stunned that she has finally said this. The table erupts into excited chatter.

"That's amazing, Gia! I can't think of anyone better quali-fied." I am enthusiastic but a little sad as I also know this will mean the unit will break. I wonder if Tom will finally—"

"I'm putting my commission on hold." Tom's voice inter-rupts my thought. "W-Mech is taking off. I want to give it my full attention."

Our eyes meet, and we share a bittersweet look, both of us wishing Will could be a part of the excitement and planning.

Demery slaps Bailey on the shoulder. "Damn. Looks like we will need to find another unit to shoot for." Bailey nods in agreement. Those two have been gunners together for years. Demery turns to me. "What about you, Kat? You gonna fly us?"

"Nope. She isn't." Bailey grins at me.

"Don't start with me...." Bailey and I have been talking over the past weeks since Tabonne about trafficking and what the solution is. I know I can't go back to ignoring it like I had been trying to do, but what can one person do?

Their eyes are serious even though their face still has a

smile. "What did you tell me Teddy said you needed to break up trafficking?"

They remember what I have said too well. I nod and think of my first graduation talk with Teddy and Miles. "Strength. Power. Allies."

They nod and look intently at my face and then at the faces of our unit members. "Kat is going to figure out how to marshal those things. And then she's going after the traders." Bailey says this as if it is already decided. Then they add, "And Abernathy."

All faces at the table go dark, and five jaws clench.

I nod. "You are right. That is what I have decided to do." *And a few other things.*

I walk across base to the BIB, the Bosch Intelligence Building, on a Tuesday morning after our night at Barton's. I am eating an apple and a piece of cheese that I buried in my pocket before leaving the house. I need to get groceries this evening before I head home. The kids seem to mow through the food I buy like sweet-faced little locusts.

I haven't been inside of the BIB, or as I think of it, the Details building, for years. Usually, a unit or a solo trooper requests the data, and it is sent over either electronically or by courier. But I want to find some information myself without having everyone on base see what I am looking for.

I arrive at the two-story brick building that looks small and unassuming; inside, the ground floor is still small, with several offices off of a narrow hall. I walk toward the stairs glancing at the offices. I pause for just a moment as I see the "Colonel Michelle Romero, Assistant Director/Bosch Intelligence" written in gold on a door. My old annoyance flares slightly. I had heard she had gone to officer training after my first graduation. So she went into intelligence, huh. That fits; she, Waverly, and Petra were always in other people's business during recruitment. I still remember how good it felt to pop her one that day she called me Teddy's pet. I decide not to stop in and say hello.

I descend the steps to the first basement floor of the building. I show the guard my ID and am let into a large, open room lined with the fairly up-to-date Obis with multiple screens, each staffed by an engaged officer. There are several small, labeled rooms off this large one, each lined with file cabinets and arranged with a simple table in the center and a few chairs surrounding it. I am looking for some map data to start my project.

I find the room marked *Maps* and step inside. Since I don't usually collect the details myself, I'm uncertain where to start. I see a red-haired man flipping through a file drawer with his back to me. He moves efficiently and effectively from drawer to drawer, pulling some maps and filing others. Seems like someone who can tell me where to start.

"Excuse me." I come near but not too near, so I don't startle him. The man turns around to respond, and my jaw drops open and my eyes widen. I see the same expression mirrored in his face. "Cal? Cal Greene? What the fuck are you doing here?" I move closer and see he still has the mass of freckles just as I remember. The blue-gray eyes are the same, but now the face sports a neat red beard and mustache.

"Kat Wallace! I haven't talked with you in…what? Eight? No, nine years? And it's Major Calvin Greene, now!" He extends his arm to take mine.

"To hell with that." I push his hand aside and wrap my arms around him in a hug. He hugs back, and when we part, his cheeks are very pink under the freckles. I slap his back. "A major, working in intelligence? That's a long way from serving Teddy his whiskey neat!"

I see the familiar grin, although the teeth are no longer overly large. "Yeah, I was sixteen when he gave me that job after my dad died. He gave me dispensation to enlist the next year. And I've been with BI for the last six years."

"Amazing!" I grin back. "How about family?"

He holds up a ringed hand. "Yep. Married to Eva just last year, and a baby coming this winter!"

"That is exciting! I'll have to meet this Eva." I can't stop smiling at seeing the kid I knew as a grown-up man.

He smiles back at me. "You have three kids, right?"

My smile falters a bit. "Um, yeah. How do you know that?"

"I work as an intelligence officer. I know everything." He says this with an air of mystery and a completely straight face until he sees my face shift into worry. Then he laughs. "Do you think I didn't keep up with you through Teddy? You were my first crush. I had to know what happened to you."

Now I blush. "Cal, I didn't know..."

He laughs again. "Oh, you did too. Who always kept your glass filled?"

"Okay, I kinda knew." I am laughing now. I look at him and consider. "Can you help me in here?" I motion around the room.

"Sure. What are you looking for?" Cal asks.

"Can we keep this just between us?" I tip my head questioningly to the side.

Now I see a smile that reminds me of Teddy spread over Cal's face. "All right, Kat Wallace, this sounds like you. We can keep it private. What's up?"

So, Cal and I sit down, and I share my little project plan with him.

The late afternoon has just a hint of breeze in it as I walk to the little building just before seventeen bells and open the door. I stand in the open waiting room and start to head to the window to check in but then hesitate. Maybe I'll just head home. I start to turn, and a door opens and Ruth the therapist steps out.

"Ah, there you are, Kat. Right on time. Come in and get comfortable." She smiles a warm smile.

That's pretty fucking unlikely. But I promised Mama and Miles I'd try. I nod as I step into her office and look at the comfortable chairs and the table in between. There's a stack of interesting books and a box of disposable tissues. *I bet I know which gets more use here.* "Hi, Ruth. I decided to come here today."

TWENTY-EIGHT

Senator-Elect

Rob Abernathy stood at the door of his mountain cabin and watched as the auto pulled up. He had sent Paddy Owens to the field to pick up Alejandro DeLeon from the airfield. As he reasoned, Owens was somewhat responsible for his loss of an assistant and so would fill that role until Rob found a candidate he felt was suitable.

Paddy stepped from the driver's side of the auto and walked around to open the back passenger door. Rob could tell by the set of the man's jaw he felt the task was beneath him. That made Rob smile. The man needed to know his place.

DeLeon stepped out of the auto and raised a hand to Rob in greeting. "Hello, Senator." Rob was glad to have that title back and equally as determined to move it to the next level as soon as possible. He raised his cup of coffee slightly in response. He had no desire to be social with either of these men. He would get to the point and see that they both did as he wished.

He turned and walked back into the luxurious log home he thought of as his "cabin."

~

Senator Abernathy came into the large, open section of the cabin, where the elegantly rustic furnishings complemented the large fireplace and the animal heads he had mounted from his hunts. It was a relic of the excesses of the Old Days, and he happily embraced it. He glanced at the two men seated in two widely spaced chairs. "Mr. Owens, if you would please step outside for a moment?"

Paddy Owens scowled but nodded. He stood up and stepped out of the open French doors to the stone patio and waited quietly.

Rob watched as the Glitter dealer walked away and then turned to DeLeon. "A report on the cartels, please."

Rob listened carefully as DeLeon gave a rundown on the financials of each trafficking cartel as well as details regarding any difficulties with personnel or law enforcement. After the report, Rob gave several brief instructions for how he wished people and issues to be dealt with and then verified that all funds were being appropriately deposited into his accounts in the New Caribbean and in Sarapion. He had DeLeon repeat the account numbers back to him to be certain there would be no mistakes.

He then turned toward the patio where Paddy Owens stood with his back to the room, idly gazing at the landscape. Only lazy men or very wealthy men had time to gaze so casually. And Rob knew that Paddy was not among the very wealthy.

"Mr. Owens." No response. Senator-Elect Rob Abernathy raised his voice. "Mr. Owens." He saw the soft, somewhat round man jump slightly at the second call and turn around.

Paddy came quickly back and said obsequiously, "So very sorry, Mr. Abernathy, I was caught up in the bird calls outside. What can I do for you and Mr. DeLeon?"

Rob wanted to strike the man, both for his servile behavior

and for not responding the first time. He did not like to ask for things more than once. But unfortunately, he needed this little man to provide a service.

"Mr. DeLeon, Mr. Owens has a contact in Bosch. He will connect you with a Mr. Howard Archer. Archer is part of the Bosch council and therefore is well placed to provide information. He is also deeply in debt. Archer will provide us with an opportunity to 'do business with him.' He has stated that he can circumvent the BPF and their monopoly of Glitter, and he can arrange for some portion of the Force to provide transport of thralls."

DeLeon looked with surprise at the man he thought was simply Abernathy's driver. "What is the point of using Bosch forces for transport? We have our own soldiers."

Abernathy's face darkened. He did not like being questioned. "By paying some pirates better than what they make now, they become loyal to us and complicit in our activities and therefore vulnerable to blackmail. They will then be loyal not to Bosch but to our cartel and to me, though my name is never to be mentioned."

DeLeon nodded. "I see. Yes. That could work."

"It certainly will work," Rob said with clear conviction. "Eventually we will seize control of the Glitter trade and transfer the monopoly from the pirate nation to us. It will need to be a slow and careful process as the pirates are a suspicious group, but this Archer will get us in the door." Rob smiled to himself as he considered how delightful it was going to be to crush Mary's home when he took control of her. It would also be quite profitable. He was going to like having an inside man in Bosch. And he was definitely going to like having Mary.

TWENTY-NINE

Decisions, Well Wishes, and Guarantees

BOSCH & TRUVALE, SEPTEMBER 2362

I can't keep my foot still. I am sitting in my usual seat in front of Miles' desk, and I have created a relaxed pose: shoulders down, Mona Lisa smile, head tipped to the side, elbows comfortably on the chair arms, hands soft and open and laying one on top of the other over my belly. But my damned left foot just won't cooperate. It continues to bounce up and down as I wait for Miles to finish with his call. I yell at it silently to *calm the fuck down*, and it does for a moment and then takes up rhythm again until I feel my whole body start to quiver.

"Okay. Sorry about that, Kat. It's a busy day today. What did you want to talk to me about?" Miles sets down his office comm and looks over at me with a pleasant but distracted smile.

I see an out. "I can come back later if you are busy...." *No, Kat. You've made this decision. It's a good one. It's time to go public with it.* "Actually, no. This won't take long."

Miles can tell something is up because his eyes narrow and he gives me his half-pursed lips/half-smile look. "What are you up to now, Kat?" His voice drips with genial suspicion.

I sit up in my chair and lean forward, placing my forearms

on the beautifully inlaid desk. "First: Any hint of any version of 'I told you so' will be met with the appropriate level of violence." Miles' eyebrows go up. I take a deep breath in. "Second, I need a recommendation from you. I have decided to enroll in the next Officer Training School class."

And now I've said it.

I watch as Miles' face goes through several shifts. I see it start with eye-widening surprise that shifts to his eyes narrowing. That's likely a *Did I hear that correctly?* look. Then a smile starts on his face. Notably, he has still said nothing. Probably because he is afraid that "I knew it all along!" would count as an "I told you so" and would be dealt with swiftly. He is correct.

He pushes his high-backed chair away from the desk, stands, and comes over to me, putting his big brown hand on my shoulder. "Trooper Wallace, I would be proud to write such a letter. May I say, congratulations on an excellent career choice."

I start to laugh as I have heard him and Teddy before him say essentially the same thing over and over at graduations. I stand and find myself wrapped up in a bear hug from this man who has so patiently guided me through the years. Fucking OTS. I am shaking my head and grinning at the same time. I pull back from the hug and look at him. "I figured if I'm going to be the captain of my own ship, I'd better be an Officer. But, just for the record, I refuse to take any of the How to Be a Tool classes."

Miles laughs. "I think we can assume you have already achieved mastery there!"

I pull back, look fake-offended, and semi-softly punch him in the shoulder. I incline my head over toward the bar. "Buy you a drink?"

He glances at the pile of papers on his desk and looks back

at me, showing me his hand with about three centimeters between his thumb and forefinger. "A small one. And just one. I have a letter I need to write."

Takai sat at his desk in the small study in the captain's quarters of the *FA Venturer* and picked up his comm to return the call to his wife as promised. He planned to be back in Bosch the following week to watch Grey's performance in her school play, but Kat had insisted that they talk tonight.

He thought of Kat and the events of the past few months. He had been ready to end his marriage back in May but found upon arrival that Kat captivated him still. Of course, seeing that handsome, young man equally as captivated with her helped Takai clarify his position and hers: She was his wife, the mother of his children, and she was a desirable woman. His desirable woman. He suspected that the young lieutenant had discovered for himself just how desirable Kat was and had intended to press Kat more on the issue, but the officer's untimely death had rendered that issue moot. It had also thrown his wife into a tailspin the likes of which Takai had never before seen, and he had seen her through many ups and downs. But she was now back to herself, almost, something for which he took the lion's share of the credit. He didn't like how jealousy felt; it was not part of The Way. He was glad it was an issue that could now be put behind him. Behind them. He did love Kat, and that was that.

He dialed the comm. She picked up on the first ring.

"Good morning, love!" Her voice sounded strong and happy. "Well, good evening to you. Have you had a good day?"

They exchanged some small talk about their days, past and upcoming, until Kat said, "I have some news for you."

Takai waited as she inhaled deeply before continuing.

"I have decided to enroll in OTS. It's a six-month program. Sweet New Earth, Takai, you know how many times I have railed against the notion, but I've decided, if I want to make any changes to Bosch, any inroads to end trafficking, I have to be an officer." He heard her pause after saying this in what seemed to be all one breath.

"Kat, I...I don't know what to say." He kept his voice even. He had agreed that Bosch would be the home of record for at least a few years. He was assuming it would be the two-year commitment that Kat needed to keep to regain her citizenship. But this, this sounded more permanent. "Are you sure this is what you want?"

"Totally. I have wanted to end enslavement since before I ever came to Bosch. I have been working to do just that, but I couldn't see that I need the rank to go along with the drive." He could hear the commitment in her voice, and he knew there would be no convincing her otherwise.

He drew a breath in and shook his head, but his face was relaxed. It would be fine. "Then I am delighted at the decision. You will excel. I hope they know what they are in for!" He heard her laugh ring through the comm.

"Thank you, love. I can't wait to see you next week. I miss you."

Takai glanced at the closed door to his study and smiled. "And I miss you. Only a few more days, and I'll be back in our bed for four nights."

"Mmmmm, that sounds lovely." Kat's voice had taken on a deeper tone. "I love you, Takai." There was a holler in the background, and she sighed. "I have to go. Your children are expecting breakfast!"

"Kiss them for me. I love you."

They clicked off, and Takai set the comm down and considered the news.

He was lost in thought when a knock came on the door. "Takai?" A soft, melodious voice came through the door. "Tea?"

Takai stood and went to the door and opened it. Hayami stood in her pink Sakura blossom dressing gown holding his evening tea. "Thank you, my love." He leaned to kiss this graceful, petite, and exquisite woman whose raven black hair was pinned back, just begging for him to release it.

"How is Kat?" she asked solicitously. "Any better?"

Takai rubbed at his hairline near his ear with his right hand. "A bit. Her doctors have a new six-month plan for her. I have high hopes."

Hayami smiled sweetly. "You are a kind husband. We can wait to see how she fares through this treatment. And then, perhaps, she will be strong enough for you to tell her."

"Yes. That is what I hope. But in the meantime..." He took the tea from her hand and set it on the table just inside his study, then wrapped his arms around this rare beauty and kissed her with increasing passion.

I am sitting on the couch at Mama's after the Friday "Say Goodbye to Ray's" party. I had made it quite clear that even though I would now qualify to go to Barton's, Ray's was my first and greatest love and would not be cast away so easily.

Peter and Paul had laughed and slapped Ray on the back. "Looks like those shutters will have to stay put."

It had been a festive event with food, wine, and beer. The children had played all afternoon with cousins and Gia's girls as well as some friends from school and the neighborhood who had appeared. Now they are settled on blankets outside watching some movie Mama selected. The siblings, my unit, and I are scattered over the floor and the furniture of the front room. Mama sits in her chair near the window and is smiling at the houseful of people. She loves a good party. Carisa sits on an oversized pillow near Mama and is chatting with Elise. She doesn't like large crowds but did well tonight.

I reach over and pick up the wooden letterbox that holds cards from my friends and family and start to flip through them, reading them aloud to no one in particular, smiling at the good wishes, like the delightful one from Priestess Aiko that reads,

Now you shall be the captain of your ship, in word and deed.

Just under that one is one from Kenichi, congratulating me,

You shall lead in Bosch, just as your Teddy-Papa would have wanted. Just as you have chosen. Then he added something odd. *Please inform me when you plan to travel to Kiharu so I can provide you with Riki's services. One can't be too careful with family.*

I wrinkle my brow and shrug, thinking that something was lost in his translation from Edoan. I continue reading other notes, laughing at the saltier comments and the several "but you said you'd never..." I figure I'd better get used to that as I have changed my course significantly. But the important part there is that *I* am at the helm: I am captaining my own ship. So, I can take a bit of ribbing about my past statements.

Then I see an unopened envelope tucked at the very bottom of the box. I pull it from its spot and regard it. The paper is thick and feels expensive: single-use, not recycled. And unlike the other cards just dropped in, sans envelope for all to see, it is sealed. I hold it aloft. "Who is this one from?"

Peter, the expert on all things, leans in and peers at it. "I don't know. Never seen it before."

Mimi calls from where she leans on Ryann, "Open it and find out."

So, I do. I break the seal and open the envelope and pull out a card with a short note.

Mary,

So, you are going to be an officer in your little pirate troop. How very charming. It seems we are both moving up in ranks now that I have taken my Senate seat a second time. It won't be long now until I reach the office I am meant to hold. I will be watching your progress. And as you take each step up the ladder, remember, you are mine. Now and always. I like the idea of an officer of the BPF bringing me my breakfast. So, carry on.

RA

PS I do hope that young man of yours wasn't too damaged by my errant shot. Perhaps you should guard your precious things more closely.

"Are you going to read it out loud?" Gia prods me with her foot.

I slip it back into its envelope and feel the smile of satisfaction slip across my face. "Nope."

Paul scrambles up. "Oooh, why not? Somebody have a crush on you? Who is it from?"

I chuckle and lean back on the couch, pleased with the timing. "It appears that Senator Rob Abernathy and I are now correspondents. How delightful is that?"

I see Carisa grasp Elise's hand, and the rest of the room begins to buzz. Peter comes up and takes the note, which I surrender willingly. There are questions flying, but I am lost in my own thoughts. I stand and go to Carisa. "Don't worry. I have this under control." She looks up at me and I smile reassuringly, and I see her nod and relax a tiny bit.

~

Senator Abernathy sat down in his office late Friday afternoon in Truvale and began to meticulously arrange the items on his desk. He heard a small "eh-hem" and looked up to see a young man with dark hair and rather dark skin standing nearby. Rob hated breaking in new assistants. He sighed. "Yes, what is it, uhh…?"

"Pierce, sir." The man's tone was even.

"Pierce, then. What do you have for me?" Rob was a busy man.

"Some mail has come in for you. Most were regular congratulatory wishes on your seating that I can answer, but I thought you'd want to see this one yourself." He held out a rather large envelope to the new senator.

Rob looked curiously at this Pierce fellow and narrowed his eyes. He took the envelope even as he contemplated that this was why he had an assistant—so he didn't have to look at mail. He reached in through the neatly slit top and withdrew a large document that had a smaller photograph and a card attached to it with a clip.

The large one was a map of the local Appalachian region. There was a red circle on it right at the location of his safe house. The photograph was of him, sitting on the back porch of his safehouse as a fire crackled in the firepit and he smoked a cigar and drank a glass of wine. The bottle sat nearby, and the photograph was so clear, he could read the label: Three Fires Pinot Noir 2352. He had consumed that particular bottle just two nights ago. His breath was coming faster. Now he looked at the card. It was short and to the point.

Rob,

Congrats on the Senate seating. Watch your fucking back. Tick-tock.

Kat

Acknowledgments

I am grateful, once again, to so many folks for their support as *Navigating the Storm, Book Two of Pirates of New Earth* came to fruition.

The usual crew: Martha Bullen, best book coach ever and Kat Wallace fan, for keeping me organized and focused and for making sure my paragraphs don't run on for pages; David Aretha and Andrea Vanryken, editors extraordinaire without whose two sets of eyes and insightful comments, the story would never run as smoothly as it does; Alan Hebel and Ian Koviak, patient and gifted cover designers who have the instincts and the visual gifts to portray Kat just enough for readers. Elias Othitis, talented producer, for being on board to create the audiobook and Helen Laser, an amazing actress whose narrative voice captures Kat Wallace's persona perfectly.

And the new mates: Maggie McLaughlin, who made sure the transfer of both *A Merry Life* and *Navigating the Storm* to distributors ran seamlessly and patiently repeated the process as I made corrections; Joe LeMonnier, mapmaker and careful listener, for translating my vision onto paper; Mary Ann Sabo and Claire Driscol, who have marshaled their public relations talents to get me in front of so many readers that may not have heard about Kat without their efforts.

And a special shout out to Fight Camp and the trainers: Tommy, Shanie, Flo, Aaron, PJ, Jess, and Rocky. I started Fight Camp in the early days, when I was just getting to know Kat, to understand how she might fight. I did not anticipate the gift of strength in mind and body it would give me. Thank you each and all.

To Jane Woodward, your enthusiastic in-the-moment text reactions as you read *A Merry Life* brought me joy and kept me writing for readers like you.

And, of course, my everlasting appreciation to my husband, Rick, for everything, and to my adult children, David, Megan and Daniel, and their partners, Jana, Josh and Jansu, for their unflagging and enthusiastic support of my writing and me.

About the Author

Sarah Branson started conjuring stories of pirates when her family hopped a freighter to Australia when she was seven. She has since grown up, traveling the globe, raising a family, and working as a receptionist, retail clerk, writing tutor, and certified nurse midwife. She also taught science and history to middle school and high school students in the U.S., Brazil and Japan. Through these myriad experiences, she has developed a deep appreciation for people's strength and endurance and believes that badass women will inherit the earth.

Sarah is still weaving pirate tales in her head and now, on paper, phone and computer, for your reading enjoyment. She draws on all of these experiences when creating stories about strong women and men finding adventure, love and their paths in worlds that are constantly changing. She lives with her husband in Connecticut.

For more information and updates:
www.sarahbranson.com

Coming Soon:

Pirates of New Earth, Book Three: Burn the Ship

No looking back.

Kat Wallace is rising in the ranks as the officer she never imagined she would be. Her position allows her to mobilize the Bosch Pirate Force in a war against human trafficking and its shadowy kingpin, and her commitment to Bosch brings with it important new friendships, but also reopens old wounds. When tragedy strikes, Kat's response will rock not only the Bosch but her own personal life.

Burn the Ship

BOOK 3 PIRATES OF NEW EARTH

Revenge Denied: Safehaven Point & Bosch, July 2365

I didn't kill today, and that means I failed.

The sky that surrounds the Coupe and me is a deep and peaceful July blue with only a few puffs of clouds off to the east. The engines purr contentedly as I return from Safehaven Point, a small city just south of Truvale and a block of sunshine falls onto my left forearm, even now the little bit of heat causes my thrall brand a twinge of pain. I swing the Coupe around to complete my base leg before coming into my final approach of the old airstrip. The Coupe, both cockpit and cabin, is silent and seemingly serene. But it belies the cacophony in my brain: *Dammit, dammit, dammit, Kat Wallace! Half a bell late. You couldn't have flown faster? Bet Papa never was late because the kids were sick. Kik had to pick this morning to wake up vomiting and crying? So like a six-year-old. Not his fault, poor kiddo, but still. Dammit! And you know Mac will be right behind him: twins share everything. Fuck! I was within arm's reach of that bastard.*

My brain continues its enraged rant; my victory playlist remains unused, and my mouth is set in a tight line. As I come in toward the runway, pilot Kat takes over, quieting the noise in my head in order to negotiate a small bit of crosswind. I sideslip to touchdown and then roll and brake until I am near the end of the strip closest to the cave. Then I allow the racket of my anger to return.

"Sweet New Earth! Not again!!" I slam my hands onto my arm rests and let my head loll back against the headrest, but my neck muscles remain taut and I continue to feel the adrenaline flow through me from my momentary confrontation with Senator Rob Abernathy. How could I have missed him this time? The plan was flawless. I had collected all the details, just as Teddy taught me. And I was set to orchestrate my revenge.

The Senator was scheduled for a campaign speech to the Bluest, the informal name of the CNE: Chosen of New Earth, a group of religious fanatics that wore blue hooded robes of varying hues depending on their position in the church. Everyone actually calls them the Bluies, though not to their hooded faces. To my way of thinking, it is a real waste of a palette of a beautiful color. The Bluies influence in the upcoming Federal Alliance presidential election had escalated as the Abernathy campaign embraced their stance on mandatory population increase (of the right sort, to be sure), and, in turn, they had championed the key plank in his platform on "the economic necessity and humanitarian benefit of thraldom". They were all bastards as far as I was concerned, but having an easy disguise like a blue cloak was too good an opportunity to pass up.

By the time I had wheeled Mama to come over to the house this morning to tend my sick boy and his likely-soon-to-follow brother, I was three-quarters of a bell late. I made up a quarter bell in flight, but I was still behind. As I flew, I slurped down my hastily prepared coffee, the beans for which I had liberated on my last extraction campaign, and ran over the plan.

Get to Abernathy's office before his meeting with the Bluie Patrician of Doctrine. Stroll in, bedecked in my lovely blue cloak styled appropriately out of rough fabric to demonstrate humility. This concept was ludicrous given the expensive shoes on the feet and the exquisite hand jewelry that adorned the mostly pale hands and arms that extended from the "humble" coverings. Nonetheless, my humility cloak was the proper shade for a mid-level assistant who may be verifying details before the event and was to be my ticket to my past enslaver's office. I'd be let in after showing my properly pilfered ID, and then I'd kill Senator Rob Abernathy, foiling his plan to be FA president once again and this time for good. And as a bonus, the blame would be pinned on the Bluies.

Except I was late. And the event had already begun by the time I water landed off Safehaven Point and then maneuvered my small, inflatable boat quietly to shore and moored it there. But I had to see if I could still achieve my goal, though I had no intention of cutting it too close. I had to get safely home. I had commitments.

I planned to pick up some of my sick boys' favorite frozen juice slushies on the way home. In addition, Grey was singing, a talent that she surely had not inherited from me, on stage for the first time this afternoon at Bonnet camp. Bonnet camp is an on-base program for children ten and up to learn a bit of Bosch Pirate Force, or BPF, boxing, marksmanship, and flight simulator use as well as singing, dancing, playing instruments, and theater. Ever popular, it always closed in late August with a full pirate musical that drew spectators from all over Bosch. This was Grey's first year attending and today was the first showcase leading up to the big event. Takai was scheduled to arrive home from Edo where he was ministering to his supposedly ill father in time to attend as well. So, no cutting it close. Either I would get my target or I wouldn't.

I am not nearly so phlegmatic now, however. I throw open the Coupe door and leap to the ground, not even waiting to drop the ramp. I grab the first rock I find and lob it at the rocky bank nearest the edge of the runway with a "Fuck!" It lands with a satisfying crack. Five more rocks, curses and cracks later and I am breathing hard and not even slightly mollified. I stand and blow an angry breath out.

Once I arrived at the event enrobed in my cloak, I had been jostled through the crowd of Bluies and ended up in the section closest to the hopeful candidate. The almost late Senator was greeting the fortunate members, pressing his knuckles together and then clasping his fingers in the CNE gesture of the joining of forces for strength. As he moved along the margins of the crowd, he took care to charm every believer with his charisma, making sure to speak softly to each person, demonstrating his indisputable compassion for each of his constituency. Fools. One moment I was watching this charade and the next, he was in front of me, so close I could have shanked him, and I seriously considered that move. But I would never have gotten away. Our eyes met and the old fury rose in me as I saw him smirk.

"You get to continue to draw breath today, Senator." My voice was low as I hissed this through my teeth.

His smug smile broadened and he leaned in to murmur in my ear, "And you have failed. Again. Mary. Tsk-tsk. Not much of a pirate after all, are you, Captain Wallace? At least you don't have anyone with you that's going to die this time."

I felt my jaw clench and my right hand clutched at the bone handle of my blade strapped on my thigh as his taunts hit their mark. Even after more than three years, the pain of Will's death was razor sharp and caused my old friend, Remorse, to remind me why I ran these missions solo. I pulled back and met his eyes in a steely glare. I gave a slight growl, pulled phlegm into the back of my throat and spat it in his face.

Time spiraled to a stop for an instant as I watched his expression shift from shock to revulsion and then toward dangerous anger. But neither he nor his anger frightened me any longer. When time restarted, he had turned to order his surprised bodyguards to take me in custody, but I had already melted back into the pool of blue, my face covered with my hood as I began to echo the murmurs of dismay of the other Bluies. I shuffled along the perimeter of the crowd, staying just deep enough to be obscured. My eyes darted about as I assessed my best path for exfil.

After a few minutes I saw my opening: a large vehicle with a logo of a massive black obelisk and the words *Obi: We Cover Your Life* written in block letters on its side was parked near the congregation. The red-headed cameraperson had their video camera focused on a young dark skinned woman costumed in a butter colored dress as she spoke earnestly to the lens in front of her as the sea of blue ebbed and flowed behind her. I slipped to the edge of the mass of fanatics and then stepped a meter or so away from them, seeming to lean down to fix my shoe.

A quick glance at the Obi reporter and then I dodged to the back door of the vehicle and was rewarded when it opened easily. There I shed my blue cloak and sat on the floor, eyeing the various electronic contraptions and cursing my failure for a good half-bell before the rumble of the Bluies slowly subsided into silence and the door swung open. I stood and nodded at the astonished camera person, who looked to be about twenty years old and stood, mouth agape.

"Thanks for the haven." I patted his cheek as I hopped out.

He recovered enough to start to protest, but by the time he

had set his heavy gear down and turned to confront me, I was far down the street making my way to the bay and my waiting inflatable.

Now I sigh, climb back into the Coupe, pull out my purple pen from my sling bag and reluctantly put a fourth mark in the Failure column of the tally sheet I have posted just above my primary display. Four attempts to end him in three years and none successful. Teddy used to say, "Don't matter how often you fall, girl. As long as you can get up, you'll make it."

I stroke the area under the word Success. I will make my mark there. One day.

Also by Sarah Branson

A Merry Life: Book 1 Pirates of New Earth

Published by Sooner Started Press

Made in the USA
Middletown, DE
15 March 2024

50871347R00175